FIVE DECADES OF THE X-MEN

FIVE DECADES OF THE X-MEN

Stan Lee, Editor

MARVEL®

BP BOOKS, INC.

ibooks
new york
www.ibooksinc.com

DISTRIBUTED BY SIMON & SCHUSTER, INC

Special thanks to Bob Greenberger, Bobbie Chase, and Andrew Lis

X-MEN
FIVE DECADES OF THE X-MEN

A BP Books, Inc. Book
An ibooks, inc. Book

PRINTING HISTORY
BP Books, Inc. trade paperback edition / February 2002
BP Books, Inc. mass market edition / April 2003

CONTENTS

INTRODUCTION

By Stan Lee

LISTEN UP, True Believers. Here's a challenge for you . . .

Put yourself in the editor's shoes. Countless fans are demanding more, more, and still more X-Men anthologies. That's the good part. But here's the bad part. You (the editor) have already compiled and produced enough X-Men anthologies to wallpaper a dozen Danger Rooms with them. And, since we're quite sure that you've got better things to do with your time than wallpapering Danger Rooms, here's your challenge . . .

What new angle can you come up with for a new anthology? What can you think of to make it seem truly different than all the previous anthologies?

Not too easy, huh? Well, you're in luck. That's the exact challenge that was handed to The Mighty Marvel Bullpen and the erudite editors here at BP Books and, in order to save you from wracking your mutant-loving brain with such a complex and confounding conundrum, they have generously solved the problem for you.

Yes, to show how much they care, they've worked night and day until coming up with a practically priceless, prize-winning idea; a truly unique theme that will resonate throughout the halls of comicdom and make this very book, which you're now so

1

proudly holding, a volume to be treasured and cherished for years to come.

Think of it. They've decided to give you a separate epic tale featuring the most colorful heroes and villains from each of the five decades of the X-Men's titanic triumphs! That's right, five decades. It's almost hard to believe, but our magnificent mutants first took the comicbook world by storm in the early sixties—fifty long and thrilling years ago!

Now, a full half-century later, the indomitable and powerful playmates of Professor X are still the best-selling group of comicbook titles on Earth! In fact, I'm probably being too modest. They're probably the best-selling comics in all the known galaxies—and the unknown ones, as well.

And, because all this reminiscing has put me in a mellow, somewhat generous mood, I've decided to do you a great favor. I'll herewith present, for your eyes only, a brief sample of the spectacular thrillers awaiting you on the pages ahead. But bear in mind that what follows is just a teaser, just the slightest hint of the reading pleasure that awaits you; for no mere words of mine can begin to do justice to the awesome artwork and spellbinding stories that our heroic editors have so carefully culled from five decades of literary triumphs.

Okay. The stage is set. The time has come. Let the wonderment begin . . .

We begin with the decade of the swinging Sixties, and the first masterwork that you'll soon be thrilling to is titled "Baptism of Fire, Baptism of Ice," by John J. Ordover and Susan Wright. And if that doesn't qualify as one of the best movie-type titles of the year, I'll resign my membership in Magneto's Merry Miscreants' Society. But this yarn has lots more to offer than its dynamite title. It features the first battle between the X-Men and Magneto, and as a bonus, it also deals with everyone's favorite frozen teenager, Bobby Drake, who resents his mutant power because he thinks the girls will consider him a freak. Hey, how many females wanna to date a human ice cube?

Well, as luck would have it (luck, my foot! It's the result of clever plotting on Ordover and Wright's part) Bobby actually gets a date with a great looking girl. Now our fearless young super hero who has calmly faced death countless times is scared stiff. What if he has to turn into Iceman while he's with her? You can guess the rest. A new mutant super-villain makes the scene right in the middle of poor Bobby's date. Naturally, he has to become Iceman to save the girl as well as all the other people on the scene. That's where magnanimous Marvel treats you to some great action scenes as Iceman does what Iceman does best. After the villain is vanquished, Bobby figures he blew his cover as well as his chances with the wide-eyed, astonished girl he was with. Now, if you're wondering about the rest of the X-Men team, they're in it too, but if I say any more about this titanic tale, I'll spoil the fun.

Next we come to the savage Seventies. This is where we lay "Firm Commitments" on you, scripted by Sholly Fisch. In this nail-biter, you'll find the Beast, Cyclops, Angel, Marvel Girl, and of course Professor X prominently featured.

You'll witness the plight of a Genetech scientist who discovers that his biogenetic research is being used by the Secret Empire, a covert organization whose purpose is pure evil. Unwittingly, the trapped scientist finds himself helping to kidnap the X-Men. But, when things look blackest, that's when our fighting-mad mutants strike back, and when you'll feel like standing up and cheering as we see that heroism comes in many forms, even to those who haven't super powers.

Now, the Eighties. Ah, the extraordinary 1980s. What a time it was. And what better time than to publish "Up the Hill Backwards," written by Tom Deja and starring Banshee, Havok, Longshot, Dazzler, Psylock and Callisto. With a great cast like that you almost don't even need a plot, but you lucked out—you actually get a story, too. After the infamous Mutant Massacre, Banshee forms a new X-Men team, but the chosen leader, Havok, doesn't want the job and things go from bad to worse until Havok finds himself, and his team, in life and death combat against one of the most dangerous foes in the history of the X-Men.

One of the best and most unique X-Men stories was "God

Loves, Man Kills." Well, you lucked out again. In this great volume you'll find in the decade of the Nineties, "The Cause," by Glenn Greenberg, the gripping sequel to that now-classic tale. It re-introduces the murderous Reverend William Stryker as he's about to be released from prison. You'll watch, wide-eyed, as tensions mount between humans and mutants, tensions which keep escalating until Stryker himself becomes a target for assassination. Question: Should the X-Men try to save the man who would destroy them? Fear not, frantic one, we won't keep you waiting too long; you'll find the answer in this drama-drenched tale.

Finally, we come to the turn of the century, the fateful year 2000! This is where the intriguing story "Gifts" by Madeleine Robins presents Rogue, Nightcrawler and Psylock up against a different menace than any X-Men have ever faced before. At first, it seems no more than an attack at La Guardia airport in New York City by some evil mutants. But then, as airplanes, runways and buildings themselves become torn apart, we realize it's a far different menace, a far more deadly one. Trapped in one of the airport's terminals is a high school drama class returning from a class trip. At a fateful moment, the X-Men learn the danger they face is from two people in that group—but how can the X-Men fight people who are victims themselves?

There you have it, Bunky. If that doesn't sound like the greatest gaggle of thrillers ever assembled between two covers, it's only because my poor powers of description aren't equal to the daunting task of accurately describing all the fun and excitement awaiting you on the pages ahead.

So let's not waste another minute, hear? Five decades of America's most popular super team are waiting to enthrall you, and it isn't polite to keep fifty years waiting!

Excelsior!
Stan

1960s

BAPTISM OF FIRE, BAPTISM OF ICE

by John J. Ordover and Susan Wright

BOBBY DRAKE stood naked on the balcony outside his bedroom. He cared nothing about the nippy breeze or the chirping of the busy songbirds that wintered on the grounds of his exclusive private school in New York's Westchester county. He was in a life-or-death struggle—even if it was only in his own mind!

It was just like any other morning that Bobby had spent since he came to live at Professor Xavier's school for what could euphemistically be called "gifted students" or "exceptional children" or any of a dozen other terms for "oddball." The correct term, of course, was one that Bobby would never use in polite company: mutant.

"Take that, you dirty rat!" he swore in his most threatening super-hero voice, practiced daily in the bathroom mirror.

With a deep breath, he mustered his power as Iceman, a gift from an odd tweak in his DNA that let him control his body temperature and the consistency of the water molecules so abundant in the air around him.

A crackling ripped round him as water molecules snapped together into rigid ice crystals, rushing inward to form a thick "ice-armor" enveloping his body. Even his eyes and mouth were coated by a protective layer of ice. Yet he could still see and breathe, something that continued to amaze him. He could understand why others thought it was frightening and impossible.

But right now the Iceman had more important things on his mind. Focused on his quarry, he cupped his right hand. By force of thought, a ball of ice grew rapidly in his hand until he had a solid rock-hard iceball.

He hefted it, feeling its comforting weight. Bobby had never been good at throwing a ball, but that was one skill he had managed to perfect during the past few months while he'd been hanging around the school. Leaning into it, he snapped his missile through the air.

The iceball flew straight and true, smashing right into the base of the tree limb. With a sharp crack! the limb was jolted back and the entire tree shook from the collision.

For a second he thought the tree had beaten him again. He had tried everything to get rid of the pesky limb that made such a racket scrapping against his window at night. But the trunk was too smooth for him to climb, and the head gardener thought it would ruin the "line" of the tree if he cut the limb off.

Bobby formed another iceball, ready to do whatever it took to get some sleep, but the limb shuddered and didn't swing back into place. The entire thing, as big around as his arm, swung down with a mighty groan and hung by a few fibrous threads of bark.

As the weight of the limb pulled it from the tree, Iceman leaped into the air, shouting, "Got ya!"

Now he wouldn't be woken at night whenever it was windy.

It wasn't the most glamorous battle he'd ever imagined having, but what the heck! He had to make do with what he had.

Frankly, he was bored out of his skull. He had been promised big things by Scott Summers, a fellow student at the school and whose X-Men code-name was Cyclops, when he had rescued

Bobby from the good citizens and his former friends in Port Washington, New York.

He could almost hear Cyclops now, telling him, "Never within the memory of man, has there been a class like this! Never was there a teacher like Professor X. And never were there students like us . . ."

It sounded like exactly what Bobby Drake had been looking for. But instead of being turned into the man he knew he could be—Iceman!—he was being babied by Professor X and the other guys who lived at the school. Bobby knew he was only sixteen, the youngest of the four "special" students, but his power was strong.

His fist cracked, shattering the ice around his tightened fingers. Instantly more ice swarmed over his hand, exposing none of his skin to danger. He was ready for action—

A sharp command thought rang through Bobby's mind, echoing in the great halls of the building.

"*Attention, X-Men! This is Professor Xavier calling! Repeat, this is Professor X calling!*"

Bobby shivered at the odd sensation of having another person's voice in his mind. He wasn't sure if he would ever get used to it, but that was Professor X's special gift.

"*You are ordered to appear at once!*" the Professor continued. "*Class is now in session! Tardiness will be punished!*"

Bobby was glad he was already iced up and ready to go. He would show them. He would get there first and Professor X would have to see that he was ready for the big leagues.

Spinning around, he held his hand over the edge of the balcony. Steadying himself, a solid column of ice shot straight down, forming a fireman's pole directly to the small patio outside the danger room where the X-Men trained.

"Nothing to it," Bobby muttered as he jumped over the railing of the balcony, squeezing the slippery pole between his legs.

He spiraled down the ice pole, not bothering to break his descent at the bottom. Bounding into the training room with its high ceiling and even higher-tech equipment concealed in the walls, Bobby announced, "Iceman right on schedule, sir!"

Professor X's nod acknowledged his quick arrival. Bobby smirked behind his ice-mask as Cyclops, Angel and the Beast arrived right after him. It was a good thing they couldn't see his expression, but he swaggered a bit in his boots at the thought of beating the older boys. Scott "Slim" Summers, Warren Worthington III, and Hank McCoy had joked with him a few times too often about being the youngest kid on the block. It wouldn't have bothered Bobby so much if only Professor X stopped taking it easy on him.

"Cyclops present and accounted for, sir!" Slim was tall and well-built with a reserved aura to him.

"Angel reporting, sir!" Warren didn't sound like the others. He was more outgoing and confident, thanks to his rich upbringing and pretty boy looks.

"The Beast is here, sir!" Hank gave him a wry grin, the only one who seemed to notice that Bobby had arrived first. At least Hank had a sense of humor, but he was so darn smart that it was sometimes hard to follow what he was saying.

The Professor surveyed them all from his usual chair. Bobby wasn't exactly sure why the Professor never left it, but he could feel the old man's power even from across the room. His bald head and deeply slanted brows could have seemed forbidding, but Bobby had already grown to love the Professor because of how much he cared about all of them.

Before the Professor could speak, Cyclops leaped forward. "C'mon, Angel, let's tilt the Professor's chair back and make him more comfortable!"

"With pleasure, Cyclops, old man!" Angel flew forward, snagging the lap rug before it could fall from the Professor's inert legs. Cyclops adjusted the leather chair to lounge back. "We want the Professor comfortable while he puts us through our paces!"

Bobby thought they were sucking up to the Professor just because he had reached the Danger Room first. Cyclops treated their mission as a call from god, and heaven help the would-be X-Men who ever took anything less than seriously around Slim. Angel seemed to treat being a hero as something to be done to help the little people out of *noblesse oblige*, a term Hank had explained to Bobby once.

Since the Beast wasn't joining in their fussing, Bobby saw an opportunity to impress the Professor himself.

"Hey, Beast, come here!" Bobby crossed the rug to his side. "I wanna show you a new stunt I learned with my frosting power."

He grabbed Beast's massive arm with both hands, feeling the muscles flex beneath the hairy pelt. With one smooth thought, ice ran down Beast's sleeve and covered his clawed fingers.

"Leggo my arm, you blasted walking icicle! You want me to freeze to death?" Beast shook Bobby off like he was clump of wet snow. With a couple of hasty swipes of his hand, the ice broke off and fell to the floor. "Brrr! I don't mind ice cubes, but I like 'em in a Coke, not tickling my arm!"

"Nah!" Bobby struck a stance he had secretly been practicing along with his impressive Iceman voice—his arms akimbo on his hips with his legs spread wide. "With all your super-powers, you guys are just a bunch of softies! Can't even stand a refreshing dose of freezing ice cubes."

"Softies, are we?" Beast growled. But there was a twinkle in his eye as he chaffed his arm. "Just wait'll my arm thaws out. I'll make you eat those words, little fella."

"Yeah? You and what other army?" Bobby shot back, not to be outdone.

Angel flew in and grabbed Beast's belt, like he had to save Bobby or something. "Hold it, lads! No fighting during class, re-member?"

Bobby was ready take the battle to Angel's corner by calling their high-class classmate a swarmy goody-two-shoes, but the Professor took control.

Using his mental power, he sent his thoughts into each of their minds. *"Thank you, Angel! And now, it is time to begin your lessons. The Beast will be first. Prepare to operate the training machine, Cyclops."*

"Yes, sir, Professor!" Usually the Professor mentally operated the training devices in the danger room, but Cyclops opened up the complex control board that could also control the gadgets used in their daily sessions. Bobby edged closer, wishing he could run the danger room sometime. But he'd probably have to wait until he was draft-age to get any real work handed to him around here.

"Everything is ready," Cyclops reported.

"Allow me to congratulate all of you," the Professor continued, as Beast did a couple of deep lunges to loosen up for the session. *"You are receiving my thoughts perfectly. Soon there will be no need for me to speak aloud to you at all."*

"And now, Beast . . ." The Professor folded his hands calmly in his lap. *"Grab the taut wire above you with your toes. You have exactly a second and a half. Go!"*

The words were hardly formed in Bobby's mind when the Beast was in the air and hanging upside-down from the wire by his long and hairy toes.

"I can do this in my sleep by now!" Beast exclaimed, dangling his arms above the ground.

"Excellent!" the Professor projected. *"Now spin around."*

The Beast began to swing and quickly looped up and over the wire. As his momentum grew, he spun in one continuous motion.

"Faster!" the Professor urged mentally. *"Pretend an enemy is shooting at you. You must make yourself an impossible target."*

The Beast spun so fast that he turned into a blur. Bobby swayed just from watching him.

"And now, at my command, release yourself from the wire and execute maneuver 'G'! You have exactly three seconds." There was a tense pause as the Beast continued to spin. *"Go!"*

The Beast let go, shooting like a bullet through a free-standing hoop that rose from a hole in the ground. He bounced against the far wall without slowing and dove through a small square bracket that emerged from its hiding spot just as he passed by. Then he ricocheted against two other walls before landing on the floor next to the Professor.

It looked like fun to Bobby.

"Three seconds exactly!" The Professor's thought was tinged with approval at the difficult maneuver. *"Well done, Beast!"*

The Beast wasn't even winded, and the Professor seemed eager to push him. *"Now for your balance drill."*

The Beast nimbly flipped into the air and came down head-first on top of a ten foot rod not much bigger around than a TV antennae. The Beast stopped his fall with one finger, balancing high up next to the ceiling. His legs spread wide and he held out his other arm to help keep his equilibrium on the slender rod.

"Steady . . . steady . . ." the Professor urged calmly. *"Now, slacken the tension, Cyclops!"*

The Beast shifted as the rod grew wobbly beneath him.

"Good!" the professor commended him. *"Now, as the rod begins to sag, maintain your balance . . . on one finger! Hold it . . . hold it . . ."*

The rod bent far over. The Beast pulled in his legs, trying to center himself perfectly over the treacherous rod.

"Too fast!" the Professor chided. *"You're swaying too much. Recover . . . quickly!"*

As the Beast steadied himself, the rod sagged all the way over, pointed back to the ground in a steep arch. Bobby realized he was holding his breath.

"Now land on your feet before the rod snaps back. Careful . . . careful . . ."

The Beast seemed to gather himself like a spring. With absolute focus, he flicked his mighty finger and propelled himself off the sagging rod. He covered an impressive distance considering he had no leverage, and landed halfway across the danger room.

"Whew!" the Beast exclaimed. "How'd I do, sir?"

*"You'll be receiving your grade tomorrow, Beast. All right, Angel . . .
it's your turn."*

Bobby felt the familiar disappointment when the Professor
didn't call on him. He never got to play during these sessions. Every
time he iced up and got ready to go, he ended acting as audience
while the other guys showed off.

Angel leaped into the air and took a few practice turns around
the cavernous danger room on his huge white wings. Bobby noticed
that Angel was making special effort to point his toes and keep a
perfect line. The guy really cared too much about how he looked . . .
if only Professor X would let Iceman could show them a thing or
two! He wouldn't be so worried about how pretty he looked doing it.

"Are you receiving my thoughts clearly?" the Professor asked.

Angel banked and snapped out a salute in reply.

*"Good! Now be sharp . . . today we test your wing reflex. You
dare not make a mistake."*

From up in the air, Angel replied, "Mistakes are for homo sapiens, sir . . . not the Angel!"

Bobby started to roll his eyes when a tower of fire blasted high
into the room. It caught Angel off guard. He dipped one wing and
swerved sharply around the blazing inferno. He even managed to
keep his toes pointed, Bobby noted with a snort of disgust.

The Professor warned, *"Don't be overconfident, Angel. You almost singed your wing on that unexpected flame jet."*

"You're right, sir," Angel admitted, gliding to the end of the
room. "I'll do better next time."

Once again proving that no matter how much of a prig Warren
Worthington III could be, the Angel was a decent guy.

A large jagged crusher emerged from the walls and smashed shut
as Angel flew through its jaws. It made a resoundingly loud *Klack!*
when it closed. Angel put his arms out in front of him to maneuver
better.

"Good! You avoided the second obstacle with seconds to spare."

"Ahhh!" Angel sighed, ruffling the air as he swooped over them. "Now I'm getting warmed up."

Unlike the silent Beast, Angel kept up a running commentary as he ran through his training session. When he dipped up and down through the rapidly revolving spanner, avoiding its sharp-edged arms, he even bragged, "First time I ever flew the spanner without a slip!"

Angel made it look easy, but as he prepared to dive back into the spanner a sudden burst of pure sound knocked him up and away.

"Wha . . . what's this?" Angel exclaimed, flailing in the air.

"I warned you against over-confidence," the Professor reminded him. *"This sudden sound concussion is to test your survival ability. You must not fall to the ground!"*

Angel's arms were wind-milling as his wings folded into limp strands. Bobby instinctively raised his hands as if to keep Angel from falling. He had never seen Angel so helpless in the air before. The Professor really had a lot of tricks in his bag.

"Hold on Angel! Flap your wings. Keep flapping . . . don't stop! You can do it, boy. You mustn't fall."

Angel did several flips in the air, trying to get his wings back under him. When they finally furled open, catching solid air, Angel's expression was tense with deep lines of concentration creasing his forehead.

"That was a close one, sir. But I think I'm all right now." Angel hovered over them, his wings a flapping blur. Chagrin was clear in his expression, and for once Bobby didn't feel glad to see the older boy cut down to size. That had really looked like a tough test.

"Yes, you're beginning to master the hovering maneuver . . . ," the Professor acknowledged. *"It may save your life someday. That will be all now."*

Bobby couldn't contain himself any longer. If the Professor passed over him one more time, what would he have to do? Set fire to himself to get their attention?

"Professor!" Bobby exclaimed. "When are you gonna stop taking it easy with me just because I'm younger than the others? How am I ever gonna graduate at this rate?"

"*Some things cannot be rushed, Iceman,*" the Professor thought soothingly. "*You may have five minutes of free play, doing what you wish.*"

Free play! Bobby thought indignantly. *What kind of training was that?*

Well, if the Professor was going to treat him like a kid, he might as well act like one. He snagged a carrot and a banana peel off the snack tray next to the door, then ripped a couple of buttons off the coat Hank had dropped near the door.

The others were waiting, not sure what he was up to. Bobby hunched over so they couldn't see him press the buttons into the icy mask over his face exactly where his eyes should be. He stuck the carrot straight in and twisted to make sure it was secure. He had to freeze on the banana peel in place of a smile.

At least he was going to get a few laughs out of this!

Something tickled his mind, almost as if the Professor was trying to send him something that he couldn't quite receive. But Bobby was too busy with his gag to pay attention.

Jamming an old hat on his head, Iceman whirled around to face everyone. "Taaa . . . ta! Look at me! I'm a snowman!"

He struck a pose any respectable snowman would be proud of. Angel and Cyclops stared at him open-mouthed.

Bobby threatened, "I'm gonna go stand on someone's lawn if I don't get something to do around here pretty soon."

Something started moving in from one side of the room. A black bowling ball was flying through the air directly towards him!

"Watch yourself, Iceman!" the Beast called out as he recovered from his throw. "This thing is no soap bubble."

Hot diggity! Bobby thought. *A test for me at last . . .*

The bowling ball seemed to slow, as if giving him plenty of time to respond. With his next breath, Bobby formed an ice shield, blowing it into a curved shaped almost as large as his own body. The snowman gear was flung away as he lifted the heavy shield to catch the bowling ball at the perfect angle.

"Right back at you, partner!" Bobby laughed as the ball caught the shield and rolled up the curve, sling-shotting back at the Beast.

"*Good work, Iceman.*" The Professor's thought was full of warmth. "*Your reflexes are astonishing for a sixteen year old.*"

The Beast caught the bowling ball one-handed behind his back. "Right in the ol' pocket, kid! Hey, maybe we'll challenge the Harlem Globe Trotters some day, eh?"

The Professor turned his head. "*Silence Beast! The lesson is not yet over. Cyclops is still to be tested.*"

Cyclops was frowning with his arms crossed. Of course he had to criticize Bobby's first training attempt. "Look, you two clowns, be more careful next time. That bowling ball just missed the Professor by a whisker. That kind of horseplay isn't funny."

Bobby took up his super-hero stance, proudly puffing out his chest. But before he could take Cyclops down a notch, the Beast was bawling, "Quit grandstanding, Cyclops! We know what we were doing. And the Professor knows we don't want him to get hurt any more than you do."

Cyclops was ready to shout back, but the Professor cut him off. "*Cyclops! Attention! This is your test. Assume the Beast and Iceman are your enemies. Put them out of action without causing serious injury.*"

"As you say, sir," Cyclops replied.

Bobby was thrilled that the Professor had chosen to pit Cyclops against him and Beast. Finally he was one of the X-Men team! He wasn't about to fail.

Slowly, silently, Cyclops adjusted the small lever at the side of his head shield. As he did, his eye visor opened wider . . . and wider . . . until . . .

"You're the oldest, Beast, so you're first," Cyclops announced.

A ray of light shot out from Cyclops' eyes, striking the Beast in the chest. The Beast was lifted off his feet and thrust back, shouting out, "Yeow!"

He crashed into the wall so hard that the reinforced concrete shattered into a Beast-shaped indentation. Bobby knew that wall would be proof of Cyclops' power over Beast for many weeks to come. He wasn't going to let that happen to him.

"Hey, turn down that blasted visor of yours, will ya?" Beast complained good-naturedly, even though he was stuck like a pinned butterfly. "You almost knocked me clean through the wall!"

"Sorry, Beast. I just wanted to show the Professor what I can do."

Bobby was already reacting, ready for Cyclops' attack. With the ease of a thought, he formed a solid cube of ice around himself. He made it plenty thick to keep that probing energy beam away from his body.

"And now for the Iceman," Cyclops announced with glee. "You're just wasting your time, Junior... that ice-cube shield can't block out my energy ray."

"Maybe not," Bobby retorted. "But it'll sure slow it down a lot."

Cyclops' ray beamed into the ice, making it sizzle and smoke. But Bobby kept reforming the ice. That would teach him! He would show them all that he was just as good as they were.

The energy ray couldn't pierce his ice-shield. Bobby was ready to cry victory when Cyclops reached up and adjusted his visor again. The beam opened wider, almost engulfing his shield.

"Hey, that's not fair!" Bobby exclaimed. "You're opening that cotton-picking visor of yours wider."

"Iceman, for the kind of career we're training for, there is no such word as 'fair'!"

Bobby held on, willing the ice to harden faster. At least Cyclops had stopped calling him "Junior".

The ice began to crack, groaning and splitting under the bombardment.

"Now protect yourself," Cyclops called. "My energy beam is smashing through."

"This is one day I shoulda stayed in bed," Bobby blurted out.

As ice chunks exploded in every direction, the energy beam

caught Bobby right in his icy chest. He flew back and landed on the floor with a hard whap!

"Okay, turn that blamed beam off, willya?" Bobby called out, glad he still had his ice armor to protect himself.

"*Angel! Beast! Join Iceman!*" the Professor urged. "*Try to sub-due Cyclops.*"

As the Beast knocked Cyclops off his feet, the beam swung away from Iceman. He leaped onto the pile of tangled limbs along with Angel. "Thanks, Prof! I could use a little help."

They all wrestled in a rolling pile, laughing but serious about getting the best of each other. The Professor calmly sent them his thoughts, "*It's not for your sake alone, lad. A few minutes of rough-house is good for all of you. It helps you let off steam.*"

Iceman let out a whoop as the Beast clobbered Cyclops. It sure felt good to be one of the gang at last. They were finally treating him like he could hold his own, like he was worth sparring with. Iceman felt like he was on top of the world, even as Angel pressed his icy mask into the padded floor.

With a slippery twist, he got behind the winged X-Men and formed a ball of snow in one hand. Iceman smeared it right into Angel's pretty face, open mouth and all . . . it was one of the most satisfying moments he'd had since he came to Professor Xavier's school . . .

Suddenly a sharp commanding thought pierced the brain of the four rampaging youths. "Enough! The lesson is over. We must turn our energies to different matters. Return to your places at once."

Stunned by the force and explosive power of Professor Xavier's mental command, the X-Men recoiled and drew back, their friendly free-for-all completely forgotten.

"Whew, he almost bowled me over with that one," the Beast muttered under his breath.

"Let's simmer down and see what happens next," Angel urged.

One thing Bobby could say for Angel, he wasn't holding his reddened, ice-smeared face against him.

The Professor waited until they had settled into a line in front of his chair. "*I congratulate you all. You have mastered reading my thoughts perfectly. Now I shall return to normal communication.*"

Lifting one hand, the Professor gave them a rare smile of approval. "You may be interested to learn that at this very moment I sense a taxi approaching our main gate. Within that vehicle is a new pupil . . . a most attractive young lady."

Young lady! A girl? Coming here? Bobby stared at the other X-Men, not sure that Professor X could be serious. But the old man nodded at them with a slight smile of amusement.

At the sound of gravel crunching in the driveway, Angel, Beast and Cyclops ran to the window outside the danger room. They leaned through it to see as if their lives depended on it.

"You're right, sir!" Cyclops exclaimed. "Wow! She's a real living doll."

"A redhead," Angel added. "Look at that face . . . and the rest of her!"

Beast was shoving under Angel's wing to catch a glimpse. "All of a sudden I'm in no hurry to graduate from this place . . ."

Bobby turned on his heel and walked away in disgust. "A girl . . . big deal! I'm glad I'm not a wolf like you guys."

"I'm glad too," Angel laughed over his shoulder. "Who needs the extra competition from Iceman?"

That sounded a bit too sarcastic for Bobby. But before he could retort, Cyclops was saying, "I wonder what super-human powers she possesses. She looks normal enough."

Beast pulled away from the window. "Well, let's go up and change so we don't scare her when she first sees us."

Bobby would have preferred to meet her behind the anonymity of his ice-armor, but the Professor agreed and sent them to change out of their X-Men uniforms. Grumbling a bit at the weird ending to his first training session, Bobby followed the others upstairs while Professor X stayed below to greet their new classmate.

Bobby broke out of his ice-suit quickly and threw on his usual school-day chinos and sweater. The other guys were primping in their rooms, so he reached Professor X's study before they did. This was the place where Professor X talked to them about their powers, where he gave them their grades and encouraged them to work harder. It was a somber brown-leather place with stuffed bookshelves lining three of the walls.

Pausing outside the door, Bobby heard the Professor's knowing answer, "I think you already suspect what kind of school this is, Miss Grey. You see, I can read your thoughts quite clearly, and I know all about your unusual talents."

Bobby blushed at how frustrated he had been earlier—Professor X must have known he was going to pull that little snowman stunt. That was why he had sicced the Beast on him. Oh well, at least it had encouraged Professor X to include him in the training sessions—

A mental message from the Professor hit him like a cold gust of wind. "*If you're going to eavesdrop, Bobby, you might as well come in.*"

Sheepishly, Bobby opened the door, chiding himself for his stupidity. Of course the Professor always knew what he was thinking . . .

"You, Miss Grey," the Professor was saying, "like the other four students at this exclusive school, are a mutant. You possess an extra power, one which ordinary humans do not. That is why I call my students X-men, for ex-tra power."

The other X-Men came in behind Bobby. They were spruced up and slicked back within an inch of their lives. The Beast was even wearing his Sunday suit, and he looked mighty uncomfortable. Bobby snickered at him.

"And here they are now," the Professor finished. "Allow me to present them to you. From left to right we have Hank McCoy, whose codename is Beast. Bobby Drake, Iceman; Scott Summers, Cyclops; and Warren Worthington III, whose codename is Angel. Boys, this is Miss Jean Grey. Her codename is Marvel Girl."

Warren stepped forward first, while Slim was still struggling with the button on his collar. "Welcome to the X-Men, Miss Grey."

Jean Grey was wearing a pillbox hat and white gloves with her calf-length skirt and a suspicious attitude. *Not,* Bobby thought, *that her attitude wasn't justified. The way Warren and Hank were bearing down on her, it was no wonder she was stand-offish.*

"How come he's calling you Marvel Girl, Miss Grey?" Hank was quick to ask. "What power do you have?"

Warren was hovering not much further away. "She has one very obvious power . . . the power to make a man's heart beat faster."

Bobby groaned. "Y'know something, Warren, if I had your line, I'd shoot myself."

In response, Jean lifted her rectangular purse and gazed at the little mirror inside the lid. She adjusted a lock of hair that was out of place. "You'll learn more about me, boys, in time."

Bobby grinned at her use of the word "boys." That should put them in their place.

But Hank couldn't contain himself, as usual. "Well, no time like the present. C'mon, Cyke, bring the little lady a chair."

Jean frowned slightly. "That's really not necessary."

The chair suddenly shot straight toward Jean.

"Th . . . the chair!" Scott exclaimed as Hank leaped into the air, grabbing onto the chandelier to get out of the path of the wayward chair. "It's—."

"Yiii!" Hank exclaimed, swinging slightly up above. "Holy smoke! What's going on?"

The chair stopped neatly in front of Jean. "Don't be alarmed, boys. I just thought I'd save you the trouble."

She seated herself as Hank sheepishly dropped back down to the floor. Slim acted like he didn't know what to do with his hands.

"Now, then, Professor," Jean finished. "I believe we can continue our interview. As you were saying . . ."

But Scott interrupted, saying, "I don't get it, sir. What happened to that moving chair?"

The Professor rubbed his chin with one finger. "Perhaps you'd better demonstrate a bit more, Jean."

"Very well, sir." She glanced at the older boys, and Bobby felt his frustration edging back up. Just because he was younger and smaller didn't mean he wasn't a full-fledged X-Man! Wait 'til she got a load of him when he was bulked up as Iceman!

"All my life I've had to conceal this power of mine," she continued. "Now I must admit it's a pleasure to be able to practice telekinesis openly, without fear of being discovered." She nodded toward the Professor's desk. "Observe that book."

One of the heavy tomes lifted off the stack, floating in the air.

The other boys exclaimed under their breath at the sight. It wasn't as impressive as seeing the large chair whiz across the room, but Bobby had to admit that her control was good. Jean held the book in the air and ruffled through the pages, stopping on any she wished.

"By the power of thought, I'm able to move objects at will," she told them. "But it gets boring after a while, so I'll return the book, like this!"

The book snapped shut and slipped through the air, inserting itself neatly into the bookshelf.

"Thank you, Jean," the professor said with a smile. "And now let me tell you about my school. I was born of parents who had worked on the first atomic bomb project. Like yourselves, I am a mutant. I have the power to read minds, and to project my own thoughts into the brains of others. But when I was young, normal people feared me, distrusted me."

Bobby remembered when Professor X had told him the same thing on his first day at school, in this very study. He had felt so relieved to know he wasn't the only one who had been rejected by his people; to know that he would be accepted here.

"Here we stay," the Professor told Jean. "Unsuspected by normal humans, as we learn to use our powers for the benefit of mankind ... to help those who distrust us if they knew of our existence."

Jean was looking very serious, so the Professor gently reached out and took her gloved hand. "Due to an accident, I myself must remain in this chair, but I have many devices at my command, and through my mind, I am always in touch with my X-Men."

Jean smiled in return, clearly as relieved by the Professor's fatherly attitude as Bobby had been when he arrived several months ago.

The Professor nodded to the X-Men, his chair backing up slightly. "And now I leave you to get to know each other better."

Hank didn't even wait for Professor X to go before he made his move. He leaned over the back of Jean's chair.

"Let me be the first to welcome you to the X-Men, Beautiful! Mmmmm . . ."

"Oh!" Jean startled as Hank held her face with one large hand and planted a wet kiss on her cheek.

"Hank!" Warren protested, reaching out to grab the big hulk. "Take your paws off her."

Jean's eyes flashed in anger. "Don't worry, Warren! I'm not exactly helpless, as you can see."

Hank's feet flew out from under him as he was carried high up to the ceiling. His arms and legs wind-milled as he tried to catch his balance, hanging on nothing.

"For the luvva Pete!" Hank shouted as his head banged into the ceiling, making a hollow boom like the striking of a drum.

The expression on his face was so funny that Bobby laughed until he could hardly speak. He hung onto Warren for support. "Oh boy, what a gal! I hope she keeps that big ape up there forever."

Jean stood up, her fists clenched as she stared at Hank. His body started moving in little circles up near the ceiling, going faster and faster. It reminded Bobby of the training session earlier, but that time the Beast had been in control. Now he was tumbling and shouting for it to stop.

"Hey, c'mon!" Hank pleaded. "Have a heart! I was only trying to be friendly."

Jean spun him around faster until he was a blur. The other

guys were laughing now, and even Professor X was smiling. Bobby had never seen anything so funny.

"A fella could get dizzy up here," Hank cried out plaintively. "Lemme down, huh? This is embarrassing!"

Jean crossed her arms as if judging whether Hank had learned his lesson. "Very well, I'll let you down."

Hank spun one more time then his body did a complete somersault as Jean dropped him onto the couch. "There, you're down."

"Oooff!" Hank exclaimed as he hit the couch full force. It sounded like the impact broke all the springs.

Jean turned to Professor X, daintily adjusting her pillbox hat. "I hope I wasn't too rough on the poor dear."

"Not at all, Jean," the Professor assured her. "We don't use kid gloves here."

Not anymore, Bobby swore to himself, *at least not with me anymore. Not after that little display by the newest student!*

The Professor added, "We have to make our training as rough as possible to prepare ourselves for our mission in the outside world."

"That's what I've wanted to ask," Jean insisted. "Just what exactly is our real mission, sir?"

The Professor's smile faded, as serious issues crowded in again. "Jean there are many mutants walking the Earth and more are born each year. Not all of them want to help mankind. Some hate the human race and want to destroy it. Some feel that mutants should be the real rulers of Earth. It is our job to protect mankind from the evil mutants."

It was a pretty speech, Bobby thought. He had no reason to doubt Professor X's word, neither had he encountered any evil mutants. He had also wondered what the label "evil mutant" truly meant; after all, if he had unleashed his power and full strength on the people in his home town who wanted to hang him, and had killed many of them, would they have labeled him an "evil mutant?"

He didn't feel comfortable asking. He'd finally been allowed to join in the X-Men games after being left out for so long. Then this girl walks in the door and he was back to being the low man on the totem pole!

Something had better change soon, Bobby thought to himself. *I thought I was supposed to be some kind of super hero, not an ordinary schoolboy.*

Meanwhile just such a mutant prepared to strike a secret government laboratory known as Cape Citadel. Magneto had planned for months to unveil his power, to show the human race that it no longer held dominion over planet Earth—that the Day of the Mutants had dawned!

In the first phase of Magneto's plan, he parked his armored van outside Cape Citadel to monitor the launch of the mightiest rocket the government had ever built. He knew the government technicians were confident that nothing could prevent its successful flight. Magneto intended to make a mockery of their greatest effort and force homo sapiens bow to homo superior.

With an earth-shattering rumble, the rocket rose from its launch pad, the umbilicals falling away. White billowing smoke engulfed the launch tower as the rocket disappeared into the sky.

"Ahh!" Magneto drew on his power. "I can feel the irresistible waves of pure magnetic energy surging from me."

The energy gathered force and flowed from the horned helmet protecting his face and skull. His bulging muscles flexed under his skin-suit, sustaining the current.

"Now by exerting every iota of power, I can direct that energy upward . . . upward . . ."

Magneto could feel the path of the magnetic energy as it shot straight into the air, seeking the speeding missile. When the energy beam hit, the rocket was shoved off course, and began to wobble and dive.

Magneto shouted in victory as the missile sped back to Earth as fast as it had tried to leave, crashing into the nearby ocean. The dismay and confusion caused by his interference pleased him enough to continue his plan.

Over the next two days, using his magnetic power, Magneto wrecked havoc on the base. He shot down the missiles the base tried to launch and forced others missiles to ignite in their silos and explode overhead. The guns of the security officers went off by themselves. The seemingly magical acts unnerved the personnel on the base, and more security were brought in, giving Magneto more toys to play with.

He enjoyed their fear so much that he even wrote a warning in the sky and signed it so they would know who controlled them: "Surrender the base or I'll take it by force! Magneto."

When the military men didn't come out, Magneto boldly walked through the front gate, his cape flaring out behind him. The puny homo sapiens couldn't understand why their guns didn't fire and why they couldn't touch him.

Reinforcements could do nothing, there was no stopping Magneto. He could exert his will over them, containing them within a magnetic forcefield, moving them about at will. Quicker than even Magneto had imagined was possible, he took command of Cape Citadel.

Back at the world's most exclusive private school . . . the four male X-Men were sneaking up on their new team-mate, trying to find out what she was doing. She had pretty much kept to herself since her arrival the day before. But the door to her room was open, so they edged inside and down the short corridor.

"Where did the new doll go?" Hank whispered as he went first. "Oh, there she is!"

Bobby peered around the corner into Jean's room. She was absorbed in her reflection in the full-length mirror; wearing her new Marvel Girl outfit. Complete with mask, gloves, tights and high-heeled boots . . . it was enough to make Bobby's jaw drop.

Jean was talking to herself, "Mmmm . . . whoever designed this uniform could have given Christian Dior a run for his money."

"Wowee!" Bobby exclaimed under his breath. "Looks like she was poured into that uniform."

Jean whirled on them. "You again! Honestly, can't a girl have any privacy around here?"

Bobby sat back hard on his butt at the disdain in her eyes. He was relieved when Hank hustled to defend them. Both his hands were held out, as if to ward off Jean's wrath.

"Easy, gorgeous," Hank urged. "We were just passing by. Don't go getting mad..."

Jean was advancing on them, focused on the older boys, naturally! Bobby almost wanted to make a jerk out of himself like they were doing just to get her attention. Even if he ended up on the ceiling, at least he wouldn't be passed over—

A sharp command thought registered in his brain. From the expression on the others, they were receiving it too.

"Attention, X-Men! This is Professor Xavier. Report to my study immediately ... you have fifteen seconds. No excuses will be tolerated."

Warren was shaking his head. "Wow! Did all of you receive that mental blast?"

"And how!" Hank agreed. "It sounded like a trumpet's blare. Let's go!"

Jean was trying to hide her surprise at the telepathic communication. Bobby figured it was the mask that helped make her look cool and collected.

Exactly fifteen seconds later, they were all down in the Professor's study. The quiet room seemed different somehow. As if the Professor's tension was making everything look sharper and clearer.

He was oddly still. "I commend you for your punctuality. I have just heard a bulletin on the radio which concerns you."

"You're speaking aloud," Warren put in. "That means it's important."

Bobby thought to himself, *I never saw the Professor like this before ... so grim, so intense!*

28

The Professor raised one finger, looking at each of them in turn. "A crisis has occurred at Cape Citadel which leads me to believe the first of the evil mutants has made his appearance. This will be your baptism of fire!"

Fire! Bobby thought wildly. *Does that mean the Iceman isn't going?*

But the Professor was looking right at Bobby as he finished, "You are to go to the Cape and defeat him!"

"Yahhoo!" Bobby shouted out. "Action at last!"

"Gangway!" Angel called out as he raced past Bobby toward the stairs. Hank and Scott were right behind.

"Hah!" Bobby taunted after them. He instantly froze the molecules in the air of the study, drawing them to his body so they would cover him from head to foot. "I can get ready faster than the rest of you. All I have to do is ice up and put on my boots!"

He had the pleasure of seeing Jean Grey gasp in shock when she saw him covered in a thick layer of ice. Maybe that would teach her not to ignore him!

They piled into Professor X's fancy Rolls Royce which zipped them through traffic, finding gaps and gaining ground despite all barriers, taking them rapidly to the airport. On the way, Bobby couldn't think of anything but the mysterious evil mutant that waited for them down in Cape Citadel. They were off on their first mission as X-Men!

Bobby didn't want to seem nervous, so he nonchalantly commented, "It must have taken a heap of green stamps to buy a chariot like this."

Professor X's thoughts broke through to them all, "*No joking, please! Concentrate on your mission. Review your powers. Your foe is certain to be highly dangerous.*"

Minutes later, in the Professor's remote-control private jet, the X-Men and Marvel Girl were winging toward Cape Citadel at nearly the speed of sound.

Marvel Girl had her face pressed to the window. "You mean the Professor is guiding this plane from the ground ... by thought impulses? It's unbelievable!"

Even in the midst of their first mission, the Beast of course had to leer at Marvel Girl. "Look, doll ... when you join the X-Men, you realize nothing's unbelievable."

At Cape Citadel, Bobby saw military men huddled behind their tanks and mobile guns outside the gates. Grown men were quaking in fear as their artillery bombarded the installation. But he was Iceman, and he wasn't going to fail in his first mission. He would prove to the others that they needed him.

The hum of the magnetic barrier over the base became louder as they drew closer. They approached the head honcho wearing a metal helmet with one star, as the general ordered, "Cease firing! It's useless! We haven't anything in our arsenal that'll penetrate Magneto's magnetic forcefield."

The general looked tired with dirt streaks on his face from the sweat. It appeared the battle had been going on all night. His men looked even worse, bleary-eyed and desperate.

Cyclops took the lead, stepping into the ring of military men. "With due respect, General, I represent the X-Men. Perhaps we can help."

The general's aide tried to stop them, confusion filling his eyes. "X-Men? What the ... ?"

The general was obviously a practical man, not used to magical happenings on his watch. "Look, we're having enough trouble with one guy in a cornball costume. Who or what are the X-Men?"

"No time to explain, sir!" Cyclops replied. "I respectfully request you hold your fire for fifteen minutes while my partners and I go into action."

The general shook his head, but finally he motioned to his aid to let them through. "All right, we've nothing to lose. But I feel like a danged fool."

"You won't regret it, sir!" Cyclops thrust his fist into the air. "X-Men attack!"

That was the call to charge. Iceman ran through the ranks of men, using his freezing power to gently hustle them out of his way.

"Sorry men!" Bobby exclaimed. "I'll be out of here in a second and then you can warm up again. I'm saving my real big freeze for whoever's hiding behind that force field."

The Angel took wing above him, adding, "At last we'll have a chance to use all the training the Professor gave us."

Bobby had to admit that the Angel was an impressive sight, his curved wings spreading over their heads.

The soldiers cried out in surprise. "A walking snowman!" "That guy is flying above us!" Most of the others were ogling Marvel Girl in her remarkable uniform as she sprinted past them.

"What's next?" another moaned as the Beast jumped over his head.

"You'll see in a sec, soldier," the Beast laughed, "when I play leapfrog over you!"

Cyclops finished making his own way through the rank and file soldiers, using the power of his eyes to repel them away. "Sorry, boys! I'm in a hurry and this is the easiest way to clear a path for myself."

As they reached the forcefield, Professor X sent his thoughts into their minds. *"Use your energy beam at greater power, Cyclops! That magnetic field is stronger than it seems."*

Bobby was amazed at the strength of Professor X who was still in touch with them mentally despite the distance between them.

"Yes, sir, Professor!" Cyclops acknowledged out loud. "I'll increase the beam's intensity."

Kneeling down on one knee, Cyclops stared at the nearly invisible barrier between the X-Men and the base. He toggled the switch on the side of his visor opening it wider until it was almost at full intensity.

Bobby threw up an icy eye-shade, flinching back at the brightness of the beam. He had never seen Cyclops' power at this magnitude.

"I'm getting through!" Cyclops exclaimed. "That's what was needed . . . a natural counterforce to batter the unnatural magnetic field."

The brilliance was so blinding that Bobby had to turn away.

"And now I'll switch to maximum power!" Cyclops shouted.

Bobby could still see the bright spots of light despite his closed eyes. He didn't know how Cyclops could stand it . . .

"I can only maintain this for a few seconds, but . . ." Cyclops let out a cry. "I did it!"

The humming tension of the magnetic forcefield shattered. Bobby felt a surge of confidence. They were the X-Men, and they could beat this rogue mutant with one hand tied behind their backs!

But Cyclops slumped to the ground groaning. The Beast picked up his limp body in one arm and started running toward the base. "Cyclops almost knocked himself out but he got us in here! Now let's prove we can carry the ball."

Marvel Girl was right by Iceman's side as they sprinted toward the launch towers. He gave her a victorious grin, but she was looking down at Cyclops in concern. The Angel glided ahead as their advance force, keeping a sharp eye out for their foe.

The shaking of the ground was their only warning.

Fiery blasts abruptly shot from the ground as the silos opened up. Five of the most sophisticated heat-seeking weapons ever created soared into the air. Their white contrails dipped through the perfect blue sky as the missiles dived and zeroed in on the X-Men.

"Angel!" Iceman called out, but the winged man had already seen his danger.

Folding his wings, Angel dived and swerved. "Got to dodge them somehow!" Despite his efforts, the missiles stayed on target. "It's no use, they're too fast—gaining on me!"

Bobby couldn't just stand there! Summoning his power, Iceman forced his hands to grow several large grenades of ice that were pressure-packed for extra punch. "Hang on, Angel! I can help you while they're still in range."

Bobby hurled the ice grenades at the missiles as they shot overhead. He willed them to connect with the heat-seeking weapons. They couldn't miss—it was Angel's only chance!

The grenades exploded on impact, expanding exponentially until the missiles were nearly covered by ice. Two, three . . . no, four of the missiles were hit.

"Bulls-eye!" Bobby exclaimed.

Marvel Girl was shrieking in delight along with the Beast's bellows. Even Cyclops had recovered enough to admire his work.

The ice-coated missiles began to fall.

"The ice covered their noses, keeping 'em from exploding," Bobby told them. "Now with their guidance systems knocked out, they've got to drop to the ground."

"Oh, no!" Marvel Girl exclaimed, pointing into the sky. "Watch out, Angel!"

Iceman turned away from the satisfying sight of the missiles falling harmlessly to the ground. But there was one missile he had missed. His heart sank when he saw it was homing in on Angel, who was coming back around in his losing battle with the high-tech weapon.

"Can't keep dodging it much longer!" Angel shouted.

Iceman smashed his icy fists together. It was too far away for him to hit it with an ice grenade! He had failed . . . he had let his team down and now Angel was going to die—

"Angel!" the Beast bellowed. With a few agile leaps, he was climbing the main launch tower. "Lower . . . fly lower! Come towards me! Hurry!"

With a great push, the Beast soared into the air, grabbing onto the top arm of the launch tower. The umbilicals fell down as he swung around a few times, knocking everything out of his way.

Angel was dipping and swooping, forcing the missile to overshoot him and return. "Okay Beast! But what . . . ?"

As he dived past the launch tower, the Beast swung up and over the launch arm. The missile was a streak in the air; it looked too fast for the Beast.

"Just wait and see, pal!" Beast cried out as he caught the missile.

Iceman thought it was going to explode, and he prepared to fling a shield of ice over the other X-Men to protect them from falling flames.

The Beast's grunt was audible even from that height. "Nah!"

As he swung back down the launch arm, the slender heat-seeking missile was clutched between his prehensile feet. "Got it!" the Beast cried out triumphantly.

"Good work, Beast," Marvel Girl called. "Now, release it! I'll take over now."

Using her amazing telekinetic power, Marvel Girl mentally hurled the missile into the ocean. It looped high into the air and when it crashed into the waves almost beyond sight, a tremendous explosion reached into the sky.

Iceman shuddered at the thought of what would have happened if it had exploded in the Beast's clutches. He might look like a clumsy hulk, but that catch said a lot for his control!

Angel was gliding overhead, keeping an eagle eye out for the next attack. "There he is! I've found him!"

The other X-Men turned to look, trying to locate Magneto. But Angel didn't wait. "X-Men attack!"

Iceman, Cyclops and Marvel Girl ran around the launch tower as the Beast nimbly scurried across the upper catwalk. "There he is!"

Iceman heard a strangely deep voice, intoning, "Wrong, you flying fool! It is I, Magneto, who have found you!"

Always sensitive to the air molecules, Iceman could feel the disturbance rippling around him. Things began streaking past them and rising into the air; empty canisters and barrels, construction material, I-beams and metal struts, loose hardware and even old tires rushed inward.

"See how I can stop your flight by magnetically hurling every nearby object which is not bolted down!" Magneto bragged.

"This guy is starting to get on my nerves," Bobby muttered. If only he could see this elusive Magneto, he could show him a thing or two about hell freezing over...

Angel was surrounded by the stuff, imprisoned by the interlocking pieces. His wings folded and he began to tumble along with the tangled mess.

"Don't congratulate yourself too soon, Magneto," Cyclops shouted. "See how easily I can remove your magnetized junk with my energy beam!"

At one beam from his blazing eyes, and the bits of refuse burst apart like they were confetti, releasing Angel. Marvel Girl was kept busy catching falling debris with her telekinesis and tossing it away from the X-Men below.

"Much obliged, Cyclops." Angel came low to hover over their heads. "Magneto can't have gone far. Let's find him now."

From behind the launch tower came a low and ominous laugh as Magneto stepped out from behind a huge rocket fuel booster. Iceman almost choked in surprise—amusement not fear. It was just some nutball mutant in a funny helmet and a costume a mad dictator would wear to fight Captain America in a World War II newsreel.

"Not all those with mutant powers are fit to rule the earth," Magneto announced. "You must be destroyed!"

Then Bobby saw it just like he had seen that bowling ball rushing at him yesterday during his first training session. Everything seemed to slow and the massive rocket fuel booster looked as if was moving toward him through a vat of molasses.

"Heads up, X-Men!" Iceman called. "Here comes trouble."

Professor X had been right, Bobby thought. *This was indeed the baptism of fire for the X-Men. Why oh why, couldn't the Professor have called it something else? An initiation, a debut, an entrance, an unveiling . . . , but no, the good old Professor had to use the word "fire.* It may have sounded okay at the time but it wasn't

35

making Iceman happy, especially if those words came true in the form of a highly explosive gasoline mixture rushing toward the X-Men.

Well, I swore yesterday that something better happen to change things or I'd die of boredom. I'm not bored right now. Terrified, maybe, but not bored.

And everyone was watching, not just his classmates, but all those soldiers with their infrared and spy devices, and the newsmen with their video cameras and zoom lenses. No doubt they were wondering if they could get their hands on him to find out why he was different. After all, the last time he had been forced to use his powers where people could see him, he had been chased through the streets by angry citizens bearing torches like he was in some bad horror movie.

Then—it was almost laughable, Bobby thought, if it weren't so painful—then they had tried to hang him, along with Cyclops who had come to convince him to join Professor X's little coffee clatch. They had known him for years around that town, and they still called him a monster. Bobby had just wanted to have fun with his power, and maybe help out a friend or two in a bad spot. What was with people?

And with that rocket fuel rushing towards all of them, Bobby thought, isn't it a bad sign that my life is flashing before my eyes?

"Can't get out of the way in time!" Bobby said. Then he did what he did best; he created a ice shield to protect them. "Only one thing to do. Stay close together and I'll cover us with an ice igloo shield."

Cyclops crouched next to him as the shield hardened over their heads. "He's ignited the rocket fuel. It's going to blow up!"

Iceman got the shield sealed just before the canister collided. Cyclops aimed his eyes downward and punched a hole directly into the concrete pad, opening up a path into the vast control room below.

"Jump!" Marvel Girl cried out.

A blazing inferno hit them along with the shock wave of the explosion.

Bobby was falling, but he realized Marvel Girl was holding them all up, gently wafting them down. Cyclops focused his eyes on the hole above them, blocking the flames from shooting in after them.

"Nice catch," the Beast said admiringly. For once he didn't call her "doll" or "gorgeous." Iceman figured he wasn't the only X-Men who had to "sink or swim" or "run the gauntlet" today—or any of the other metaphors Professor X could have used other than "trial by fire!"

"Now, let's get back up there and finish this guy off!" Cyclops announced. He turned his eyes toward another part of the ceiling, and began to blast his way through. "Marvel Girl, take us up!"

They could hear Magneto gloating up above, "The heat is so intense! Wait . . . that beam . . . from beneath the ground! What . . . what does it mean?"

With a final flick of his visor, Cyclops burst through the concrete pad, sending a shower of debris over Magneto. The X-Men emerged, each fighting in their own way; Cyclops hit him with the full force of his eyes while Iceman tossed a barrage of ice grenades, hitting Magneto in the chest.

Angel flew directly towards him. "It means you're finished, Magneto!"

Magneto shot straight into the air. "You haven't defeated me yet! I can still escape you, flying by means of magnetic repulsion."

Angel took off after Magneto, but he immediately crashed into an invisible barrier.

"Ugh! He created another magnetic forcefield." Angel pushed against it, straining his wings. "Can't get through!"

"Don't worry, Angel," Marvel Girl called. "We'll breach it in no time."

Cyclops was already boring his eye-beam into the magnetic field, causing it to ripple under the onslaught. It only took them a few minutes to breach the barrier, but by that time . . .

"He's gone," Angel exclaimed in dismay. "But where?"

"A mutant with his powers?" Cyclops asked wearily. "He could be anywhere. But at least we've beaten him for now."

The X-men reformed at the general's side. Angel landed last, having taken a final reconnaissance flight to be sure the base was cleared of all evil mutants. "Your base is operational again, General. Magneto is gone."

"Uncanny!" The general looked years younger with his eyes open wide in shock. "Your fifteen minutes aren't up yet."

Iceman shuffled his feet modestly as the media moved in, their cameras flashing.

The general recovered himself and took control in front of his troops and the viewing public. "You call yourselves the X-Men! I will not ask you to reveal your true identities, but I promise you that before this day is over, the name X-Men will be the most honored in my command."

"Thank you sir," Angel replied for them. He was the most photogenic, after all, with Marvel Girl posing by his side. "And should America's security ever again be threatened, the X-Men will be back."

Iceman harumphed to himself, wondering why Jean never looked in his direction. So what if his ice-suit was a little lumpy? He had saved them all with his ice shield—he was part of the team. What did it take to impress a girl these days?

It wasn't until they were back in the remote controlled jet that Bobby began to appreciate what he had accomplished. He felt pretty good when Professor X mentally told them, *"Well done, students. You have justified all our long hours of training . . . all our sacrifices . . . all our dreams! Now, return to me, my X-Men!"*

A few weeks later, one dreary December Saturday, Bobby Drake walked through the snow-covered streets of Manhattan, strongly resenting the warm down overcoat he wore. The last thing he had to worry about was cold weather, not since his Iceman powers had shown up. *But,* he thought sadly, *going outside in five degree weather in shorts and a T-shirt was about the same as wearing a sign that said "I'm A Mutant. Kick Me."*

So he walked north toward Central Park, the unnecessary collar of his unnecessary coat turned up, unnecessarily, against the cold.

When he thought about why he was going to the park he cheered up a bit. Cheryl Fenn was gong to meet him there. Since he had finally been accepted as one of the X-Men team and was being included in the regular training sessions, Bobby had been able to focus on the other dissatisfaction in life—no girls. With the one girl at Professor X's school kept busy fending off the three older guys, Bobby was feeling left out again.

So when he ran into Cheryl last week, at an ice cream shop of all places, he'd turned on all of what he liked to think of as his natural charm.

Amazingly, far more amazing to Bobby than being able to form ice out of thin air, she had said yes, and suggested they meet for a walk in Central Park, to enjoy the cool air and look at the icicles hanging from the trees. *She seems to like ice,* Bobby thought as he walked up sixth avenue toward the park, *and that has to be a good sign.*

When he got to the park Cheryl wasn't around. *But then I'm early,* he thought. *When you have only one date every six months, you don't take any chances.* He breathed deeply, enjoying the cool air and the scenery.

"Hi, stranger!" a voice said from behind him, and he turned to see Cheryl, right on time. She had brown hair, was almost as tall as he was, and her wide smile made her pretty face momentarily stunning.

"Hi there!" Bobby said, turning on his charm switch, "cold enough for you?"

"Almost." Cheryl smiled again. "I like the cold. But I'm getting chilly standing here. Shall we walk?"

"Sure."

Bobby lead the way, his feet sure as they walked across the snow-and-ice covered paths of the park. There was gentle wind blowing, enough to make the icicles hanging from the tree branches chime gently in the breeze. Everything was coated in silvery ice and white show, with only the dark gray tree trunks and wrought iron fences forming an underlying structure. The temperature began to fall a bit, although the sun was still out.

"So, where do you go to school?" Bobby asked.

"Hunter High School," Cheryl answered, and started in about classes, her friends, and her teachers, a detailed description of the kind of normal high school like Bobby could only read about in Archie comic books.

"Sorry," she said, after a minute. "This stuff must be really boring to you. Tell me about your school."

They walked on for a minute in silence, as Bobby thought about what to say. He noticed it was getting still colder, even though the breeze was gentle. But cold wasn't something he cared about that much.

What can I tell her, he thought. *See, I go to school with this guy with wings, and this other guy who wears glasses all the time not 'cause he's a geek but because if he didn't he'd wreck the place with power beams, and this other guy who's a genius but looks kind of like a gorilla and walks on the ceiling. And the only girl there is so gorgeous that she wouldn't even look at him—but at last he thought of something he could say.*

"Well, these guys I hang out with are all loony over this one girl, Jean. Especially my friend Slim, but I'm not sure what she thinks—" That seemed to do the trick.

It kept getting colder as he talked. He wasn't sure how it happened, but Cheryl put her arm around him and started cuddling close for warmth. It made him feel like he was ten feet tall.

"You're a really nice guy," Cheryl said, snuggling closer and looking up at him. "You listen, and you're funny. Why don't we go someplace warmer and—"

Cheryl stopped, looking at something behind Bobby. With quick reflexes, he turned and saw what it was at once: A naked man stood on the great lawn. He was hairy but human, his long shaggy locks flowing down the back of his neck, and his beard covered with ice. As they watched, the naked man started screaming that he was cold.

"Put something on, then!" a man jogging by shouted back. "You'll freeze your chestnuts off!"

"I will be warm!" the man screamed, and raised his hands. An electric blue light surrounded him in a sphere, then expanded over the snowy meadow.

Where the blue field touched, things suddenly froze like they were dipped in liquid Nitrogen. The ground cracked open, trees shattered, a fire hydrant exploded into plumes of water that first froze into ice, then shattered into dust.

As Bobby and Cheryl watched, the blue field slipped toward them. "Run!" Bobby shouted, giving Cheryl a shove back down the path. He hoped she'd just keep running. He hoped she wouldn't turn and see what he had to do next.

But she did.

"Come on!" she shouted at him. "What are you doing?"

"What I can," Bobby said sadly. He raised his own hands, and at once they were covered with ice.

Cheryl screamed. *Of course she did*, Bobby thought, *what else do you do when you see a mutant?* The ice flowed down his body, freezing and then shattering his clothes until they fell away, leaving his body covered with a thick, icy armor.

He turned toward Cheryl. "Let me get you out of here," he said. She was frozen, not with cold but with fear. Bobby—Iceman—gestured and an iceslide formed under his feet. He moved toward Cheryl faster than the freezing field coming after them. He grabbed her and held her to him, as he slid quickly past the trees and screaming people to the edge of the park. He dropped her off and turned back.

"Wait," she said, "I'm sorry I screamed. I thought you were frozen. You're a mutant, right? Iceman?"

"Yup." *I'd deny it if I could,* Bobby thought. *But right now, that would be a little hard to believe.*

"Cool."

"What?" The noise exploding trees drowned out what Cheryl was trying to say. "Listen, I have to go deal with this guy; I'll be right back."

"Okay."

Iceman turned back to the park. The blue field was fading, leaving devastation behind. The park looked unearthly, like the plains of a dead and frozen world. Trees were splintered with their limbs scattered around them. Benches and fences were torn up and twisted like a tornado had come through Central Park.

With the field now down, Bobby slid gracefully toward the hairy, naked man at the center of it all. He was huddled around himself like a man trying to keep warm.

"I'm cold," he muttered, "So cold."

"Excuse me," Iceman said to him. "Could I get you some hot cocoa or something? Or would you rather just sit here in the park freezing things?"

For a moment, it seemed the man didn't hear him. *Maybe I can just pack him in ice and getting him out of here,* Bobby thought. Professor X will know what to do with him.

Then the man turned. "You!" he shouted, "Frost Giant! You who stole the heat from my body! You have dared to follow me! Well, you have taken my heat, so now I will take yours!"

Uh-oh, Bobby thought, *this guy's crazy. Why do they all have to be crazy?*

The man pointed a finger at Bobby, and blue light started to glow on the tip. An ice-shield formed in front of Bobby almost faster than he thought of it. Good reflexes, he congratulated himself. Always had good reflexes.

The blue light leapt from the man's finger and struck Bobby's shield, which cracked in the cold. Bobby concentrated. The shield became a wall of ice but still the blue beamed poured on, not just freezing the ice-block in its path but taking all heat from it, stopping all the motion of its molecules, destroying its atomic cohesion.

Bobby kept the ice forming in front of him, just barely holding back the cold blue light. It reminded him of their trial by fire a few weeks ago, but then he had the other X-Men to rely on. Now, it was just him. Would he find out that being Iceman was not enough in a crisis?

The field began to spread, to circle around the iceblocks he put up.

Iceman got cold.

Bobby had always loved the cold. Even as a kid, a three-year-old, he'd run naked into the snow, worrying his poor mother to distraction. On a Boy Scout trip at the age of ten he'd gotten lost and fallen into an ice-fed mountain stream—and freaked out the Troop Leader who found his clothes drying on bank while Bobby swam happily in the frigid water.

It had taken him a long time to realize that other people hated the cold, found it fearful and threatening. When at puberty his ice-powers manifested he actually hadn't been very surprised. . . .

Once again proving that when his life was threatened, he would sit back viewing home movies for a while until he pulled himself together. He's have to mention this little freak to Professor X . . . it could be costly some time.

Now the cold of the blue light surrounded him, drawing heat from his body. For the first time cold was his enemy.

I am not *going to freeze to death*, Bobby thought, *I am* not. That would just be too damn ironic. He could feel himself getting colder, being chilled to the bone. Each breath he took sucked even more heat out of him. He dropped the icewall and surrounded himself with a white sphere of ice. It won't hold long, Bobby thought, but maybe long enough for me to think of something.

Okay, he thought, this guy eats heat. Where's Jonny Storm when you need him? Maybe the Human Torch could feed him more heat than he could swallow. But how could an Iceman out-ice him?

An idea came to him. Before he could talk himself out of it, Bobby dropped the sphere that was his only protection and threw himself directly into the blue field.

It got colder, and still colder, and colder still. Bobby could feel his arms and legs getting number with cold, but still he slid toward the man. The naked man's eyes went wild. He concentrated, and the blue field took even more heat from Bobby's body. But still Iceman kept on. This was his only chance. Cut the crazy off from all sources of heat, and keep it up until he froze. *Mano a mano* . . . or rather, mutant against mutant. . . .

When he stood in the air only inches from the man, Bobby raised his hands and called to the ice. Called to it more strongly than he ever had before. It came. The ice covered the man, then shattered and the man broke free. Bobby covered him again, head to toe. Again he broke free, and again Bobby covered him in ice.

At last the crazy mutant tired. The ice covered him and he stayed covered. But Bobby didn't stop, he didn't dare. He piled the ice taller and deep and wider. The blue field cut off but still Bobby added ice to what was first a tower, then a hill, then a small mountain. Frozen to the spot he added ice until there was a tap on his shoulder. It was Cheryl. He stopped, and turned to her.

"It's over," she said.

"I'm cold," Bobby answer, and collapsed to his knees as the ice shield fell from his body. Cheryl pulled him to her and shared her warmth with him. Finally, Bobby was satisfied.

"You handled that very well, Bobby." Praise from Professor Charles Xavier was rare. "You saved the park, and hundreds of lives. I'm proud of you. Have you recovered from your ordeal? Is there anything more we can do for you?"

"Well, there is one thing—" Bobby started to say.

"Yes?"

Wrapped in thick down blankets, Bobby sat huddled near the

radiator in the school's living room, holding a near-boiling mug of herb tea. Under his blankets he was wearing a warm woolen sweater, and under that thermal underwear.

"Could you turn the heat up around here?"

1970s

FIRM COMMITMENTS

by Sholly Fisch

For the fourth time in ten minutes, Jay Sanford checked his watch. There was more than an hour left until the interview, but he'd figured that it would make a better impression to be an hour early than a minute late. He shifted in his chair and, for the eighth time, pulled his tight collar away from his neck and adjusted his tie. Five years of graduate school hadn't exactly left him comfortable wearing a suit and tie.

Of course, it wasn't just the tie that was making Jay uncomfortable. It wasn't every day that a newly-minted Ph.D. landed a job interview with a company as prestigious as Genetech. In its relatively brief history, the New York-based company had already built a reputation among those in the field as a leader in cutting-edge research. In the right circles, the name "Genetech" carried almost as much weight as the Brand Corporation or Stark Enterprises. The word was that they took only the best and the brightest, and competition for any opening was fierce. A position with Genetech would open doors for Jay, where otherwise, it could take years for him to even reach the threshold.

And besides, he needed a job.

Pretending to adjust the briefcase on his lap, Jay snuck a glance at the one other candidate who was sitting in the Human Resources waiting area, a few chairs down from his own. Jay assumed that the stranger was scheduled for the appointment that preceded his. The only question was whether he was up for the same job.

Jay hoped not. He found his neighbor intimidating, and not just because of the air of sheer confidence and ease that he radiated. No, the intimidation came at least as much from the sheer size of the guy. Even based on only a few surreptitious glances, Jay estimated that he must have weighed at least three hundred pounds, and it looked like it was all muscle. If he'd had fur, the guy would have borne a striking resemblance to a gorilla—a gorilla with close-cut hair and glasses. Not to mention the book he was reading . . .

"It's Latin," his neighbor said with a smile.

Jay recoiled in his chair.

The man's smile turned into a broad grin. "My heartfelt apologies for startling you," he said, "but I couldn't help noticing your gaze resting on the cover. It's Latin. A facsimile edition of Gregor Mendel's records, documenting his original experiments in herbaceous genetics, to be precise. Naturally, I had previously encountered excerpts in English, but with a seminal work such as this, no translation can take the place of the original vernacular, don't you think?"

Jay tried to form words, but somehow, none came to mind.

"Oh, but where are my manners?" The man extended the most enormous hand Jay had ever seen in his life. "Allow me to introduce myself. Henry P. McCoy."

Jay shook his hand, watching his own hand disappear into McCoy's surprisingly gentle grip. "I'm, uh, Jay. Jay Sanford." He paused, waiting until his hand reappeared, then asked the question that he dreaded: "Are you, uh . . . are you interviewing for the research slot, Mister McCoy?"

"Hank, please. Yes, I fear I am. I take it that means we find ourselves in competition, eh?"

"Uh, yeah, I guess so." Jay felt as though his IQ had just dropped fifty points by comparison.

"Well, may the best man win. Would your field of endeavor lie in genetics as well?"

"No, neurology. Actually, my dissertation research had to do with action potentials of efferent cells." Now that the conversation was turning onto familiar ground, Jay found himself warming to his subject. "You know, the electrical-chemical transfer of messages between nerve cells? But I guess you're more interested in genetics, huh?"

"Yes, although I must say your work sounds fascinating as well. My particular specialization lies in the study of mutation. If all goes well, I hope one day to isolate the genetic cause of mutation."

"Uh . . . really?" Jay felt his IQ starting to dip again. "Where— uh, where did you study?"

"Oh, a small private academy. Not an institution whose name would prove familiar. However . . ."

"Mister McCoy?" said the receptionist, interrupting. "Mister Willis will see you now."

"Right on the dot," Hank said. He rose from his seat and smoothed out his jacket. "Well, once more into the fray. The utmost good fortune to you, Jay. It has been a pleasure to make your acquaintance."

"Yeah, you too," said Jay. And much to his own surprise, he discovered that he really meant it. Hank seemed like such a genuinely nice guy that, even if he was the competition, Jay just couldn't bring himself to hate him.

Of course, when Hank still hadn't emerged from the inner office after more than an hour, and Jay's appointment was running twenty minutes late, he started to reconsider his opinion. He was almost ready to give up and leave when the office door finally opened.

To Jay's dismay, the smiling Hank was being escorted out of the room by a middle-aged man who looked as though he'd spent the better part of the last hour in a very good mood. ". . . really hold *thirty-seven* patents, Hank?"

"Blushingly, I would have to respond in the affirmative. Chalk it up to an overly active penchant for tinkering. However, that's not to say that all of the devices proved equally useful," Hank said with a chuckle. "For instance, I once invented an apparatus to open popcorn bags noiselessly in movie theaters.

"It had only one flaw—it occupied three rows of the theater!"

Willis laughed heartily and clasped Hank's hand with both of his own. "Well, thanks so much for coming down today, Hank. I expect that we'll be in touch very soon."

"I anticipate it eagerly, Marty. Best of luck with that golf game." Hank gave a friendly wave to Jay, turned toward the door, and left.

Willis shook his head with a smile as he watched Hank leave. He took a breath, composing himself, and turned to Jay. "Now, then, Mister . . . Stamford?"

"Sanford."

"Oh yes, Sanford. I'm sorry. Won't you come in?"

I'm dead, thought Jay as he followed Willis into the office.

A few days later, Jay was sprawled across the sofabed in his studio apartment, lounging in his underwear and watching cartoons, when the phone rang. He struggled to swallow a mouthful of peanut butter and stuck the spoon back in the jar as he reached for the phone.

"Huwwow?" he mumbled into the phone, swallowing.

"Jay? This is Martin Willis at Genetech."

In a flash, Jay leaped to his feet and forced the peanut butter down his throat. "Oh, Mister Willis! How are you?" He hit the "mute" button on the remote control just as the anvil landed on the coyote.

"Fine, fine, thank you. Jay, how would you like a job with Genetech?"

Jay's mouth responded before his brain could even register what was happening. "Absolutely! Yes, sir! Thank you!"

Even through the telephone, he could hear the chuckle in Willis's voice. "Well, we should probably discuss salary and terms before you make any final decisions..."

Jay smacked himself in the head and cursed himself silently: *Of course you should! Idiot!*

"But," Willis continued, "I think you'll be very happy with our offer."

Jay took a moment to pull himself together before he spoke. He felt a little wary of appearing too desperate or sounding like a total moron. "I'm sure you're right," he said, "but absolutely, let's discuss it further. I'm very interested in the possibility."

Jay hesitated for a moment, considering whether to ask the question that was burning in his brain. His common sense told him that it was inappropriate.

But then, his curiosity got the best of him. "Uh, Mister Willis, I'm sorry if this is out of place, but I have to ask..."

"Certainly. What would you like to know?"

"Well... uh... why me?"

"Why... you're a very talented young man, you show a great deal of potential, you made an excellent impression on the team here..."

"No, I understand that—I mean, thank you. But I was certain that Hank McCoy was a shoo-in for the job."

"Ah. Naturally, I can't discuss other candidates in any detail. Let's just say that your research interests fit more closely into our current agenda." Willis paused for a beat. "Also, I gather that Mister McCoy has taken a position with the Brand Corporation."

Ohhhhh, thought Jay, the light dawning. Well, sloppy seconds was better than not getting invited to the table at all. Besides, if Hank had landed himself a job at Brand, then it was good news all around, wasn't it?

Jay's first few weeks at Genetech flew by in a happy blur. The staff was small—no more than one hundred people—which was small enough for him to have come to know pretty much everyone by face, if not by name. The small size also meant that, as he quickly found, Genetech's reputation for "the best and the brightest" was no exaggeration. Even walking the hallways, he could feel the air thick with ideas and inspiration. Sure, some of his colleagues might have been a little odd, but he found himself routinely impressed by the sheer brainpower of everyone around him. And when he needed a break from being an intellectual, there were enough folks with whom Jay could also talk about baseball or cartoons to keep him satisfied.

In Jay's opinion, though, the thing that still kept him feeling like a kid on Christmas morning was the remarkable facilities that Genetech had for research. As section manager, Marty Willis proved to be a boss who provided support when needed but otherwise preferred to back off and give his people the necessary latitude to pursue their research. Jay enjoyed total access to equipment that made his grad school tools look like antiques. Best of all, Genetech's enormous bank of donor cells provided endless opportunities for new discovery. The secrets were just waiting to be unlocked, and Jay had everything he'd need to find the keys.

When Willis first introduced Jay to the facility and gave him a tour of the donor bank, he called special attention to the area that housed a collection of mutant cells. Much as the newscasts about the "Mutant Menace" made it seem otherwise, Jay knew that the true incidence of mutation among the general population was extremely low. That fact, coupled with the fraction of people who typically donate cells to research, meant that Genetech's mutant cells were a rare treasure. Jay had been handed an opportunity that few scientists ever got to experience. It was no wonder that Jay gravitated straight toward these cells as the focus of his neurological research.

It was that very research that sent Jay racing into Willis's office that morning. Seconds later, he was pulling Willis back to the lab to show him what he had found.

"All right, Jay," said Willis, an edge of amusement in his voice.

"Now, what's so important that you had to pull me away from the annual report?"

"I . . . well, it'll be easier to show you. Take a look at this," Jay said. He gestured toward a fairly simple set-up. A set of tiny electrodes were connected to one end of a single neuron. A second set of electrodes had been carefully attached at the other end as well. "Now, we know that every neuron has a certain resting potential —a minimal level of electrical charge—and exhibits a slightly higher charge when it conducts a message."

"The action potential. Right."

"Okay, now, normally, the resting potential of many axons ranges around negative 70 millivolts, right? And the action potential peaks around 30 millivolts."

"All right, still nothing new."

"But here's the thing. Over the past few weeks, I've been playing around with some of the mutant cells. Know what I found?"

"What?"

Jay shrugged. "Nothing. They acted just like the normal cells. Same basic effects and ranges.

"*But*," he said, pausing for dramatic effect, "today, I tried a mutant cell from a different donor. An efferent cell that would be connected to effectors in the body.

"Watch this. I've got this set of probes set up here to deliver a standard 30 millivolt charge to simulate neural transmission, and the second set connected down at the end of the axon to measure the charge it would pass on to the neighboring cell."

Willis glanced at the equipment and tried to hide a pained smile. "Um, Jay, before you go on, maybe you should change the meter. You've got the wrong one hooked up." He pointed at the device connected at the far end of the cell. "This one's calibrated much too high. You need to be measuring in millivolts, not volts."

Jay grinned. "You'd think so, wouldn't you?" he said. He set the probe to a charge of 30 millivolts and gave the cell a quick jolt. Instantly, the readout on the second meter jumped as well.

"One thousand volts!" Jay read. "A *thirty-six hundred percent increase* from the stimulus!"

Willis's jaw hung open. "But . . . but that's not possible . . ."

"I know," said Jay. "Conservation of energy says that the output can't exceed the input. But that's exactly what it's doing! Which means the additional charge has to be coming from somewhere else."

"But where?"

"I'm guessing the cell itself. Clearly, this cell isn't just transmitting electrochemical messages. It's adding to them somehow. See, if I try it again—" He gave the cell a second jolt. "—it doesn't happen. It needs time to regenerate. Maybe it's drawing energy from the light like a solar battery, or who knows what.

"So then I asked myself, why only *this* cell? Why not the other mutant cells?"

"Good question."

"I checked the donor records. They're anonymous, of course, but they do include information on the particular manifestation of the mutation in each donor. Some of the others came either from latent mutants, who exhibited genetic abnormalities but no noticeable signs. The others came from donors whose manifestations were primarily physical. Enhanced strength, flight, that sort of thing.

"This was the first one from someone whose mutation involves the ability to discharge energy."

Willis nodded quietly. He eyed the neuron carefully for a moment, considering it, then looked back at Jay.

"Jay," he said, "this is big. Neurons that produce more energy than they take in . . . No one's ever even thought of such a thing."

Willis clapped him on the shoulder. "I'll pass on word to the people upstairs. They'll want to talk to you, I'm sure," Willis said. "But in the meantime, you need to keep working on this. See what else you can find out. Figure out how it works."

Willis walked to the door, then turned back to face Jay with a grin. "You know," he said, "it's too bad you can't hook mutants up to car engines. We could solve the energy crisis!"

"Working late again, eh, dear?"

"Oh, hi, Rosa." Jay straightened up in his chair and stretched with a grunt. He hit "print" on his computer and shoveled a last bite of Chinese food into his mouth before dropping the empty cardboard container into the garbage. He handed the waste basket to the elderly cleaning woman. "Yeah, 'fraid so."

Jay had been working late a lot lately. In the months since he made his big discovery, he'd started to appreciate just how much more there was to know. Now that he knew what to look for, the discoveries were coming fast and furious. The "Sanford Effect," as Willis had taken to calling it—mostly to tease Jay—was true of cells in all of the mutant donors. You just had to know where to look. For mutants with mental powers like telepathy, it was in the brain cells. For those with enhanced physical abilities, it was in the efferent cells that controlled their muscles. And so on.

However, for every question that Jay's research answered, it also raised a dozen more that begged to be investigated. One by one, the puzzle pieces seemed like they were finally starting to fall into place.

"Well, you should go home soon, dear. You're too young to spend your whole life at work."

"Don't worry, I'm heading out in a couple of minutes," he replied. "I just need to drop off this report, and then I'm outta here."

They walked out into the hall together. "That's the spirit," Rosa said. "Do you need me to open up Mister Willis's office for you?"

"Sure, thanks. I'll just leave this for him to read in the morning."

Reaching into the deep pocket of her smock, Rosa produced a ring of passkeys and opened the door marked "Martin Willis" before moving on down the hall. Jay thanked her again and wished her a good night before stepping into the darkened office. He scribbled a brief note at the top of the cover page and lay the report down on the cluttered desk.

Which is when the open folder on Willis's desk caught his eye. Jay stared at the papers for a moment, his brow furrowed in thought. A moment later, he was skimming through the other papers beneath them. By the time he absently laid it all back on the desk, his face looked drawn and ashen.

"Oh, my God . . ."

"Federal Bureau of Investigation," said the crisp, authoritative voice on the phone. "Special Agent Burke."

"Uh, yes, hi," said Jay. "I need to report something."

"I can take that report for you, sir. Let's start with your name."

The words spilled out in a rush as Jay spoke quickly in a hushed tone. Even though he was back home and calling from the safety of his apartment, he couldn't shake the feeling of dread that had followed him for the past few hours, ever since he read the confidential file on Willis's desk. The sooner someone took care of this, and the sooner Jay was out of it, the better he'd like it.

"Let me confirm that I've understood your account correctly, Doctor Sanford," Burke said, after Jay had finished his story. "You say that you have reason to believe that your employer, Genetech, is involved in a covert plot involving mutants."

"Yes."

"Specifically, that Genetech is using mutants as . . . human power sources?"

"Yes, that's right. I found blueprints for a device powered by living mutants."

"You further believe that these mutants would be unwilling participants in this process."

"Well, I can't imagine anyone just letting themselves be turned into a battery, can you? I'd been assuming that all the mutant donor cells at Genetech had been given by voluntary donors. But now, I'm not so sure."

"Doctor Sanford, do you have copies of these blueprints in your possession?"

"No, I didn't think to make any. I was so shocked when I found out what was going on, I just didn't think. I was too worried about getting out of there before someone found me."

"I understand. Did anyone else see these plans?"

"Well, I'm sure that the people who are in on it have seen them, of course. But anyone else?" Jay thought for a moment and shook his head. "No, not that I know of. The cleaning woman, Rosa, let me into the office, but she left before I read the file."

Burke sighed. "Doctor, you seem like an intelligent man. I'm sure you know how this must sound."

"What do you mean?" Jay said, a little indignant. "I'm not crazy!"

"I never said you were, sir. However, you have no hard evidence. There are no corroborating witnesses. You don't even know for certain whether such a device has been built, or whether the 'power sources' involved would be willing participants. I'm afraid that, with the information currently on hand, there's very little we can do."

Jay was quiet for a while. "I see," he said. "So what do you suggest?"

"Go back to work in the morning," Burke replied. "Don't say anything about this yet to anyone else. Not to your co-workers, and not even to your family or friends. Keep your eyes and ears open for anything that might serve to corroborate your story or add missing details. Then, once you have concrete evidence in hand, contact me again, and we'll take it from there."

Go back to work? Jay thought with a shudder. *Go back to those people? Just keep on helping them, like nothing's happened?*

Still, the realistic side of his brain saw Burke's point. Leaving wouldn't solve anything. At least, if he was still at Genetech, he could try to dig up some evidence. Other than that, there wasn't much else he could do.

"Doctor Sanford?" asked Burke. "Are you still there?"

"Yeah, I'm here," Jay said. "Okay, I get it. Thanks for your time."

He hung up the phone.

The next day dragged on for an eternity as Jay forced himself through the paces at Genetech. Objectively speaking, nothing had changed since yesterday. Everyone still acted the same, and everything proceeded in much the same way as it had been all along. But every time Jay touched his equipment, he found himself plagued by visions of human beings trapped inside machines he'd helped to create. And every time his smiling colleagues met him in the hall with a comment about last night's ball game, Jay couldn't help searching their eyes for some sign as to whether they were willing parties in these atrocities, or just unknowing dupes like himself. From an impartial perspective, maybe nothing had changed. But to Jay, everything had.

It was mid-afternoon when Willis stuck his head in Jay's lab. "Jay, could you come by my office for a minute, please?"

"Uh, sure," Jay said.

Jay followed Willis to his office, trying to reconcile the impression of the man that he had formed over the past few months with what he now knew. Once inside, he sat down in the chair in front of Willis's desk, the same one he had sat in when he had eagerly tried his best to impress Willis into giving him a job. Involuntarily, Jay glanced over at the top of the desk. He wasn't surprised to see that the file was no longer there.

What did surprise Jay a bit was the anxiety that he felt when Willis closed the door. Rationally, he told himself, he had no cause to be nervous. There was no reason to think that they were onto him so soon, and it wasn't as though it was the first time that Willis had closed the door. But the tingling sensation at the back of Jay's neck wouldn't leave, and he had to force himself to stay calm. Particularly when he noticed that Willis was making no move to sit down himself, and was leaning against the door instead.

"So," Willis said, "I hear you had quite the adventure last night."

The effect was like an electric shock through Jay's body. A thousand thoughts raced through his mind at once. Did Willis know? Was he talking about something else? How could Jay get out of the office when Willis was blocking the door? Jay tried, without success, to keep his emotions off his face as he stammered out a response.

"Uh, wha-what do you mean, Marty?"

"Oh, you know. Maybe you saw something you shouldn't have seen. Made a phone call that shouldn't have been made . . ."

Jay could feel himself starting to sweat. "I, uh, I don't know what you're talking about."

Willis frowned at Jay like a father whose child had just claimed not to know who broke the cookie jar. "Come on, Jay. This will go much more quickly if you don't try to lie. Besides, you're not very good at it."

Jay was silent, so Willis continued. "Oh, stop acting like a deer caught in the headlights. There's really nothing to worry about. In fact, this could prove to be quite an opportunity for you."

Jay cocked his head to the side, not certain whether he'd heard correctly. "An . . . opportunity?"

"Absolutely. Now, I'm not saying you didn't ruffle a few feathers upstairs. Not everyone shared my opinion at first. But I pointed out the quality of the contributions that you've made to the organization in your short time here, and that carried considerable weight. I'm not sure you realize it, but you're a highly valued employee. It was a completely different situation than, say, with Ms. Cortez."

"Ms. Cortez?" Jay asked, puzzled. Then, he got it. "You mean Rosa?"

"Yes, that's right, the cleaning woman. A shame, really. Still, she knew that it's strictly against company policy to provide access to restricted areas for anyone other than the people working in those areas. I'm afraid there wasn't any choice in her case but to institute disciplinary action."

"For opening a door? What kind of 'disciplinary action?'"

Willis waved his hand dismissively. "Don't worry about it. You won't be seeing her anymore, anyway."

Jay wondered what that meant, but he was starting to suspect that it was better not to ask.

For his own part, Willis hardly paused. "What you *should* be thinking about right now," he told Jay, extending a finger toward him, "is *you*."

Yes, Jay thought. *Definitely better not to ask.*

Willis eyed him with a serious expression. "Jay," he said, "what I'm about to tell you cannot leave this room. Frankly, some of it may sound . . . odd. But it is deadly serious, and known only to a very select few. By sharing in this knowledge, you will become one of that select few. Do you understand?"

Jay nodded, transfixed.

Willis returned the nod with a satisfied air. "Good. As you know, Genetech is engaged in the business of research. Probing the mysteries of the human body to create a better future."

Jay nodded again. So far, all of this came right out of Genetech's publicity brochures.

"What you don't know—and almost no one does—is that Genetech is actually the research arm of a much larger . . . shall we say, parent company." Willis took a breath. "You see, Jay, we live in a dangerous world, and it's getting more dangerous every day. We face threats that would have been unimaginable only a few years ago: mutants, super beings, creatures that can destroy a city as easily as you or I would swat a fly.

"Now, as sobering as all that may be, it's still not the biggest threat we face. Look around you. Drugs, promiscuity, riots pitting neighbor against neighbor . . . The very moral fiber of this nation is disintegrating before our eyes.

"And why? Where are the authorities who are supposed to be holding it all together and preserving our society? They're impotent, held back by a system that overregulates and tangles everything up in such a mass of red tape that it's a miracle when anything gets done. Tell me, how can you possibly instill order in a society where getting a law passed requires three hundred politicians to agree?"

Jay stayed quiet, assuming the question to be rhetorical.

"That's why a group of powerful, well-placed men and women has taken it upon themselves to set the country back on course. Their plan is to centralize the power in an elite group with the commitment to get things done. In fact, they've already begun. You'd be surprised at how much they control already, even if the general public doesn't realize it."

This was starting to sound vaguely familiar to Jay, from some far-fetched conspiracy theory he'd heard or read somewhere. "The . . . Trilateral Commission?" he ventured.

Willis laughed. "The Trilateral Commission! No, that's all just a smoke screen to keep people looking in the wrong direction. Do you honestly think that a venture of this subtlety and magnitude would be run by David Rockefeller?

"No, the real organization goes by the rather unlikely name of the Secret Empire."

Jay said nothing, but the disbelief must have registered on his face.

"Oh, I know," said Willis. "It sounds like it belongs in an old movie serial. *'Flash Gordon Versus the Secret Empire.'* But the Empire is real, and it may just be our best hope for saving America."

All of this was getting to be too much for Jay. It felt like being buried under an avalanche. Either Willis was crazy, or Jay was in so far over his head that he'd better start digging out now, or he'd never see the surface.

"Look," Jay said hurriedly, "I've already filed a report with the

FBI. People know where I am. If anything happens to me, they're going to come looking, and—"

"No one will come looking, Jay. There is no report."

"No, I'm serious! There's a file right now at the FBI—"

Willis looked Jay straight in the eye. "No, Jay. I'm not making myself clear. I didn't mean that I don't believe you. I meant that there *is*. No. *Report*."

It took a moment for Willis's words to sink in. As the full enormity of the situation began to come clear, Jay's jaw slowly went slack and it felt as though the strength was draining out of his body.

"I told you, you'd be surprised how much the Empire already controls," Willis said. "Its reach extends to the highest offices of the government.

"Cementing the Empire's position will take technology—technology at a level beyond what's available today. As you saw last night, your research is already helping to carry us toward that goal, by providing alternate energy sources that can accomplish things that standard gasoline or electricity can't.

"That's why you're being offered a choice. Join the Secret Empire. Become a knowing participant in the process, and enjoy a position of privilege within our ranks. Help us work toward a better tomorrow.

"Or say no. And we'll part company for good. It's your choice. But I'm afraid I need an answer *now*."

Jay's head was swimming. The logical part of his brain told him that this all had to be a dream, or some kind of massive joke. Secret Empires, mutants . . . the whole thing was so absurd as to be laughable. But there was nothing laughable about the plans he'd seen last night. Or the fact that Willis knew that he had made the call. Or the look on Willis's face.

Jay thought about Rosa. He thought about his parents and kid sister out in the suburbs. He thought about his odds of making it through the door. He hung his head and, silently, made the only decision he could.

"I need that answer, Jay," said Willis.

Jay smiled without mirth. "Guess it isn't much of a choice, is it?" he said. "I'm happy to accept your generous offer."

Willis offered a knowing smile in return. "Good choice," he said. "Welcome to the team."

For the first time, Willis removed his right hand from his jacket pocket. It held a small pistol with a silencer attached. Willis walked over to the desk, dropped the gun in a drawer, and slid the drawer closed. He picked up the receiver of his phone and pressed a button. After a moment, he simply said, "Doctor Sanford has accepted our offer," and replaced the receiver in its cradle.

With that hurdle past, Willis smiled and extended a hand to Jay, who took it in a half-hearted shake. Willis sat down behind his desk and leaned back in his chair. "Now, you'll be getting a full orientation shortly," Willis said. "In the meantime, though, there are some ground rules that you need to know.

"The Empire's greatest strength lies in secrecy. No one can stop us if they don't know to try. Even most of our members don't know each other's names, so if one of us should ever be captured and forced to talk, the damage would be minimal. Instead, we operate by code numbers. Yours is sixty-three."

"Sixty-three," Jay repeated.

"When the appropriate situations arise, you'll need this." Jay jumped a bit in his chair as Willis reached back into the drawer. When his hand reappeared, though, it didn't hold the gun. Instead, Willis took out a piece of purplish black cloth that he tossed across the desk to Jay. Jay spread the cloth out in his hands. It was a cowl designed to hide the wearer's features completely, except for a simple pair of eyeholes. On the forehead was the number sixty-three.

Jay's mind was filled with visions of Klan rallies and burning crosses. "You can't be serious," he said, staring at the cowl.

Willis leaned forward toward Jay. "Oh, this is serious, Jay. More serious than anything you've ever experienced. Your anonymity will be your shield. Without it, no matter how valuable your contributions might be, you become a liability."

Willis sighed, once again becoming more like the man that Jay had known before today. "Look, Jay, I know this is a lot to absorb. And I know I'm not giving you much time to digest it. But I can't emphasize the point enough: This is no game. It's bigger than you, me, or any one person. If you let any of this slip to anyone— friends, family, anyone—you'll not only endanger your own life, but theirs as well. Do you understand that?"

Jay stared at the floor. His eyes moved to the cowl in his hands, then back to Willis's face. "Yes. I get it," said Number Sixty-Three. "So is that it?"

"Not quite," Willis replied. "There's still the matter of your entrance exam."

Jay's head was still swimming an hour later, as he sat in the back of the dark blue van that roared north up the Henry Hudson Parkway. He stared out the window at the Hudson River and the New Jersey shoreline beyond it, imagining freedom beyond the distant cliffs of the Palisades. His emotions warred within him. On the one hand, the whole thing still felt as though it couldn't possibly be happening. On the other hand, it also felt all too real.

Not that he bothered voicing his emotions, of course. He figured his companions wouldn't be terribly sympathetic. When they arrived with the van, they introduced themselves only as Number Eighty-One and Number Ninety-Four, which wasn't much in the way of introduction. In fact, they hadn't said much at all, although their beefy builds and rough demeanors suggested that they weren't exactly science geeks like Jay. They weren't wearing cowls, and Jay assumed it was because, even in New York, a van full of men in hoods would attract attention. This line of thinking did little to relieve his nervousness.

Nor was his nervousness helped by the fact that Jay still had no idea where they were going, or what they were going to do. The way Willis had explained it, this outing would be something of an exception for Jay. For the most part, his duties would be confined to the lab, and basically consist of continuing the same work he'd been doing all along. Before he could be accepted, though, he had to do something to demonstrate his loyalty and prove that he could be trusted. Willis hadn't said what the "something" was, and the uncertainty left Jay imagining the worst. But then again, he suspected that he was probably better off not knowing.

Whatever their mission was, though, Number Eighty-One made a couple of things painfully clear. The first was that he and Ninety-Four were in charge. Jay's job was basically to follow orders, keep his mouth shut, and stay out of their way.

The second was that if he didn't, there wouldn't be any second chances.

The van pulled off the highway deep in Westchester County, with Number Ninety-Four reading directions off a map and feeding them to his partner. As Number Eighty-One drove the van through the streets of Salem Center, Jay pulled himself together and tried to prepare himself for the unknown events to come. Now that they were on local streets, Jay assumed that whatever was going to happen would happen soon.

"Graymalkin Lane," said Number Ninety-Four. "Over there."

Sure enough, after making the turn, the van pulled over and stopped behind a sedan that was parked on the quiet, tree-lined street. Beyond the bushes and shrubs, Jay could just barely make out a hint of the sizable mansion that stood in the distance.

Number Eighty-One turned off the engine, as a man in a rumpled, ill-fitting suit stepped out of the sedan and turned to face them. He wasn't quite as massively tall as Jay's companions, and he was a bit rounder, but his crooked nose and the way he carried himself still didn't make him someone Jay would have wanted to meet in a dark alley.

Number Eighty-One climbed out of the van, and Number Ninety-Four began to follow. Ninety-Four paused long enough to look back at Jay with an expression of distaste.

"C'mon," the thug growled before walking over to Number Eighty-One and joining in the conversation.

Jay fumbled nervously with his seat belt and the door handle. Freeing himself from the van, he half-jogged to catch up with the others.

The man from the sedan was talking animatedly. ". . . So this guy in a helmet comes flyin' in out of the sky, right? An' I'm not close enough to see nothin', but I can tell from the noise that him an' the X-Men are tearin' the freakin' joint apart! So I'm just stickin' to orders an' sittin' tight, waitin' ta see what happens, right?

"So then it gets reeeeal quiet. An' I call it in, 'cause I figger whoever won, we probably got a clear field for a pickup on the losers, right? But then, while I'm waitin' for backup, who do ya think shows?"

Jay's companions listened quietly with impassive expressions.

"The Avengers! The freakin' Avengers!" said the man from the sedan. "So I'm thinkin' no way am I gettin' mixed up with the Avengers. I figger call in an abort order an' get outta there. But then the helmet guy starts fightin' the Avengers! And there's, like, rocks—*big* rocks—shootin' around in the air! An' *dinosaurs*! Real, live freakin' dinosaurs! An' by the time the whole thing's over, the helmet guy *wins*! He beats the whole freakin' Avengers! So he loads the X-Men an' some o' the Avengers into the Avengers' ship an' flies away with 'em."

Jay stared, incredulous. The guy had to be exaggerating. Otherwise, where were the police cars? Either he was exaggerating, or Westchester had the most apathetic, uninvolved neighbors in the world.

But Numbers Eighty-One and Ninety-Four never changed expression. With an edge in his voice, Eighty-One simply asked, "He took them away?"

"Yeah. An' the other Avengers took off after him."

"Then why'd you drag us all the way out here?"

The man from the sedan raised a finger and smiled knowingly.

"Because," he said, "one of 'em never came out. That wing guy, Angel. He's still in there."

Jay's companions registered the information and glanced at each other with a quick nod. "Right," said Number Eighty-One. "Let's go."

Number Ninety-Four stepped briskly to the back of the van and took out a black, rectangular case about four feet long. The others had already started walking through the bushes in the direction of the mansion. Mesmerized, Jay had almost forgotten to follow them when Number Ninety-Four snidely asked if he was coming.

Twenty-six minutes later, the four were wearing their cowls and still crouching among the bushes near the front of the mansion. No sound came from the building. However, the broken windows, the scorched patches of earth, and the front door that lay twisted on the ground all seemed to support the story he had heard.

The twenty-six minutes had passed slowly for Jay, since his companions still weren't big believers in conversation. Numbers Eighty-One and Ninety-Four sat quietly and watched the mansion intently. The man from the sedan (Number Eighty-Seven, now that Jay could see the number on his cowl) lay on his back in the grass with his knees bent. As near as Jay could tell through the cowl, Number Eighty-Seven's eyes were closed.

The waiting time had given Jay the opportunity to think, which wasn't good. Because now that the black case was open and Jay saw the high-tech cannon that it had held, he could only imagine that they were there for one purpose:

To commit murder.

Jay thought about making a break for it, but he knew it was no use. He was outnumbered by well-armed men who, he had no doubt, could snap him in two like a dry twig. If he ran, he'd be dead before he reached the street. All he could do was wait and see how it all played out.

Jay's reverie was interrupted as Number Ninety-Four got Number Eighty-One's attention with a smack in the arm. Number

Eighty-Seven sat up with a grunt. Jay looked over to see signs of motion through the doorway of the mansion.

A young, muscular man staggered a bit as he stepped out of the doorway and looked around at the signs of destruction. He was dressed in a close-fitting, blue and gold costume with a blue mask. The costume looked as though it would be more at home in a circus than here in the middle of Westchester. But that wasn't the thing that made the biggest impression on Jay.

No, it was his wings.

This had to be the "Angel" that Number Eighty-Seven had mentioned. An angel was exactly what he looked like, with white, feathery, six-foot wings extending from his back. At first, Jay assumed that the wings had to be artificial. But the subtle, fluid way they moved as he stepped outside quickly convinced Jay that they were natural.

Then, he started to fly.

Without meaning to, Jay held his breath at the glorious sight . . . only to see the Angel cut down by a beam of coherent light that blasted him out of the sky before he was fifteen feet off the ground. The Angel fell to Earth, where his body lay sprawled across the ground.

Jay's head jerked around to see the heat still rising from the high-tech laser cannon on Number Ninety-Four's shoulder.

"Right," Number Eighty-One said tersely. "Let's go get him."

This time, the anxious Jay was out in front as the group moved quickly toward the Angel's position. As he got in close, he was relieved to see that the Angel was still breathing. Apparently, despite his fears, the cannon had been set to stun, rather than kill.

Number Eighty-One pointed to Jay. "You take his legs," he said. With only a moment's hesitation, Jay did as he was told. Number Eighty-One hefted the weight of the Angel's upper body —a task that, Jay figured, probably wasn't made any easier by the Angel's light but cumbersome wings. At the same time, Numbers Ninety-Four and Eighty-Seven were packing the cannon back into its case.

Within a matter of moments, the Angel was loaded into the back of the van, the group from the Secret Empire climbed into their respective vehicles, their cowls were off, and they were gone.

It was dark by the time the van pulled up to the rear loading bay at Genetech. As they pulled up, Numbers Eighty-One and Ninety-Four put their hoods back on. Jay followed their lead. Three more cowled figures waited for them by the open door. Jay thought he recognized one as Willis from his build, but he had no idea whom the other two were. Not only were they masked, but they were also wearing loose-fitting robes that concealed the shapes of their bodies. For all he knew, they could be total strangers or people he saw every day.

Jay climbed out of the van and walked to the back to help unload their human cargo. As one of Jay's companions opened the rear door, though, Willis stepped up behind Jay to lay a hand on his shoulder.

"Let them do it," said Willis. "We should debrief."

Out of the corner of his eye, Jay spotted Number Eighty-One giving Willis a subtle nod.

"Okay," Jay said, a little tentatively. He stepped away from the van, pausing briefly to look on as the two thugs in robes hefted the Angel's limp form out of the vehicle.

"Tell me, how was it?" Willis asked.

"Fine," Jay replied with an unconvincing attempt at a nonchalant shrug. Even though he couldn't see anyone's face, he suspected that Number Ninety-Four was smirking beneath his hood. There was no way to know, however, because with their delivery completed, Numbers Eighty-One and Ninety-Four got back in the van and drove off without a word.

Jay watched them leave. Under his breath, he muttered, "Pleasure working with you."

Willis chuckled.

Jay and Willis followed the thugs as they carried the Angel

through the door and into the building. They walked down a short hall to where a third masked man in a robe held an elevator door open.

He stayed at his post, keeping watch, as Jay and the rest of the group entered the elevator. Willis inserted an electronic card into a slot, and the door slid closed. The elevator descended past the basement and sub-basement to a level whose presence Jay hadn't suspected before.

When the doors opened again, they revealed another corridor. The hallway lined with sheets of sturdy-looking metal that had been polished to a vaguely reflective shine. There were no signs or ornaments of any kind. Clearly, the corridor had been designed for function and security, not comfort. As if to confirm the impression, two more hooded members of the Empire stood waiting with semiautomatic rifles in hand. They looked over the arrivals in the elevator, then stepped back to let them pass.

Stepping off the elevator, Willis gestured to Jay to hold back as the others carried the Angel toward a door at the far end of the corridor. "Seriously, now," he said quietly. "How was it?"

"Well, it's not exactly what I'm used to."

"I didn't think you were. Well, if it helps, I'll assure you that it's not the sort of thing you'll be doing all the time. We just had to gauge your level of commitment. Having second thoughts?"

Jay looked at his masked employer. "I was under the impression that second thoughts wouldn't be a good idea."

"They wouldn't," Willis agreed. "Especially now that you're an accessory to kidnapping. Consider it another incentive to keep all of this to yourself."

"Oh, thanks. I was feeling a little undermotivated." Jay knew that he wasn't using a whole lot of common sense to censor what he said. It made him realize just how exhausted he was. "Listen, Marty, I'm sorry, but this has been a really, really long day. I've done everything you wanted. Can I go home now?"

"Sure," Willis said in a paternal tone. "But first, I think you've earned something. Come with me."

They walked to the door at the end of the hall, and Willis pushed it open. Inside, there was a large, yellow disc, approximately twenty feet in diameter. The two thugs had fastened steel manacles around the Angel's wrists and ankles to secure him to one end of disc like the minute hand on the face of a clock. One of the robed figures was in the process of covering the top of the Angel's head with a metal cap that was attached to a cable.

Beside the Angel, three other figures were strapped to the disc as well. One was a slender man with green skin who wore a purple cape. The second was a young man in a skintight black costume adorned with white, concentric circles. Next to him was a young woman with green hair. All three appeared to be unconscious but alive, and all wore matching metal caps on their heads. A thick cable ran from the center of the disc to a high-tech bank of machinery that glowed softly with energy.

"And to think," Willis said with a proud tone and a close eye on Jay, "all this grew out of your discoveries with a single cell."

Jay couldn't believe his eyes. The horrifying spectacle before him was unlike anything he'd ever imagined. Yet, it wasn't the massive machinery that made the biggest impact on Jay. It wasn't even the sight of the helpless captives manacled in place. No, he was most struck by something else entirely:

Half of the spaces on the disc were still waiting to be filled.

The Secret Empire wasn't done yet.

I've gotta get out of here! I've gotta do something! Jay thought desperately as he paced briskly around and around his apartment. It had been bad enough when the whole thing existed only as abstract lines on paper. But now, it was real! Living, breathing human beings were being kidnapped and imprisoned, with a nightmarish machine sucking the energy from their bodies like a giant leech.

And it was all because of Jay. Jay and his research. The same research that had made him so proud and seemed so wonderful just a couple of days earlier. If only he had never stumbled onto his discovery, then none of this would be happening.

The whole thing seemed some like mad fever dream—like a merry-go-round run amok, spinning so fast that there was no way to get off.

But there *had* to be. There had to be a way off. Because Jay simply couldn't handle this. He couldn't continue this way and keep living with himself. If he tried, he'd go insane.

If there was a way out, though, Jay couldn't see it. And he'd been wracking his brain from the moment he got home until now, when it was already (Jay glanced at the Mickey Mouse clock on the wall) almost three A.M. The Secret Empire was just too powerful. It seemed like they could be anywhere ... and there was simply no way to know. Was his phone tapped? His apartment bugged? Were the obnoxious youths drinking and carrying on loudly on the stoop across the street just a bunch of punk kids, or were they really there to keep an eye on him? Hanging in limbo like this, not knowing, was even harder than having his fears confirmed.

Jay wanted to fight back. He wanted to break away. But the Empire was just too big. And Jay was only one man.

For probably the fortieth time that night, Jay told himself that he needed help. But whom could he call? Whom could he trust? The police? The newspapers? If the Secret Empire had agents planted in the FBI (*the FBI!*), then what would stop them from controlling the media or the cops, too? If he went to any of them, it might lead to nothing more than signing his own death warrant. There was simply no way to know whom to trust. Anyone could be connected to the Secret Empire.

Unless ...

Jay stopped pacing. His expression slowly changed. His eyes grew clear as an idea blossomed in his mind. Of course. Suddenly, it was all so obvious.

He couldn't understand why he hadn't seen it before.

* * *

For the next two weeks, Jay did what he was supposed to. He showed up for work on time, he conducted his research, and if the progress wasn't coming quite as fast as it had been, well, no one could come up with a revolutionary bombshell every day. He was producing steadily, and that's what was important.

In fact, Jay showed every sign of adjusting to the new arrangement. He treated Willis with cordial respect, if not close friendship. No one would have described Jay's mood as boundless joy, but he was acting a little less resentful each day. There had been no mention of the Secret Empire since that first night—an intentional move on Willis's part, in an attempt to help Jay acclimate more smoothly. Willis assumed that the substantial raise that showed up in Jay's paycheck after the first few days was helping to cushion the blow, too.

As Jay's mood changed, so did Willis's. As far as Jay could tell, Willis didn't seem to be watching him with the same sort of evaluative eye that he had used when Jay first joined the Empire. Willis was starting to relax around Jay again, and wasn't watching him nearly as closely anymore.

Which was exactly what Jay had been waiting for.

That evening, instead of going straight home to his Manhattan apartment, Jay took a subway downtown into deep Brooklyn. Once there, he changed trains twice, then left the subway, hailed a taxi, and rode several blocks to a bus stop. He waited for a few minutes until the bus arrived, then got on board and rode into Queens. By the time another subway train deposited him back in Manhattan beneath Grand Central Station, Jay was fairly certain that he wasn't being followed.

Jay climbed the stairs to the terminal, found the appropriate window, and bought a ticket for a commuter train. Locating the appropriate platform, he boarded the train, surveyed the seats with narrowed eyes, and chose one near the back of the car that afforded him a good view of the aisle and all of the doors. Finally comfortable that he had done everything he could to discourage pursuit, Jay sank back into the seat and settled in for the ride.

The better part of an hour later, the train pulled into Jay's station. He stepped down off the train onto the platform of the suburban station. He looked around at the few other disembarking commuters who made their way across the platform toward parked cars, waiting taxis, or simply the sidewalk beyond. Jay rubbed the back of his neck thoughtfully. His problem was that he knew approximately where he wanted to go, but he wasn't sure how to get there. Of course, it would be easy enough to ask directions, but the nagging voice at the back of his mind warned him that it was probably best not to let anyone know where he was going. He didn't think anyone had followed him, but he knew full well that he wasn't good enough at this to be sure. Not to mention the fact that anyone around him could be part of the . . .

"Need some help, sir?"

Jay jumped, startled, at the voice behind him. He turned to see a janitor in uniform, holding a broom up on his shoulder. The janitor smiled at Jay. But, Jay wondered, was the janitor smiling out of amusement over his reaction, or was it something more?

"Oh, no, thanks," Jay said, putting a smile on his own face in return. "Just trying to remember everything the wife wanted me to pick up on the way home."

The janitor nodded. "Best be careful about that one," he said with a grin. "Otherwise, you could end up sleeping in the yard."

Jay forced a chuckle. "Well, you have a good night now."

"G'night, g'night."

The janitor lowered the broom and started to sweep, but he didn't seem to be going anywhere. Trying his best to keep up appearances, Jay turned purposefully and strode toward the line of waiting cabs. He climbed in the one at the front of the line and gave the driver the name of a street.

As the cab set off, it occurred to Jay that, if the driver belonged to the Empire, Jay was pretty much at his mercy. Jay assumed they were going in the right direction, but he didn't know the area at all. For all he knew, they could have been heading somewhere else entirely. He strained to read the name on the license that the driver had posted on the dashboard: R. BERNS. Was it his real name? Probably. But still . . .

When the cab stopped at a red light, Jay experimented with the door handle to see if the door opened from the inside. It did. The door cracked open.

"Hey!" said the driver. "What're you doin'?"

"Sorry," Jay said, pulling the door shut with a bang. "It didn't look like I closed it all the way."

A few minutes later, the cab turned onto a street Jay recognized. "What's the address?" asked the driver.

"This is fine right here, actually," Jay replied. "Thanks." He paid the fare, got out, and watched the cab pull away.

In fact, there was still a block or so between Jay and the place he was going. However, he figured it was best not to leave the cab driver with the exact address. And besides, he wanted to see if anyone was watching outside.

Trying to look casual, Jay walked cautiously along the street. As far as he could tell, nothing seemed out of place. There were a few cars parked on the street, but none of the car windows were dark and no one seemed to be inside.

Finally, Jay reached his destination. He stopped on the sidewalk and took a deep breath, feeling the full weight of the pressure that threatened to crush him. He released the breath and stepped forward. It wasn't the first time he'd been here, but it was the first time he'd come through the front gate. He noticed a sign:

XAVIER'S SCHOOL FOR GIFTED CHILDREN

It's a school? he thought.

Jay walked through the gate toward the sprawling mansion that lay beyond. Making his way down the winding driveway, Jay couldn't help gazing around at his surroundings: the portico that framed the front door, the bell tower atop the main house, the multiple-car garage that dwarfed his entire apartment . . . It was a far cry from the lifestyle he was used to.

As he came closer to the mansion itself, Jay admired the thorough clean-up work that someone had done. The door had been replaced and the broken windows repaired. The scorched patches in the grass had been covered with new turf that was just starting to take root. Already, the signs of battle were barely noticeable unless you were looking for them.

Still, particularly in light of recent events, Jay was a little surprised by the lack of security around the school. Just then, however, he caught a hint of movement within a nearby hedge, and realized that he was being tracked by hidden cameras. If that was the case, Jay wasn't in any rush to find out what other surprises might be hidden around him.

Jay stepped up to the door and rang the bell. He waited, nervously shifting his weight back and forth from one foot to the other, fully aware of the unseen eyes that were sure to be checking him out. Then, the door opened. A slender, solemn-looking young man, maybe a year or so younger than Jay, held the door ajar.

"Yes?" said the young man. "May I help you?"

Jay immediately noticed two things about the young man. One was his unusual sunglasses, with their ruby red lenses, which he was wearing indoors; either he was some kind of James Dean wannabe, or there was more to him than met the eye. (*No pun intended*, Jay added to himself.) The other was his posture—at ease but slightly arched, as though ready to move at a moment's notice. Jay wouldn't be able to enter the building without either permission or a fight.

Actually, though, Jay didn't devote too much thought to the young man. He was far more intrigued by the striking, red-headed young woman who smiled brightly as she looked over the young man's shoulder and seemed to be sizing Jay up. Almost subconsciously, Jay straightened up to his full height and pulled in his stomach.

Jay had been rehearsing this conversation in his head for over a week. "My name's Jay Sanford," he said. "I've come with information about the Angel."

Jay could see the young man's jaw tighten, but the tone of his voice remained unchanged. "The what?" he asked.

Jay had expected that. "The Angel," he repeated, indulgently but (he hoped) without a condescending tone. "I can tell you who has him, and I can tell you where he is."

"Really? What makes you think you should be telling us?"

The redhead gently pushed the dour young man aside. "Don't be silly, Scott."

"Jean . . ."

She waved her hand dismissively with a disarming smile. "He obviously knows about us already. Besides, look at him. It's not like he's an evil mutant or something. Let's hear what he has to say."

"I concur," said a voice from behind the pair. "I think I can say with some certainty that we have nothing to fear from Doctor Sanford."

The two stepped aside as they turned toward the speaker, giving Jay a glimpse of a bald, intense-looking older man in a wheelchair. He rolled the chair forward and extended a hand toward Jay. "I am Professor Charles Xavier," he said. "Please come in. We can talk in my study."

Jay shook the Professor's hand and followed as Scott wheeled the Professor's chair into the mansion. Jean walked beside. He found her presence distracting—so much so that it took a minute for the thought to occur to him: *How did he know I'm a "Doctor?"*

Soon, Jay sat in an overstuffed leather chair in the panelled study. The Professor sat on the other side of a massive oak desk, while Scott and Jean sat in two matching leather chairs nearby. Jay told his story, beginning with his initial neurological discovery at Genetech and ending with the Angel and the others strapped into the machine. Occasionally, the Professor would interject with a question for clarification. And Jean took Scott's hand with a look of concern when Jay described the other mutants who were strapped in beside the Angel. (*Must be someone he knows*, Jay thought.) But for the most part, the trio listened quietly as Jay recounted his tale.

"So," Jay explained, "I knew I had to get out, but I didn't know how. I mean, where do you turn when you can't even be sure who the good guys and bad guys are?

"Then it hit me. The Empire kidnapped the Angel from this school. And the way those guys were talking, it sounded like they'd be just as happy to get all of you. If that's the case, then it has to mean that you people aren't part of the Empire. In fact, you're about the *only* ones I'm sure aren't. And you're definitely the only ones powerful enough to take them down."

A somber silence descended on the room as Jay finished the tale. The Professor sat with his fingertips pressed together lightly under his chin, deep in thought.

"It took a great deal of courage for you to come here, Doctor Sanford. I thank you for it," said the Professor. "Unfortunately, your story fits all too well with the facts we already know. Including, I'm afraid, the empty spaces on the disc. You see, yesterday, another of my students went out to search for our missing friend.

"He never returned."

Jean leaned forward in her chair. "How do we get them out, Professor?" she asked.

"I had assumed that the disappearances were the work of one of our old foes, or perhaps some anti-mutant group," the Professor replied. "Now, I see that, to this 'Secret Empire,' the mutants themselves are merely stepping stones toward their ultimate ends. Still, that makes our adversary no less dangerous.

"It seems this Secret Empire is well-equipped and highly organized, both of which imply the need for careful planning. Yet, the speed with which they're moving, along with the apparent extent of their knowledge about us, suggests that we must move quickly ourselves."

The Professor turned his piercing gaze on Jay. "Doctor Sanford, we will need the layout of the Genetech facility. Both the public areas and the hidden levels."

"Sure. Well, I haven't seen all of it, but I can show you the parts I know. Do you have a piece of paper? I'll draw a sketch."

"That won't be necessary. Simply picture it in your mind."

It sounded like a strange request, but Jay was getting to the point where nothing really sounded all that strange to him anymore. He visualized the building, taking a mental "walk" through the front door and various offices and labs. Then, he began again, this time from the rear entrance and down into the secret sub-basement. As Jay went through the exercise, the Professor closed his eyes and raised a hand in Jay's direction. Jay thought he felt a slight tingling sensation in the back of his head, but he wasn't sure whether it was just his imagination.

Once Jay was done, the Professor opened his eyes again. "Hmm," he said once again. "It won't be easy, but handled properly, there may be a way to do it. Scott, you and I will have to discuss strategy. We need to be ready to move by tomorrow night at the latest."

Scott gave a terse nod in reply.

Professor Xavier turned back toward Jay. "Once again, Doctor Sanford, thank you. Jean will drive you back into Manhattan and leave you at a subway station where you can find a train back to your home. As long as no one sees you leave our grounds, that should prevent the Secret Empire from tracing your movements back here."

"Okay," said Jay. "Then what should I do?"

"The safest course of action is probably for you to carry on with your daily routine as though nothing has happened."

"You mean . . . go back to work in the morning?" After Jay's experience with the FBI, this was starting to feel uncomfortably familiar.

"Don't worry," said the Professor, as if in response to Jay's unspoken concern. "It will only be for a short while. If you were to disappear or call in sick on the same day as our offensive, the Secret Empire would have little trouble identifying the person who gave them away."

Jay nodded. It made sense. And for some reason, even though he'd known them for only a short time, he felt he could trust these people. More than the Empire, anyway.

"Okay," said Jay. "You're the boss."

As the black limousine sped along the highway, Jean turned to the passenger seat with a bemused smile. "You can get up now," she said. "We're not being followed."

Jay sat up and rubbed his temples. "Phew."

"Are you okay?"

"Yeah. Just a little too much blood rushing to my head down there."

"Luckily, I don't think that's lethal."

Jay leaned back with an ironic smirk. "Yeah, well, it's the first thing in the past few weeks that hasn't been."

"I know. I'm sorry."

Jay sat quietly for a bit. Jean watched the road.

"So," Jay said, "what's the deal with you folks, anyway?"

"What do you mean?"

"Well, I know it's after dark, but I can't say I noticed a whole lot of gifted children around that school of yours. So, the whole thing's just a front?"

"Oh, no. The school's real. I've been a student there for years. Actually, I left and went to Metro College for a while. Their academic requirements were a breeze compared to Professor Xavier's."

"Sorry. I didn't mean any offense."

Jean shrugged. "Someone else might have set up the school that way," she acknowledged. "Just a place where mutants could hide from the outside world. But the Professor's a remarkable man. He has a dream of a world where mutants and ordinary humans can live together in peace. I'd like to see that. I'm sorry to say there are too many people out there who disagree, though."

"Huh. Never really thought about it, myself."

Jean flashed him another beaming smile. "The world could use more people like you. Lots of regular humans think about it too much. Until we change their minds, we need a school like Professor Xavier's. You know, a place where young mutants can come to learn what they need to contribute to society. Where they can get a good education without being treated like freaks, and learn to control their powers at the same time."

"Realize their potential, physically and mentally."

"Exactly."

"And if you manage to save the world along the way..."

"... So much the better."

Jay nodded. He had to admire these people. As Willis had said, there was so much wrong with the world. But while the Secret Empire was trying to help itself, Professor Xavier and his students were trying to help the world.

Jay was so wrapped up in thought that he barely noticed when the limo left the highway and stopped a few blocks away at a Manhattan street corner. "Here we are," Jean said, pointing off to the side. "That subway should get you home, right?"

"Oh. Yeah, right. Thanks." Jay opened the door and started to get out. He paused. "Listen... when all this is over, I don't suppose you'd like to get together for dinner or something..."

Jean smiled again. "That would be fun," she said, "but I don't think my boyfriend, Scott, would approve."

"Oh. I see. Well, can't blame a guy for trying."

"No, you can't. I'm flattered, though. Thanks."

Jay got out and closed the door. He watched Jean drive away with a wave. He kept watching until the limousine had vanished from sight, then looked around to be sure no one was paying attention. He walked down the stairs toward the train.

"Late night last night, Jay?" Willis asked with an almost casual tone.

Jay finished filling his paper cup and looked past the water cooler at his boss. He caught the slight edge in Willis's voice, but chose to ignore it. "Yeah, well, I decided to take advantage of my raise and eat out last night," he replied off-handedly. "There's only so much peanut butter one person can eat."

Willis's mouth curled into a smile, but his eyes didn't. "Good. I'm glad you're enjoying the raise. There are some wonderful restaurants in Brooklyn, aren't there?"

Jay nodded a greeting to one of the others researchers who was passing down the hall before he responded. "Mm-hmm," Jay said. "Lots of really interesting ethnic places. Foods I've never heard of . . . and still can't pronounce. Too bad it takes so long to get back and forth."

Okay, so there was *someone following me,* Jay thought. *They don't trust me all the way yet. And he wants me to know it.* Still, if Jay's shadow only made it as far as Brooklyn, it meant that he was probably in the clear for now. The odds were that they didn't know about his visit to Xavier's School. At least, not yet.

Willis clapped Jay on the shoulder and gave him a paternal look. "Well, be careful. Too much of that sort of thing can be bad for you, you know."

"Oh, believe me, I know."

Willis gave him a firm pat on the back, then walked down the hall and into his office.

Jay was about to head back to his own lab when it happened.

The sound rolled over Jay like a wave as a nearby wall erupted in a sea of red light. Powdered concrete and rubble rained across the hall. Jay took cover on the floor beside the water cooler as stunned Genetech employees recoiled by reflex before they even registered the fact that something had happened. Yet, strangely, no one had been struck by any of the debris. It was almost as though someone had known where everyone was standing. As though the blast had been directed precisely with that in mind.

Almost as though it was planned, Jay thought, fighting a smile.

By the time the dust cleared, alarms were ringing, people were screaming and scattering in all directions, and chaos filled the air.

Jay stuck tight where he was. As the clouds settled, he looked up to see a pair of dramatic, masked figures. Their masks weren't the violet hoods of the Secret Empire, though. The one in front wore a ruby red visor that concealed his eyes. Close behind him was a young woman whose angular mask concealed her face but not her shoulder-length red hair. Both were clad in blue and gold uniforms. Each of their red belts was emblazoned with an X.

"Genetech employees!" the young man in the visor announced loudly. "Your employers have committed illegal acts in partnership with the Secret Empire! Anyone not knowingly associated with these acts may leave now!

"As for the rest of you, the X-Men demand the release of the hostages you abducted! *Now!*"

A team of security guards armed with handguns came thundering down the hall. The young man glanced in their direction. "Marvel Girl!"

"Got it, Cyclops," his companion replied. She gestured toward the guards, and they went soaring up into the ceiling before crashing to the floor, unconscious.

"What's happening?!" cried a receptionist who was crouching behind a potted plant near Jay.

Cyclops looked down at the floor to his right and reached up to touch the side of his visor. A scarlet beam of light shot down from his eyes to rip a six-foot-wide hole through the floor as though it were nothing but paper. A second and third beam followed behind it. *The sub-basement,* thought Jay.

Enough time had elapsed that teams of guards were now coming from all sides. Cyclops and Marvel Girl clasped hands and jumped down into the hole. Even as their heads disappeared from sight, Jay noticed something strange. For some reason, they seemed to be falling just a little bit too slowly. It was almost as if something was cushioning their descent.

By the time the guards converged on the hole, the intruders were already below. "Downstairs!" yelled one of the guards. As one, they broke ranks and ran for the stairs and elevators.

Jay started to creep toward the hole to see what was happening, but the sound of rapid-fire automatic weapons sent him scurrying back. The guards had only been carrying pistols. *Guess they found the Empire,* Jay thought.

All around him, people were streaming out of the building in a panic. As the crowd subsided, things settled down on the ground floor, but the noise from below told Jay that it was far from true on the lower levels. The air was filled with shouts, screams, bursts of gunfire, explosions, and sounds that Jay couldn't even hope to identify. Still, Jay sat tight, semi-concealed on the floor beside the water cooler, waiting to see what would happen.

Jay pulled his legs in closer and tried his best to melt into the wall as he spotted Willis coming out of his office. Briskly, Willis walked in Jay's direction with a determined look. Jay glanced around, and found that the only other people still in the hall were the unconscious guards. Jay felt the fear in the pit of his stomach. But then Willis stopped walking, and Jay realized that Willis hadn't been heading toward him—he was walking toward the hole. Willis stood, his profile toward Jay, staring intently down through the hole. Then, a smile slowly crept across his lips. He reached into his jacket pocket and produced the pistol with the silencer that Jay had seen before. Willis took careful aim down into the hole.

Instantly, Jay knew in his gut what Willis's target had to be. "Noooo!" Jay shouted, leaping forth from his hiding place. His body smashed into Willis's, sending the older man sprawling and the bullet hurtling soundlessly into the wall.

The force of the collision sent Jay to the floor himself, dangerously close to the edge of the hole, even as the gun plummeted through. Out of the corner of his eye, Jay spotted a flash of red hair down below, confirming the identity of Willis's intended target. Marvel Girl looked up to flash Jay a grateful smile before continuing the fight.

"You . . . *traitor!*" Willis growled. Jay snapped his head around to see Willis rising painfully to his feet. "After all I've given you! The opportunities I opened!"

"*Gave* me?!" Jay hadn't even regained his own footing when he had to meet Willis's charge with a grunt. The impact rocked Jay as the two grappled mere inches from the three-story drop.

"You're dead!" Willis hissed through clenched teeth. "Even if you manage to get out of here with your mutie friends, the Secret Empire is everywhere! No matter how far you run! No matter where you try to hide! You. Are. *Dead!*"

Suddenly, all the fear and tension and rage that Jay had felt over the past weeks exploded in a burst of white hot fury. "No more!" Jay shouted, breaking the clinch. He leaped on top of Willis, pummelling him mercilessly. "*No more! No more! No more!*"

By the time Jay stood up, breathing heavily, Willis was lying on the floor, unconscious and bleeding. Jay stared at the prone form of his former boss until he became aware of movement behind him. He turned to see Cyclops and Marvel Girl rising up out of the hole as though gravity had ceased to exist.

Marvel Girl gently held her hand out toward him. "You'd better come with us."

The whole thing had taken less than fifteen minutes. As the three of them headed out the back, Jay could hear the sound of approaching sirens.

"Nothing," the Professor said, frowning, from the back of the limo.

"Nothing," Scott confirmed from the driver's seat. "The room was swept clean. Not a sign of the missing mutants or the machinery."

"Plenty of thugs in purple hoods and robes, though," Jean added.

"They must have moved them out the same night that Doctor Sanford saw them," the Professor said. "The Secret Empire appears to value its secrecy, indeed."

"I'll say," Jean agreed. "I tried probing the CEO's memories, but even he didn't know where they took them. All I saw was a panel truck being loaded up in the middle of the night and driving off to who knows where."

Jay stared absently out the window. He was sitting next to the Professor in the back, while Scott and Jean, their costumes concealed beneath nondescript jackets, sat up front. The limousine was driving down a side street, heading away from the Genetech building. Now that the adrenaline rush was wearing off, he was starting to realize exactly what he'd done, and just what it meant. Willis's words echoed in his mind: "*No matter how far you run! No matter where you try to hide! You. Are. Dead!*"

"So it was all for nothing," Jay said without turning toward his companions. "The Empire's still going. The mutants are still prisoners. There isn't even any evidence for the police to find and shut Genetech down."

Jean turned around to look at Jay over the seat. "Oh, Jay, no . . . "

The Professor rested a reassuring hand on Jay's arm. "Don't underestimate what you've done, Doctor Sanford," the Professor said. "True, there may not be sufficient evidence for the police to make any arrests. Nevertheless, in light of the Empire's devotion to secrecy, today's events are certain to exert a significant impact.

"Why do you suppose that we chose such a public action, instead of acting more quietly at night, when there would likely have been less resistance? The sensationalism of a 'mutant attack' is certain to draw considerable attention—attention that the Secret Empire will wish to avoid. Indeed, even if the general public never learns of the true nature of Genetech, the leaders of the Secret Empire know that the X-Men are aware of the connection, and that we can use it to track them down. There is only one logical course of action open to the Empire: to suspend Genetech's clandestine research agenda or, perhaps, to shut down the facility entirely.

"Whatever else happens, we have cost them a valuable resource today. I strongly suspect that Genetech's days as the research arm of the Secret Empire are finished."

Jay thought about that. It did provide some satisfaction. But it didn't answer the questions that were foremost in his mind.

He turned away from the window to look at the Professor. "So what happens now?"

"The X-Men continue their war on the Secret Empire. Now that you have alerted us to the threat they pose, you may rest assured that our efforts will not end until their power has been crushed.

"Our tactics will have to adapt, of course. The Secret Empire appears to have far too much knowledge about us and our base of operations. That provides them with an advantage that we cannot allow. To compensate, we will have to leave the school for the time being and become more difficult to find. I have already made the necessary preparations for Scott, Jean, and myself to go underground."

"And what about me?" Jay asked.

"I'm afraid that it would be far too dangerous for you to accompany us further."

"Like I'm going to be safe on my own," Jay said, bitterly. "So you're just cutting me loose? That's it? 'Thanks for the help, see you later, hope you don't get killed?'"

The Professor's lips tightened, then he sighed. "I won't try to minimize the danger you are in. It is considerable. The Secret Empire is still operational, and they know that you betrayed them. I would strongly advise against returning to your home or telephoning your friends or family in the immediate future.

"Nor would it be advisable for us to leave you in the hands of the authorities. Until the full reach of the Secret Empire is known, even S.H.I.E.L.D. might not be safe.

"However, I have no intention of . . . 'just cutting you loose,' as you put it, either. The X-Men are not without some connections to individuals within the government. Our contacts may not be as extensive as the Secret Empire's, perhaps, but they are generally sufficient for our needs."

The Professor reached into the inner pocket of his jacket and took out a thick envelope that he offered to Jay. Jay reached out and took it.

"What's this?" he asked. Jay flipped through the contents of the envelope. He found various pieces of identification with his photo under four different names. The envelope also contained several thousand dollars in cash.

"We will be leaving you at a bus station in Connecticut," the Professor explained. "That should be far enough from New York City so that the Empire is likely not to have agents searching for you there. Once there, you may secure transportation to the destination of your choice. I suggest that you choose someplace far away, where you have never been—and, preferably, where you never expected to go."

"That's a lot of money for a bus ticket."

"I have no way of knowing how long it will take for us to defeat the Secret Empire. Perhaps weeks, perhaps months, perhaps even longer. These funds may suffice to support you during that time. I hope they will. If not, this should at least provide you with a start."

Jay looked down at the envelope and considered the Professor's words. It was true. He couldn't go home. He couldn't even go to his bank to take out money of his own. All he had was what was in his hands and the clothes on his back. That, and a future that seemed increasingly uncertain.

Jay noticed that everything the Professor said assumed they would win in the end. Not once had he acknowledged the possibility that they might lose—that the good guys might be the ones to get crushed. Jay wondered whether the Professor was really that sure of a victory, or whether it just for his benefit. Either way, Jay wished that he could feel as confident himself.

"Thanks," Jay muttered quietly.

The limousine sped on.

Jay sat in the waiting area of the Hartford, Connecticut bus station, a one-way ticket to Chicago in his pocket. He figured that Chicago was far enough away to allow him to choose a stop somewhere earlier—at some point when it felt right—and get off the bus, leaving no record of his actual destination.

He'd said his goodbyes half an hour before. At least he'd gotten a kiss on the cheek from Jean out of the deal. Even Scott had broken his silence to shake Jay's hand, thank him for saving Jean's life, and wish him luck. But now, they were gone.

Jay watched the clock in the station, feeling horribly alone.

Just then, a heavy, older woman in a floral print dress let her battered suitcases fall to the floor and dropped down in the seat next to Jay. She was sweating heavily from the effort, and fanned herself with a magazine. "Foof!" she said. "That's better. I love to travel, but getting there can be a real bear! Don't you agree?"

Jay smiled weakly in reply, then looked back at his feet.

"But it'll be worth it," she continued, undeterred. "I've got three beautiful grandchildren waiting for me, up in Bangor. One smile from them—mmm!—it can break your heart, the little darlings. Don't get to see them near enough.

"What about you, dearie? Where are you off to?"

Jay felt a sudden chill down his spine. It was an innocent enough question. The kind people asked each other in bus stations every day. But still . . . how could Jay be sure?

"Miami," he replied. Jay stood up. "Um, would you excuse me? I just have to run to the bathroom. Too much travel food, I'm afraid."

"You poor thing! You do look a little pale. That stuff will do it to you every time. Well, you go do what you have to do. I hope you feel better."

Jay thanked her and walked away. Twenty more minutes until his bus.

Jay felt very alone.

It was almost a year later when Jay sat in a rundown diner in Albuquerque. The reddish sand of the New Mexican desert reflected a pink light through the plate glass window in the twilight hours. Jay sat quietly at a table in the corner that provided a view of both the entrance and the door to the kitchen. He ate a grilled cheese sandwich with a glass of water, mainly because it was the cheapest item on the menu. Over time, he'd supplemented the money that the Professor gave him with earnings from odd jobs here and there, but enough lean times had taught him to make his money stretch as far as he could. It was the same reason that his clothes looked scruffy and he spent so much time living in flophouses and cheap motels.

Not that it would have paid for him to take out a long-term lease on a nicer place, anyway. Jay had lost track of the number of times he'd moved since first stepping onto that bus to Chicago so long ago. It was rare that he stayed in the same place for more than a week or a month at a time. There had been a couple of occasions when he'd left town because of face-to-face encounters with the Empire—a midnight knife fight in Kansas City still showed up occasionally in his nightmares. Mostly, however, the triggers for his moves had been more subtle. A personal question from a stranger, the same face turning up more than once or twice, an apparent tourist catching him in a photo . . . Sure, any of them could have been nothing. But Jay had learned the hard way that it was better to play it safe.

At first, Jay had slavishly scoured the news every day for some sign that things had changed. Over time, though, he'd hit a critical mass of disappointment that had slowly cured him of the habit.

Which is why it took him by surprise when the television mounted on the wall at the end of the counter caught his attention. One moment, the screen showed an image of a well-dressed, female newscaster, standing in front of the White House. The next, the picture was replaced by footage of Captain America tackling a figure in a familiar purple robe and hood. Slowly, unbelievingly, Jay lowered his sandwich in mid-bite and leaned toward the set to hear what the newscaster had to say:

"—scene on the White House lawn, where just hours ago, living legend Captain America not only vindicated his name, but also saved this country once again in the process. Aided by his long-time partner, the Falcon, and members of the mutant X-Men, the

Captain defeated the so-called 'Secret Empire' to expose a conspiracy that is shocking in its scope and reach."

Jay listened as the winding, intricate story unfolded. He learned of a plot to discredit Captain America by framing him for murder. Of a new hero named Moonstone who filled the Captain's shoes as America's darling, but whom no one suspected of being a part of the Empire. Of a network of bombers prepared to destroy the major cities of the United States, unless the government handed over its power to the Secret Empire. Of the Empire's announcing itself to the nation in predictably melodramatic fashion by invading the White House grounds in a genuine flying saucer—a ship powered by energy stolen from mutants.

But most of all, he learned of Moonstone's confession on live, national television. The faux hero had pointed fingers and named names, blowing the lid off a conspiracy that reached across the country and to the very highest offices of the government.

"Authorities are declining to share too many details regarding the Secret Empire and its upper echelon tonight, citing an investigation that is still in progress," the newscaster continued. "But already, Federal agents in almost all fifty states are reported to be moving in to arrest alleged members of the organization. With so much activity underway, it is likely that nothing about the Secret Empire will remain secret for all that long . . ."

The newscaster kept talking after that, but it didn't matter. Jay had stopped hearing her words.

Jay breathed a heavy, ragged breath, feeling the weight of a world slipping down from his back. *It's over*, he thought. The Empire had been smashed. Its members were being rounded up in droves. The good guys had won. After all these months, Jay was finally safe . . .

. . . Assuming they got them all.

Jay was stunned by the thought, but he couldn't shake it. As much he wished otherwise, he couldn't help remembering what Willis had said when he'd handed Jay his hood and number. Not even most of the members of the Empire knew each other's real names. It had been a precaution in case any of them was ever captured and talked. Maybe the newscaster was right, and maybe they were arresting people all over the country. But no matter how many they caught, there would never be any way to be sure that they had really caught them all.

A cold chill seeped through Jay's flesh and straight into his bones. He cursed his own naivete. Had he really believed it would be so easy? That some hero would ride in out of nowhere and magically make it all better?

For all the time he had spent on the run, it still wasn't over. It would never be over. He could never be sure that no one was after him, or that it was safe to go home. The running would never stop, and neither would the fear.

Unless he made it stop.

For the first time in ages, Jay found himself thinking about his conversation with Jean in the limo so long ago. *Someone else might have set up the school that way,* she'd said. *Just a place where mutants could hide from the outside world.* Yet, in the face of all that hatred and all the odds against them, Jean and her friends had chosen not to hide. Instead, they chose to take action— to fight the injustice, and to try to make things better for everyone.

Jay faced a similar choice. He could continue to play it safe, stay hidden, and keep running. Or he could take the risk, stand up, and try to resume his life.

On the screen, Jay saw images of men and women in purple robes. Their hoods had been removed, and they were being led into waiting police cars in handcuffs.

They'll need people to testify, he thought.

Jay watched the television a moment longer, until the program switched over to a commercial for detergent. He got up, reached into his pocket for a coin, and walked to the pay phone in the back of the diner.

Jay dropped the coin in the slot, and prepared to take his life back.

Jay paused for a moment in front of the Federal courthouse, and gazed up the long flight of stone steps that led to its massive doors. It was hard to believe that he was the same person as the nervous fugitive who had spent so much time on the run. Jay was clean-shaven now, his hair neatly trimmed, and for the first time in months, he wore a jacket and tie. He looked up at the statue of Justice that stood near the top of the stairs and smiled to himself. Then, he started the long climb to the top.

Making his way up the stairs, Jay overtook a trio of men who were heading in the same direction. The two on the ends wore dark glasses and windbreakers emblazoned with the words, "U.S. MARSHALL." Each kept a hand on one of the arms of the man in the middle, guiding him up the stairs. Jay assumed that it was partially for security and partially just to help him keep his balance, since the man's hands were cuffed behind his back. Jay was halfway past them when he stopped and turned at the sound of his name:

"Jay!"

The man in the middle was Martin Willis.

The four of them stood there for a moment, on the steps. Willis glared at Jay with a malevolent eye. In return, Jay considered the man who, in many ways, was responsible for everything that had happened to him in the past year. Willis looked different now. Less jovial. More haggard. More tired and, most of all, more angry.

"So," Willis said, "I knew you'd be the one ratting me out."

Once, Jay would have felt a tremor of fear in the face of the confrontation. But he'd been through far too much to be intimidated anymore. "Sorry, Marty," Jay said with a dismissive gesture, "but I don't have time for this. See you inside."

Jay turned back toward the courthouse to go. Yet, before he

could turn completely away, Willis's mouth curled into a nasty smile.

"You forgot what I told you," Willis said. "We're everywhere. And you're dead."

Jay shook his head in exasperation more than disbelief. Suddenly, though, his expression was replaced by one of shock. The two "marshalls" had pulled their guns and were pointing them straight at Jay's chest!

Jay looked around. There was nowhere to go. No possible source of cover. Nobody close enough to intervene. Time seemed to slow to a crawl. Jay could see their fingers tightening on the triggers . . .

"'Bye, Jay," said Willis.

. . . when the guns flew out of their hands. The deadly weapons soared high into the air and out of sight.

"Wha—?" said one of the gunmen.

They tried to move, but stumbled awkwardly. Somehow, despite the heat of the day, mounds of ice had formed around their feet, freezing them to the steps. Then, there was a blur of motion as a figure hurtled in out of nowhere, smashing into the two phony marshalls. Seconds later, they lay sprawled across the steps, their feet still frozen in place. Before either Jay or Willis could fully register what was happening, Hank McCoy lay a huge, friendly hand across Jay's back.

"I surmised that you might appreciate the pleasure of the *coup de grâce*."

There were a million questions that Jay could have asked. But despite it all, his mind was filled with only one thing. "Thanks," he said.

Jay planted his fist straight into Willis's face. Willis bounced hard as he hit the step, and rolled down in a heap on top of his two accomplices. He was unconscious even before he stopped falling.

As Jay's head began to clear, he looked around until he spotted a familiar group at the bottom of the stairs. Four young people stood there, clustered around an older man in a wheelchair. Jay recognized Scott, Jean, and the Professor. The other two—a handsome blonde man in designer clothes and a brown-haired teenager in jeans—were a mystery.

Jay hurried down toward them, with Hank at his side. "So, you're with them, huh?" Jay asked Hank.

Hank grinned. "Until death do us part," he replied as they reached the bottom.

"My apologies for that little incident, Doctor," said the Professor. "Virtually all of the Secret Empire has been captured at this point, but there are still one or two small pockets waiting to be caught."

"But how could you know . . . ?"

"That you needed assistance? We knew in the same way that we've always known."

"'Always?'"

Jean flashed him a smile. "Sure! You didn't really think we'd just abandon you, did you?"

"Huh?"

The Professor's lips turned down a bit at the edges. "I am sorry for the distress that our earlier parting may have caused," he said. "However, as I said at the time, it would indeed have been too dangerous for you to have come with us.

"Still, having scanned your mind at the school, I was familiar with your particular mental signature. That made it simple enough to monitor your actions from afar and ensure your safety."

"You—you mean you've been watching me all this time?"

"Not all of the time, no," the Professor replied. "Merely from time to time, or when I sensed unusual levels of distress on your part. Our primary focus has been on stopping the Secret Empire, after all."

"But . . . why didn't you just tell me? My God, I thought I was all alone! If I'd only known—"

"—You wouldn't have been nearly as careful," said Scott. "You would have let your guard down, and that could have gotten you killed."

Jay thought about that for a minute. He had a point.

"Rest assured that, if the circumstances had become truly dire, then we would have stepped in, whatever the consequences," said the Professor. "In fact, on one occasion in Kansas City, I was about to halt your assailants with a long-distance mental command. However, you proved yourself to be resourceful enough to deal with the situation without my aid. You are a very capable young man."

"Maybe we should make you an honorary mutant," the teen-ager added with a grin. Hank rolled his eyes and elbowed him the ribs.

Jay let it all sink in. In a way, it did all seem to make a certain amount of sense. In fact, his initial indignation was starting to be replaced with a weird sort of relief.

"Well . . . thanks for watching out for me, I guess." Jay watched as the courthouse guards appeared, scratched their heads for a bit, then hauled Willis and the others inside. Jay expected them to approach, but they never did. It was almost as if they couldn't see Jay and his companions. "From here on out, though, I think I have to handle this one myself."

With a little salute, Jay headed back up toward the courthouse again. Once again, however, he stopped at the sound of his name:

"Oh, Jay!"

Jay turned to see Hank coming up toward him.

"By the way," Hank said, "I'm afraid that . . . unforeseen cir-cumstances have caused me to terminate my employment with the Brand Corporation. I'd suggest that you submit a resumé now, before they issue a general call for recruitment. You would be an excellent candidate."

The two shook hands with a good natured nod. However, this handshake was a bit different than their first, so long ago. To all appearances, Hank's hand looked the same as it always had. But this time, it felt . . . furry, somehow. Still, if Jay noticed the difference, he gave no sign of it.

"Well," said Jay, "once more into the fray."

"I could not have put it better myself," Hank replied.

Jay gave Hank's hand a final shake and then withdrew. With the sun warm on his back, Jay climbed the stairs to meet his destiny.

1980s

UP THE HILL BACKWARDS

by Thomas Deja

I: Sean Cassidy

SEAN, WE need your help on this."

Sean Cassidy sat back in the Comm-Room chair at the Muir Island Research Center. The lights were down to 40% capacity out of deference to the lateness of the hour, and he spoke in low, hushed tones. He sipped his black tea ('sweetened,' as was his wont, with just a touch of County MacBride's finest single-malt twelve-year-old scotch) and considered how he should answer the stunning woman he was talking to.

His first impulse was to be honest with her. *Thank you just the same, but I have more than enough trouble helping Moira care for all the Morlocks and injured friends of mine you dropped off after that massacre in New York. I was a touch too old to be part of the Game of Capes and Masks when Charles Xavier asked me to help shepherd the new team of X-Men he was putting together, and I still ache in areas I've no wish to be aching because of it. So thank you, but no.*

But it was hard to say no to Ororo Monroe, the current leader of the X-Men. Even though she had shorn her long white locks in exchange for a mohawk and seemed to have embraced an attitude more in keeping with her days as a thief in Cairo, Sean could still see the teenage mutant Charles Xavier recruited for his X-Men. When Charles found her, Ororo was worshipped as a goddess; even though she now served Xavier's dream of mutant/human integretion as Storm, he still saw a touch of imperialism in her demeanor. Whether a mutant weather 'goddess' or an earthbound, leatherclad warrior, Ororo expected her wishes to be taken seriously.

Faith, Sean, he thought to himself. *You're getting lost in yourself.* He ran his hand through his thick red hair and sighed. "Ororo," he said, his voice thickened by the brogue of his native Ireland, "you understand that if I do this, I won't be going into the field. I'm an old man, and I won't be dragged into a young man's game again."

The face on the viewscreen smiled. Once again, Sean was reminded of theregality of Storm's bearing. "I would not ask that of you, Sean. I only ask you to train these recruits. Logan and I have some personal matters to attend to, and with Magneto presently in charge of the Academy. . . ."

"I still don't believe that," Sean muttered.

"I do not think any of us does, but it is a fact, and we must deal with it."

Sean took another sip of tea. He paused; training the new X-Men would put extra stress on himself, his lover Moira MacTaggart, and on the Muir Island Research Facility itself. The place was overrun by seriously injured mutants—including a few of Sean's friends. But it needed doing.

Now more than ever, with the corridors of Muir stuffed to overflowing with the remnants of the underground community of mutants called the Morlocks—victim of the so-called 'Mutant Massacre,' there was a need for hope. After the casualties inflicted by a group of mercenaries calling themselves the Marauders—including seriously wounded X-Men Nightcrawler, Shadowcat and Colossus—it seemed to Sean that it was vital Xavier's dream was shown to stand.

If he turned down training this nascent team, the message sent to those like the Marauders wasn't just that no one cared about the cast-down fringes of the mutant community like the Morlocks; it was simply that the mutant community was broken.

Sean looked up. "Alright . . . I'll play Charles to these young ones. But you will owe me for this, Ororo lass."

Sean met the new recruits in the facility's pressroom. It wasn't much: the small auditorium could only hold ten comfortably, and it was dusty from disuse. The fact that The Muir Island Research Facility was not exactly built to serve as the headquarters to a semi-secret 'super hero' team occurred to him yet again.

Sean recognized a few. He knew the tall southern woman with the white streak in her hair was Rogue, more by reputation than anything else. He was struck by how young she appeared, only a few years older than Kitty Pryde (who in all likelihood was going to celebrate her 15th birthday here in the Muir Island Infirmary). He recognized the wiry blonde man as Alex Summers, even out of the black regulatory suit he wore as Havok. Another of the women looked familiar, a strawberry blonde with cheekbones sharp enough to wound. Even though she hunched herself down in the chair as if she didn't want to be noticed, Sean could tell the pose was unnatural, as if she was used to the spotlight.

The remaining two were decidedly odd. The woman with purple hair and shining eyes seemed to at least be human. But as much as she seemed human, the man with the long blonde hair didn't; he was leaner and lankier than the average man, and had only three fingers on his hand. The vacant look on the man's face, like he was a total stranger to this world, was icing on the cake.

Sean cleared his throat. "Thank you all for being here. For those of you who haven't met me, my name is Sean Cassidy. I was a member of the X-Men for a time. Before that, I served with Interpol as a deep cover agent, and in the New York City Police Department. I've been asked to take a hand in training you all in combat and teamwork . . . the sort of things you're going to need to survive in this world. Now Alex and ummm. . . ."

Sean looked at Rogue expectantly. She looked back, confused. "What?"

"What will I be calling you, lass?"

The pretty woman shrugged. "Rogue is fine enough, don't you think, sugah?" she said in a distinctive, molasses-thick drawl.

"Alex and Rogue I know have some experience with the types of conflict you'll be encountering as full members of the X-Men, so I will be asking them to help me during these weeks—"

"I have full STRIKE accreditation," the purple-haired woman said, citing the British arm of the international peace keeping organization SHIELD. It struck Sean how, even though her tone of voice was normal—subdued even—it seemed to command the attention of the room. "I did serve a tour of duty with them, and I was . . . had some small experience with metacrime."

Rogue laughed. "You should see how she faced down Sabretooth, Mr. Cassidy . . . had him chasing her like a blue tick after a coon."

"That's, umm, verra nice," Sean said. He paused. "I want you all to keep in mind, this is a medical and scientific research facility. I don't have a danger room like Xavier's. We'll be doing a lot of improvising, and I'm going to be requiring you to meet me half way. But together, hopefully . . . together we'll get you all ready to fill in for the team while they're recovering."

"That's what we are, fill-ins?" asked the blonde woman. Sean once again was struck at how familiar she looked—he seemed to recall she was a singer under a fanciful stage name.

Dazzler, he finally recalled. *That's right.*

"That was my impression, yes. Storm and Wolverine may have other plans for you."

"Well that certainly gives me a warm feeling," the purple-haired girl muttered under her breath. Having people muttering under their breath was never a good thing, Sean found.

"Well, what I'd like to do is meet with you individually, understand your background and powers, so I can then develop a proper training program for you lot. Would anyone care to be first in the queue?"

The blonde man with the missing digits raised his hand.

Sean smiled. "D'you want to go first, lad?"

The blonde man stared at Sean innocently. "I am hungry. When will we be fed?"

A package of chips and some of Moira's ghastly coffee seemed to keep the boy happy for a time. He ripped the foil bag open clumsily and ate the snack food two, sometimes three at a time. This led to every third or fourth word he said being punctuated by a loud 'crunch.' The boy's name, he discovered, was Longshot. And things just seemed to fall into place for him.

"That nice Dr. MacTaggart says I generate a 'probability field,' and that makes me very lucky," he explained amicably. "I don't know why she needed to poke me to discover why I am what I am . . . but I am. Lucky, I mean."

Sean tried to hide how much his head hurt following the boy's logic.

Dazzler, thankfully, was more coherent.

". . . When they outed me as a mutant, it all dried up. Oh, the weirdness that followed me around didn't dry up—I still got assaulted by jerks and lunatics in costume, not to mention jealous jerks and lunatics in costume. But no one would touch me anymore. They broke my recording contract, the movie roles never materialized. If it wasn't for Lila offering me a spot in her touring band . . ."

She shrugged. Sean found it interesting how this woman who defined herself by her performing now sported the body language of someone thoroughly withdrawn. Now that she was deprived of the one thing she yearned for her whole life, she was defeated. He was going to have to negate that; maybe if he brought her down to an amateur night or two, coaxed her to perform again. . . .

"Scott once told me you turned down membership in the X-Men, Alison. Why are you here now?"

She looked up at him. "After it all happened, I decided I needed to know how to defend myself. I should've figured it out long before that, Mr. Cassidy. Ever since Scott, Jean and Logan found me, it's like I can't take a walk to the store without some guy in a mask falling in love with me. So Peter—Colossus, he was going to help train me and . . ."

Sean nodded and put up his hand. Peter Rasputin was another of those wounded by the Maruaders during the Mutant Massacre. There was no need for further explanation.

Up close, it was a surprise to Sean that he didn't assume Rogue was older than her years. There were lines on her face prematurely earned. That they were there was understandable; Storm had filled him in on what she knew of her background, and it was hard to imagine what her terrorist 'mother' Mystique had done to her during Rogue's time as a member of the Brotherhood of Evil Mutants. But this was a young woman with a sunny disposition, as if she was determined not to let her situation drag her down.

Of course, she may be trying too hard, he thought to himself.

"I understand you used to be an outlaw," he said after their greetings were over.

For a second, there was a change in Rogue's outer demeanor—an eyeblink's worth of exasperation, a quick exhalation of breath that sounded like surrender. "Yeah, that's me," she murmured.

Sean nodded. "I spent some time on the other side of the law, lass. An undercover assignment that got a wee bit out of hand. It's how I first met the X-Men."

The tension in her face seemed to smooth away. "I'm sorry to hear that."

Sean shrugged. "I imagine the other X-Men have been giving you a difficult go of it because of your background."

"Well," Rogue said sheepishly, her southern accent making it sound like a drawn-out 'wall,' "Ah did hurt someone they were close to—but ah didn't mean it. Ah didn't know my powers and I kept contact too long—and that friend, she's still *heah*, in the back of my head, like, or her personality is, always pushing in—"

Sean raised a hand. Ororo had also told him how Rogue, during her time with the Brotherhood, had accidentally absorbed the psyche of an old friend of the X-Men named Carol Danvers. "It's fine, lass. I won't be making any pre-judgements based on who you were. I thought you might be wanting to know that."

Rogue gave him a dazzling smile and moved on to more mundane matters.

The Englishwoman, Elizabeth Braddock, would have struck Sean as a colorful character without the purple hair . . . although the purple hair, so at odds with her proper Eatonian accent, was a definite tip-off.

When she gave a brief accounting of herself, Sean's mind reeled. Here was a woman who started out as a model but then served a stint in STRIKE, served a stint as Captain Britain, and ended up aiding the X-Men in the weeks leading up to and following the Mutant Massacre.

Sean seemed to recall reports of Captain Britain being blinded at about the time Elizabeth claimed to be wearing the tights. It would have to be something to discuss with her at some point.

Despite her relative inexperience, Sean had to consider Elizabeth a veteran X-Man next to some of the others.

"I shall be relying on you a bit, Elizabeth," Sean told her.

"Whatever needs doing, sir."

"Good. We'll be needing that attitude in the coming months— especially when the new recruits get a taste of what this life really encompasses."

Elizabeth nodded. "I don't think the previous team quite expected the level of . . . well, for lack of a better term, casualties . . . that they accrued."

"Exactly, lass. And it's a pity those 'casualties' included our telepath. You should go see Moira as soon as we're done here. I'll be wanting t' know your power levels so we can gauge your limits and better apply those abilities in the field. We're going to need someone t' network our operatives, and that job will fall to you."

The woman looked at Sean levelly. Her lavender eyes seemed

unnaturally shiny in the light. "It'll need doing, so I shall do it, I suppose."

"Good lass."

"However," she continued, not missing a beat, "I do think I can be helpful in other areas. I've been able to exert a limited form of psychocoercive influence on other people, which could—"

"Ms. Braddock," Sean cut in, perhaps a bit too sharply. "I'm not denying your versatility. In many ways, I think you can be one of the top operatives in this team. But right now, I have t' concentrate on those who don't have your level of experience."

"Agreed, but—"

"But I'm relying on you t' do 'what needs doing' until we can bring the newer types up to your level." Sean gazed into Betsy Braddock's eyes. "And because you're still relatively new t' the X-Men, in spite of your overall experience, I'm going to be wanting you to concentrate on those elements you will need in a team environment you may not have developed up until this point. D'you understand?"

Betsy's lips formed a hard line. "One does what one must."

"Good," Sean said with a nod. "I'm relying on you quite a bit, Ms. Braddock—you and Mr. Summers both. And I'll be expecting you to be up to the tasks."

Betsy just nodded.

He had saved Alex for last. In a strange way, he knew Alex Summers both the most and the least of all the members of the team. During Sean's time with the X-Men, Alex always wavered at the edge of the group, never quite joining. And then there was the lengthy period of time when Alex and his girlfriend and fellow X-Man Lorna Dane, were brainwashed into aiding a Shi'ar agent. Sean had plenty of opportunities to know Alex—but it always seemed like Alex did not want to let him.

Alex was the only one of the group counted as a true 'veteran.' And Sean needed someone with that status.

Sean locked the door of the conference room as Alex settled into his chair. Alex didn't look very much like his brother, Scott

Summers, but there was a resemblance. Maybe it was something he could capitalize on. . . .

"I have to tell you, son, that I'm relieved you're here."

Alex made a face. "What do you mean?"

"I've just spent the day talking to the others," Sean replied. "It was an . . . illuminating few hours, it was. Lord in Heaven, I gathered this was a catch-as-you-can group, but this lot is not ready for what they're getting into. We've got a nice power base overall, but the personalities and lack of experience—"

"I heard that Psylocke held off Sabretooth by herself for hours," Alex offered.

"Yes. And she was a spy, and she was Captain-bleedin' Britian—but Alex lad, she only became an X-Men a short time ago. Even that Rogue girl, her time on the team is limited." Sean sighed and massaged his forehead. "But look at this team. A singer who joined up because she had nowhere else to go. A—I have no idea what Longshot is supposed to be, but he's naive in the ways of the world. And Psylocke . . . well, pluck she may have, but she seems a bit headstrong and willful to adapt to a team situation."

Alex squirmed a bit in his chair. "Sean . . . don't get me wrong. I appreciate your candor here, but why are you telling me all this?"

Sean met his gaze. "I would think that would be obvious, lad."

"Make it crystal, Sean. I've been out of touch."

"Storm asked me to train you lot while she and Logan take care of some personal business. I don't know how long you'll be working without them, which means I need a field leader. I need to train someone to take the reins, and I think you're the best choice."

Alex was silent for a long time. Sean added, "It's just guesswork at this point, lad—"

"No," Alex said, his voice very low.

"What d'you mean?"

"I mean no." Alex glanced about, his nervous energy apparent to Sean. "I . . . you know, I never asked to be an X-Man. I mean, one day I'm graduating college and this bald guy comes up to me and says, 'Hi, Alex, this is your brother, we're freedom fighters in this war for mutant civil rights, and you've just been drafted.' Nobody asked me if I wanted to be a super hero—"

"But someone's asked you now, haven't they?"

Alex laughed hollowly. "Yeah . . . and I said yes because you're the only place I can turn to right now. Every time, you know . . . every time I try to go off and lead a life—a *real* life—some goofball alien shows up at my door to enslave me, or my girlfriend gets possessed by some piece of jewelry or. . . ."

Sean reached out and took Alex's wrist. "Listen to me, lad. I've seen you in the field. You helped us when Moira's boy went insane. I know you have it in you to fight the good fight, to be an example—"

Alex pulled his arm away. "But I don't want to! Let Scott be the big macho leader man. Let me just . . . let me be in the background, carrying the spears."

A hundred retorts went through Sean's mind. One look at the anguish on Alex's face prompted him to stay quiet.

Sean needed the younger Summers boy. He needed him to serve as example and to lead the group of remnants he was entrusted with. But the moment to reach him was in the future. Alex Summers' personal pain needed to be dissipated before the leader within could be released.

"Alright, lad," Sean said finally with a sigh. "Why don't you go and get some rest. I'll talk to you later."

For a moment, Alex seemed frozen, as if expecting a trick. But then he relaxed, and he rose from his chair. "Okay."

Sean watched him make for the door. As Alex unlocked it, he said, under his breath, "I believe in you, lad."

Now to work on making you believe the same.

After the interviews were over, Sean planned to head for the personal quarters he shared with Moira. He was only a third of a way through his annual reading of *Finnegan's Wake*, a book that demanded total attention.

He barely noticed her lurking in the shadows. He lingered at the door, but did not turn to look at her.

"You have something t'say, Callisto?"

The former leader of the Morlocks was silent at first.

"Some cub scout troop you got there, Irish," she sneered. Sean listened to her footfalls retreating before going inside.

While The Muir Island Research Facility had a variety of high-tech equipment and was one of the more scientifically advanced laboratories in the world, it did lack certain amenities the X-Men needed to train.

To be precise, it was missing a Danger Room, the advanced battle-simulator that allowed the X-Men to hone teamwork and tactics. For a time, Sean had considered using the physical therapy auditorium for their training sessions. But one walk through the wards, packed wall to wall with injured mutants, changed his mind. There were still scores of ailing patients, many of them members of the Morlock tribe the Marauders almost wiped out in the Massacre. Some of them were destined to die in the facility, but Sean knew others would heal—and they would need a place to relearn functions their bodies had forgotten how to perform.

With some reluctance, Sean brought his "X-Men" (*And doesn't that feel a little bit strange*, he reflected on more than one occasion) outside to the shoals of the island. The terrain around the facility was dreary and gray, all sharp, jagged rocks and crashing surf, the sort of place one would expect to find as the setting for a Gothic Romance. The ground was slippery, and one had to tread carefully. The roar of the surf kept communication difficult.

Not a Danger Room, to be sure . . . but certainly a dangerous area.

Sean stood inside, leaning against the wall of the island's air-craft hangar, hand mike in his left fist, watching the team. Betsy—Psylocke—was nearest to him. She was the only other person to have a handset; one of the major goals of this training exercise was to strengthen her ability to 'switchboard' between the others, acting as a conduit for her teammates to communicate with each other mentally.

The rest of the team were making their way carefully along an outcropping leading to the sea. Alex and Alison—Havok and Dazzler (*Have t'keep their codenames in mind,* Sean admonished himself. *If I want them to get used to using them in the field, I have to be setting an example.*) were working their way along the jagged rocks. They looked as awkward as they must've felt, most having only met each other a few days ago. Rogue was airborne, carrying Longshot, who in turn was carrying a portable beacon. Despite the light from the Facility, the craggy shore proved a danger to passing ships. One of the beacons Sean had set up, with the help of Moira's assistant, had burned out. Turning a practical task into a training exercise was the height of efficiency in Sean's eyes.

"We're going to be needing a clear spot to fix the beacon in, lass," he told Psylocke through the Mike. "I'm thinking Havok should blast away the remaining debris from the last beacon, and Dazzler can shape the area with a precise laser emmission before placement."

"I'll convey your wishes, Mr. Cassidy," Psylocke replied in even, clipped tones.

His attention shifted to Havok and Dazzler as Psylocke 'switchboarded' the message. Havok seemed to take the telepathy in stride, but Dazzler tensed up. For a moment she seemed to lose her balance. To Havok's credit, he reached out and helped steady her. Dazzler smiled her thanks to her partner then glanced up at Rogue. There was a flickering of emotion that passed through the woman's face—jealousy? Anger?—And then it was gone.

Another of Rogue's sins I'll have to deal with, Sean said to himself. It was hard to put the whole picture together, but it seemed that Dazzler and Rogue had had several altercations during the young Southern girl's time with the Brotherhood. He made a mental note to try and defuse the tension between the two before it damaged team cohesion.

Damaged team cohesion further, he added.

He watched as Havok guided Dazzler, not seeming to lead but doing just that. Sean's instincts were right; Alex Summers *would* be a good leader with a little bit of a push.

The question was what sort of push?

* * *

Callisto was watching them again.

Sean returned from an early morning exercise, and his head was filled with notes. The exercise, "Fox and Hounds," had one member stalked by the others in a sort of mutant tag. Things went pear-shaped rather quickly when Psylocke—the "Fox" of the exercise—chose to use her psychocoercive ability to take over Dazzler's motor functions. Psylocke then proceeded to prompt the unwilling Dazzler to blind the others with a wide-area flash.

Since the whole point of Fox and Hounds was to get the "hounds" to trust each other, Sean had to believe the exercise was a disaster. If anything, Psylocke's actions would re-inforce the lack of trust between Dazzler and Rogue. He was trying to figure out a way to get Rogue and her former enemy to cooperate when he caught sight of the shape outlined in the darkened alcove leading to the machine shop.

"What do you think of my cub scouts now, lass?" Sean said.

Callisto snorted in derision and said in her thick New York accent, "Too pretty for me."

Sean nodded. "That they are." He made to walk past her, but stopped. He turned to face her. "What do you think their chances are in the world?"

Callisto came out from the shadows. She seemed genuinely surprised. "Why you asking me?"

"You know a thing or two about tactics and strategy, tracking, the sort of things I've been trying to teach them. What d'you think; do they have enough to make a go of it?"

He studied the former Morlock leader, a woman whose mutant genes made her the perfect huntress. She had been on the island for weeks now, recovering from the wounds she received during the Massacre. At first Sean thought that Callisto was too withdrawn, overwhelmed by the guilt of letting so many of her people die. But he soon learned that this was an integral part of her psyche. It wasn't that she was withdrawn as much as calculating constantly, evaluating those around her in case they had to become prey.

Callisto stared out at the woods. "They wouldn't last."

"How so?"

She paused to spit at the ground. "Well, the missy with the purple hair is too full of herself, for one. The Songbird and the Pecan Princess are ready to kill each other and the guy with the funny hands—he's got an edge, but he's like a kid. They'd all get eaten up if these games were serious."

"What about Havok?" Sean asked.

"Pretty boy? He gets over how much he hates it here, he might survive a minute longer than the others."

Sean took out his pipe from his jacket pocket. "After breakfast, I'd like you to come by for a smoke. I have an idea, if you're game."

To Sean's surprise, it was Rogue, and not Betsy, who had the loudest reaction.

"What?"

Callisto laughed, a rough, barking noise that didn't convey much mirth. "You didn't understand Irish? While I'm stuck here waiting for the butcher's bill, I'm gonna train your asses to survive."

"She does appear to have survived a lot," Longshot suggested in that open-faced innocent way of his.

Rogue shifted in her seat to face as many of the others as she could. "You ain't been around here long enough, sugah. Until she needed the X-Men to save her and her kin from the Marauders, she would've been happy slitting our throats."

"And you wouldn't have been happy killing me at one time," Alison shot back, her tone dripping icicles.

"I was out of my mind when we fought, Ali. How many times I gotta tell you?"

"I'm sure if I knew that I'd have felt better when you tried to beat the life out of me."

Sean slammed his fist on the desk before the two women's words grew more heated. "That's enough," he shouted firmly. He waited until all eyes were on him. Sean met each X-Man's gaze in turn. "You know this is not playtime. This has always been a war. And now the war's gotten worse. For you lot to survive, you're going to have to learn to fight rougher than rough—and Callisto *is* a right rough lass. That's why I've asked her on."

There was a dead silence for a moment. The five students stirred in their chair.

"We need to stand together, I would think," Betsy said quietly.

"We need to *work* together, Betsy. And your confidence in your abilities is preventing you from supporting the whole. We *need* you five . . . well, six now . . . as a whole."

A look of confusion crossed Longshot. "I am not preventing the team from supporting the whole, am I?"

Sean was about to say something, but Alex turned to face Longshot. "You're doing fine, buddy."

A slight smile broke on Sean's face, a smile he concealed almost immediately. "It's a touch hard to make plans when your ability is centered around the unexpected." As the training of the last few days had proven, Longshot had a strange lick about him—something made fortune always fall in his favor regardless of what he did.

Longshot smiled. "Thank you. I would hate to be the reason for your yelling at us."

"I don't think anyone would blame you," Allison chimed in. Her tone was a little too singsong. Sean made a mental note to keep an eye on Dazzler's growing fascination with Longshot.

"Since I will not be expecting any more objections to the addition of your new trainer," Sean said firmly. "I am going to have Callisto take you lot to the gym. And I expect her reports to be favorable."

With that, he left the room. His mind was on his private quarters, where *Finnegan's Wake* and the bottle of County MacBride he kept locked away for use in times of stress awaited him.

* * *

The combination of the stream-of-consciousness prose of James Joyce and the smoothness of the liquor had done the trick. Sean was truly relaxed again—or as relaxed as one could be in a home unfortunately surrounded by pain, misery and the threat of death.

His mind slowly drifted to the new team Storm had entrusted him with. The discord of the group was working his nerves. This was not the first dysfunctional X-Team Sean was involved with; the team he had belonged to constantly threatened to tear itself apart, especially in regards to Wolverine and Cyclops. But at least his team did pull together, especially after it suffered its first casualty during its second mission. When the situation called for decisive action, those X-Men were capable of working as a unit.

These X-Men were showing up to be such damaged goods Sean feared making them work as a unit was not possible.

Sean sat back in his overstuffed chair and took a sip of his whiskey. The lights were low, and he savored the silence. It was only a matter of time before he had to return to the world that had become the status quo in the wake of the Massacre.

There was a knock on the door. Sean dog-eared his book and put it aside. "Come in."

It was Alex. He had traded in his uniform for a worn sweats. He looked more like a graduate student than an X-Man. *And that might be th' point*, Sean reflected. He peered into Sean's room tentatively, one hand behind his back. "You got a moment?"

The Irishman waved him in and pointed out a straight-back wooden chair. As Alex took the proffered seat, Sean indicated the half-filled bottle of scotch on the nightstand and gave him a questioning look.

Alex shook his head and said, "No thanks."

Once he seemed at ease, Sean sat back. "So what do you have on your mind, lad? Was Callisto too rough on you?"

"That's one way of putting it."

"Good," Sean replied with a nod.

"Look, Sean . . . I, you know, I've known you a bit longer than the others," Alex said after pausing. He rubbed the back of his neck. "Aren't you being a bit rough?"

Sean took another sip from his tumbler. "Do I think I'm being rough, lad? In my heart I am. Honestly, I am. But in my head, I'm not by half."

"These people aren't super heroes, Sean."

"Aye, and that's the point," Sean replied before Alex could elaborate further. Sean leaned in closer to his charge. "My God, lad—look at you lot. I've got one of the women here plotting the demise of the other while making cow eyes at the one member who doesn't even know of her attraction, and that's *if* Longshot even understands romance. The other woman is too busy trying to horn herself into a position of greater strength than the one I need her in . . . and then there's you."

"I've been trying my best," Alex shot back defensively.

"You are?" Sean took a moment to gather up his thoughts. "I think you're doing the best that you are willing t' do, but you're not doing the best you can do."

It took a moment for Alex to realize where the conversation was going. But the realization, when it came, was sudden and the reaction to it came like a thunderclap. He rose from the chair. "Oh, no. We're not going there again. I thought I made myself clear— I'm not leader material, okay?"

"I don't think you realize how much you're already behaving like a leader, Alex. Why did you come to me? Why did you speak up for Longshot?"

"I spoke up for Longshot because he really didn't know if he was screwing up or not. What's there to understand?"

Sean sighed. "You do these things instinctively, Alex. You act on impulse t' keep the team cohesive. You're showing me what I already know."

Alex raised a hand. "No, no . . . you think I don't know why you're doing all this?"

"To show you your strengths as a—"

"No, I'm sorry, Sean. I've got this all figured out."

Sean threw up his hands and sat back in his chair. "Then by all means, lad, please key me in, for I obviously don't know why I'm doing this."

"It's all about Scott."

"Pardon?" Sean was stunned. Out of all the possible answers Alex Summers could give, he did not expect Alex to evoke the name of his brother, retired from the X-Men and working with the other four original members in a questionable operation called X-Factor.

"Yeah," Alex confirmed. Agitated, he paced back and forth, hand to forehead before it all came out in a torrent of words so fast Sean had trouble keeping up. "You think I don't know? Scott's like this, you know, legend to the X-Men. I mean, he *is* the X-Men to some of you guys. When Lorna and I and the others wanted to go off to live a normal life, Scott stayed to shepherd the new recruits. I know Alison has experience with him. I assume Rogue knows of him.

"What you're doing," he told Sean, his gaze level with the older man's, "is trading on my name. You don't care how I feel and what I'm doing. You're hoping that they'll follow me because I'm the super hero equivalent of I don't know, Tito Jackson or something!"

Sean closed his eyes for a moment and sighed. "Oh, Alex . . . if you could see what I see, you'd know that's bollocks."

"Bull. You're just using me."

"Tell me what I can do to convince you otherwise."

Alex shook his head. "It's not going to work like that."

Sean watched the younger man leave the room, the door closing a little harder than it should have. He did not return to Joyce, choosing instead to think long into the night.

It was another day, and another game of Fox and Hounds. This time, Havok was the fox (which was one of the few practical choices; as making Dazzler or Rogue the fox would guarantee that the exercise would degenerate into another cat fight).

And Havok, despite lacking flexibility and finesse, was good.

He stayed to the parts of the wood that were the most heavily grown, depriving Rogue of her airborne advantage. Whenever Dazzler seemed to be closing in, he would randomly fire a bolt of stored energy to lessen the impact of a dazzle-burst on his eyes. He seemed to make all the right moves; even Psylocke reported that he had found a way to blank himself to her mind scans for brief periods—probably, Sean guessed, through some form of meditation trick. Ultimately, Longshot's wild luck ended the exercise. Longshot just happened to be in the right spot just before Alex stumbled through—and tripped over Longshot's outstretched foot.

All in all, it wasn't a bad workout. Sean still put on a face nearly as stern as Callisto when addressing his students, ordering them back to the Institute for breakfast.

As they trudged their way along the cold, hard Scottish landscape, Sean asked the former Morlock leader, "How do you think they're developing?"

Callisto shrugged. "They're fine for what they are, Irish. Won't last a day in the real world, though."

Sean stopped. "What do you mean?"

"It's plain as day," Callisto said with a sneer. "All your exercises are keeping them from becoming a team. They're still pretty kids more concerned with their pretty thoughts than staying alive. You're not making them think about what it takes to survive."

She turned away from Sean and started up the path. "And since they want to stay on their own, they're going to die."

The days were not getting any warmer, and the feeling Sean was failing in his task were not lessening. Sean wondered if these feelings of inadequacy prompted him to go to Black Ned's pub in Edinborough for a meeting with Alistair Stuart the week it was Havok's turn as the fox.

The fact of the matter was he had denied himself a trip to the mainland for over a month since training began. Sean found the simple pleasure of stepping onto a wharf and into an honest-to-

God town was something he missed. He took his time getting to the pub, just breathing in the air tinged with a touch of smoke and sea salt, lingering to look in the windows of the handful of shops. But responsibility eventually overtook him; there was business to be done. With a resigned exhalation of breath, he turned onto the main street and found the pub in question.

It was late Saturday afternoon, which meant Black Ned's was preparing for its weekly Caitrian. The staff was abuzz checking the speakers and preparing the finger food; in a short time, the place would be an insane maelstrom of dancing and singing, local musicians coming from all over the town and outlying environs to perform in a massive jam session. Sean nodded to the pub owner, and scanned for Stuart.

It wasn't difficult to find him at all. The man always seemed out of place when he ventured outside of London. Handsome enough, with the sort of sandy hair that always looked like it was in danger of becoming unmanageable, Alistair ran the Weird Happenings Organization. W.H.O., as it was called, was one-half clearing house, and one-half spy organization specializing in superhuman and mutant crises. Obviously, with that specialty, the two men had crossed paths frequently. Sean walked up to his table and stood before him, hands in his pockets.

"Good day, Alistair."

Alistair nodded. "Cassidy."

Sean motioned for two stouts before sitting down. "Thanks for seeing me."

"I was planning to come and see you anyway. The Ministry still has some questions concerning that business with the Juggernaut last week."

Sean nodded. The week before, Alison had a run-in with the unstoppable Cain Marko, a criminal with a long history with the X-Men. The new group had managed to bring him down. For a brief moment Sean had had some hope for the new team configuration, but then the bickering and fractiousness returned. "Odd, that. The reason I called you here involved the lot who brought that boy in."

"The new X-Men," Alistair added.

"I'm surprised you know."

"Give the organization some credit, Cassidy." A barmaid came over and placed two pints in front of the men. When the woman left, he contined. "A grouping of mutants shows up in our back-yard, shows some evidence of paramilitary combat training, of course we put two and two together."

"It's only temporary."

"Temporary it may be," Alistair shot back, "but it's bound to be a headache down at the Ministry. We're relatively staid there, you know. We're not exactly used to world-shaking battles in our backyard, now are we?"

"True. But they're here purely for training. I can assure you personally they will be called back to the States soon enough." Sean took a sip of his bitters, his throat suddenly dry and con-stricted.

"Sooner rather than later, if you don't mind," Alistair sug-gested.

"I'm doing my best, Stuart," Sean said levelly. "And I can do a tiny bit better if I have some help from you lads."

Alistair paused for a moment. He cast his eyes downwards, and Sean imagined the thoughts going through his head. It must be hard, he reasoned, for Stuart to serve the government and still show loyalty to friends.

Finally Alistair lifted his glass, sat back, and mumbled, "I'm listening."

". . . I'm proposing a war game of sorts," Sean explained to his charges the next day. "The lot of you, working together, towards a common goal. This shan't be an exercise to show off, nor to undermine your teammates. God willing, after this is done you'll be able to see what I've been trying to tell you lot for weeks: you need to gain cohesion as a team."

Longshot straightened up and smiled ear-to-ear. "A war game? Oh, good. I like games."

"You might not like this one," Alison called out from the parallel bars, which she was using to conduct her morning stretches. Sean wondered if she chose that particular set of bars to practice on more for its proximity to Longshot than anything else.

"Like it or not, it's mandatory," Sean said. He was in full "Strict Teacher" mode, complete with arms-folded stance. It was the sort of mode that frequently got him through domestic disputes in the rougher neighborhoods of New York City when he was a detective. "I don't like pulling rank, lads and lasses, but I *am* responsible for your training, and I am aiming to make sure you're trained correctly."

"So we'll be split into teams?" asked Rogue in between reps on the special hydralic 'lifting bench' initially set up for Colossus; like the Russian, Rogue's strength made her able to lift tons. Callisto spotted her, standing over her as if daring her to make a mistake.

"Didn't you hear him right, missie?" The Morlock sneered. "You guys gotta stick together."

"Then who are we going to be up against?" This question from Havok.

Sean allowed himself a wolfish smile. "Glad someone finally asked. I pulled in a few favors, and as such, you'll be up against W.H.O."

"That is what we are asking, Mr. Cassidy—Who are we up against?" asked Longshot.

Alison looked up. "Great. We've got an Abbott and Costello thing going."

"The Weird Happenings Organization," Betsy responded. She was sitting off to the side, cooling off after running laps. "They're a secret agency specializing in supernatural and superscientific anomalies. I had dealings with them when I was with STRIKE."

Sean nodded. "That's right, Betsy. This is an organization used to dealing with people like us. They will know a thing or two about countering your powers and making things miserable for you. And they shall have the advantage; I've allowed them to choose the site you will attempt to 'liberate' from them.

I'm counting on you lot to win. If you fail, I shall be obligated to buy the participants a round, and I shall be most cross with those who make me pay out. Is this clear?"

Most of the team members chose to remain silent, or to sub-verbalize their disapproval.

Alex, however, told Sean, "Sounds okay to me. You going to buy a round for us when we beat their butts?"

"That sounds fair," Longshot chimed in. He then turned to Alison and asked, "What's a round?"

"I suppose I could be persuaded to part with some drink money," Sean answered with a faint smile.

Sean shielded his eyes against the morning sun. It was the Sunday after his initial meeting with Alistair Stuart, and they were the only people up and about this early. "That's it?"

The sandy haired agent to Alastair's right removed his glasses and rubbed his eyes. "Yes. We've determined that this will be the proper spot for the W.H.O. team to protect from your X-Men."

"O'Brien's one of our gamesmanship experts, Cassidy, special-izing in 'mutant terrorism and adventurism.' He's taken the powers and abilities of your known members into account in choosing this hill."

The spot the three of them were contemplating was an unas-suming hill in the middle of a field. The hill could not be more than thirty feet high, and if it weren't for the uneven vegetation on its surface, Sean would have mistaken it for a large pile of dirt left there by some construction crew. The forest was sparse around the area for some seventy feet, and the sun beat down upon it.

"Why this place?"

O'Brien put away the small Personal Digital Assistant he was consulting. "That would be telling . . . although I will admit to a slight case of whimsy when choosing the area."

"How so?"

Alistair made a face. "According to O'Brien, the local guide books claim this is a fairy mound."

"If we walk around the east side of the site," O'Brien suggested, "you can see an indentation that the locals used to believe was the door to the fae homeland."

"I hope your group is taking this seriously," Sean commented, glancing at O'Brien. "My people will be playing for keeps."

"As will mine," Alistair replied.

"Yes, quite," added O'Brien. "You've given us a rare chance to test some new ordinance out in field conditions. My men and I will be taking this extremely seriously, I assure you."

"See that they do."

Alistair chuckled. "See that you have our tables reserved for Black Ned's . . . and bring your wallet."

II: A Slight Intermission

There were eyes watching the three men discuss the upcoming competition. These eyes did not belong to the fairies rumored to dwell in and around the area. These eyes carried modern communications equipment and watched through high quality binoculars. The watchers were clad in ill-fitting black suits and ties, and wore lapel pins depicting a stylized yellow sun.

If they revealed themselves to Cassidy, Stuart or O'Brien, they would not be recognized. And that suited their masters in the Spire just fine; the agents of Black Air prided themselves as being one with the shadows other agencies cast.

The eavesdroppers listened in on Stuart, Cassidy and O'Brien with their hi-tech surveillance equipment, and learned of their intentions. The head eavesdropper, a bald man with the curious sun symbol tattooed on his face and answered to the code-name Scratch, made a notation in his field manual. He and his second-in-command, who was so proud of his given name of Peter Wisdom that he refused a codename, kept watch while Scratch reported in.

"We will have intruders on Project Windowbox Location Epsilon," Scratch told his superiors. "They appear to be unaware of the importance of the site. Please advise."

And in a black, obsidian room in a black, obsidian tower, plans were made to protect the personal interests of a small cadre of very black-hearted men.

III: Alex Summers

Alex Summers had to admit he had nothing against Sean Cassidy. Truth be told, Alex looked upon the man as the equivalent of the friend that seemed essential in every circle—the one person whose life was so varied and filled with adventure it was hard not to be drawn in by his every word.

Which was why it was very uncomfortable for Alex to tell him he wasn't interested in being a substitute for Scott.

His discomfort was growing with each day on Muir Island. Privately, he wondered why he had agreed to join this interim team. It wasn't that he was an enthusiastic follower of Charles Xavier's dream of mutant/human harmony. If anything, considering the number of times he or his girlfriend had been captured, subjugated, brainwashed and otherwise forced to do things against their wills, that "dream" had become a full-blown nightmare.

In this, Alex felt a kinship to Alison Blair. Alex knew who she was immediately; her debut album went platinum and was hailed as a pop masterpiece. It wasn't his sort of music, but news reports and gossip columns made her every step public knowledge for a long time. She yearned for a normal life like Alex did. Like Alex, super-villains popping up out of nowhere always prevented her from obtaining that goal.

One night after one of Callisto's sadistic 'training sessions,' Alison stopped by to borrow some blues albums he had. As he dug them out, she looked around.

When he had found the albums in question, he rose to find Alison holding a picture of his girlfriend, Lorna Dane. "Pretty damn cute, Summers. Not the type of girl I expected you to have."

"And you expected me to be with, what? Someone fifty-five and fat who lives with a legion of stray cats?"

Alison looked a little embarrassed. "No, no . . . it's just, you know—you're so straight, I didn't imagine you going with some chick with green hair." She went back to studying the photo, pointedly avoiding Alex's face. "And I tell you—that dye job's loads better than Betsy's."

"Betsy dyes her hair?"

Alison put the photo down, her cheeks reddening. "So why are you stuck here with us instead of snuggled in your four poster with her?"

Alex shifted his weight nervously. "She, umm, became possessed by this sentient cameo and is now off with the Marauders."

"Oh, that," Alison replied quietly. "I . . . I was possessed by that thing briefly."

"Sorry."

There was a heavy silence, and then tears started welling up in Alison's eyes. Alex hesitated then approached her, putting his hands on her shoulders.

"What . . . what is wrong with us? What right does God have to curse us with this kind of life?"

Alex tried to come up with a flip answer, but chose to remain silent.

That night crystallized for Alex why he felt so close to Alison; her confusion was on the surface. The others seemed to keep theirs hidden away—all but Longshot, who despite his abilities was still an innocent in this world. Alex wondered if this 'Mutant Massacre' would cast a permanent pall on all their lives. Psylocke barely escaped being shredded by Sabretooth in the aftermath, and Rogue. . . .

Rogue was a strange case. She seemed to be constantly, actively, making the attempt to keep things high-energy. But every once in a while, when she was tired, or when she thought no one was looking, Alex caught a glimpse of the pain she was struggling to keep inside her. He would have to remind himself that Rogue was the one who had actually been down in the sewers with the Morlocks, and her wounds were still fresh.

And when Alex looked at the team as a whole, all he could see was disaster.

Later that night, as Alex was listening to the CD Alison brought her, Sean came by.

"I wanted a word with you before the games, Alex," as the older man stepped inside.

The music ceased. "Fine. Might want to choose it wisely, though."

"You know you can keep trying to play the hard man with me, lad, but I know better. I know how you've been treating the others. Even Callisto has noticed it."

Alex shrugged. "They're okay, by and large. No need for me to be nasty to them."

"Agreed."

"Glad we agree on something." Alex stood there, feeling awkward. He looked around his room and asked, after a moment, "What do you want?"

"I wanted to make a bet with you, lad."

"You already did. You're buying us beer when it's over."

Sean shook his head. "Another bet, then. One between the two of us."

Alex looked down at the floor. His head was beginning to hurt. "Here it comes again."

"Look, Alex," Sean said in response. "I've spent weeks trying to explain to you what a good leader you are. You don't want to hear none of it; it's like I'm trying to lead you up a hill to see the beautiful landscape of possibilities below, but you're afraid to climb it. The only way, it seems, for me to make you climb is to make you prove to yourself you can do it."

Alex paused. He templed his hands briefly. "So you're throwing us up against a bunch of guys trained to kick our asses to prove a point to me? Boy, the others would just love to hear that."

"Not just for that," Sean replied. He moved towards Alex. "This lot needs to work as a unit, and breaking them off and asking them to hunt each other is counterproductive. But yes, I'm hoping that this will also get through to you that I'm not looking for you to be your brother, Alex . . . you *are* the best candidate to lead this crew."

The pain in Alex's head wasn't going away. He went to the bathroom and grabbed two aspirin from the medicine cabinet. "Alright, alright," he called into the living room, "you want to bet; what's the bet?"

"I'll tell you, shall I?" Alex drew a glass of water from the taps. As Sean continued, Alex tossed back the pills and drank deeply. "This war game is going to involve all of you, even Callisto. I'll be back here monitoring your actions from the Comm-Room. Callisto will be with you as a resource, but she and I agree that you'll be leading the team."

"But—"

Sean raised his hand. "I want you to give it a try, lad. This wargame is a no-worries situation. You won't end up killing a soul with a bad decision, or damning the team to Hell . . . which, considering what we've both been through with the X-Men is a real concern. If it gets too intense out there, I will authorize Callisto to take over, but I don't think that shall happen by half.

"I'm willing to bet, Alex, that you'll find out what I've been trying to get into your head for ages now: that you're a right lot more capable to lead this team than you think you are. If you find that out, all well and good. Buy me a pint and we're done."

Alex sipped the water. "And if I wash out?"

"I don't expect you to."

"But if I do."

"If you do, lad," Sean said slowly, "Then I shall personally fly on my own power to the States and drag Logan back here to lead, personal missions be damned."

Alex raised an eyebrow. He leaned back against the bathroom sink. "I'd actually pay to see that."

"I bet a damn sight that you would."

"So you let him talk you into it?"

Alex shrugged. "It seemed reasonable, Ali."

The two of them sat on the rocks down the shore from the Facility. The tide had treated them to a continual sea spray. It was not a perfect place for a conversation, but it was private enough.

Alison chuckled. "I think you wanted to be convinced."

"As if," Alex said with a chuckle, playfully elbowing his friend. Alison returned fire.

"No, seriously," She adjusted herself on the rock and looked over her shoulder. "You're making all the right moves in his eyes. Hell, you're the one guy with his head screwed on right."

"Well, there's Betsy."

"Betsy is great at being Psylocke. She's still not great at being Psylocke the X-Man . . . does that make sense?"

Alex paused. "I guess . . . but I'm feeling weird about this . . . like Sean is trying to force me into a corner."

"Or out a door into a future you don't want to experience?" Alison suggested.

Alex made a face. "Did he put you up to this?"

"Of course not," she said with a laugh. "But I think in this case, Sean may be right. You may have the stuff, kiddo."

"And you may have to trust Rogue—is Sean right about that?"

Alison tensed immediately. She moved away from her friend. "That's different."

"I'm just making a point here." Alex shifted his position. "And then there's the way you look at Longshot."

She relaxed a bit, a hesitant smile blooming on her face. "That's different, too."

"I bet."

"Seriously," she said, laughing. "I mean, look at him—he's gorgeous."

"I dunno. That three-fingered look does nothing for me." Alex returned his friend's smile.

Alison play-punched him on the back. "Well, you're not an artist, and you're not a woman, so take my word for it . . . there's something about Longshot that's gorgeous."

"You're gonna hurt my feelings, pal," Alex half-joked.

"Well, there's no future in pining over you, Alex—you're taken, and I went down that road before. Not for me." Alex let the reference go. It was one of her rare mentioning of her life as a celebrity; he suspected she only felt comfortable discussing it with him, and only as long as he never pushed.

The two friends looked out onto the sea. Alex scratched at his chin. "So you agree with the old man, huh?"

"I think we can do a lot worse," Alison replied.

. . . we can do a lot worse . . .

Alex kept thinking about those words as he slipped into his regulator suit. He had spent five minutes staring at the high-tech garment once he emerged from the shower; after all this time, his feelings about the black-and-silver outfit were decidedly mixed. On the positive side, it controlled the cosmic rays that Alex's body absorbed like a sponge. As long as he wore it, the energies were contained, preventing him from reaching critical mass and exploding like an uncontrolled nuke.

But the suit was created by the man who ultimately utilized Alex's ability to harness cosmic rays to turn himself into the gigantic powerhouse known as The Living Monolith. The Monolith was the first of a succession of beings who tried to enslave Alex, from the high placed politician who served the Secret Empire to the Shi'ar secret agent to closeted mutant Larry Trask. It always struck Alex as perverse that he still wore the suit as if he reveled in the fact that he was a frequent pawn of others.

Maybe I could get Professor X to redesi—

He knew that was impossible even before he finished the thought. Professor X, the X-Men's mentor and the man who devoted his life to the dream of mutant/human co-existence, was off in the Shi'ar Galaxy, fighting a civil war alongside his lover, Llilandra. Who knew if he was going to come back, and in what condition?

He put on the regulator suit, all the while feeling his flesh crawl under the fabric's caress.

IV: Sean Cassidy

Sean poured himself a final County MacBride's Single Malt and took his time downing it.

After he finished, he would be sending the team off to the war game on the mainland. Anxiety still clawed at his insides. He was confident that the team would coalesce into a unified fighting unit once they had to work together, and confident that Alex would realize what he'd been trying to tell him all along.

But Sean had been around the X-Men long enough; the path they took was frequently one of paranoia, fear, pain and sorrow. The team he had now had had their share. He wondered if some of the members of this team could handle any more.

He took another sip. Soon enough it would be out of his hands. He'd be a safe distance away in the Comm-Room. Once their boarded the skiff to the mainland, it was out of Sean's hands.

"What's keeping you?" came a voice from behind him, rubbed hoarse from hard living.

Sean stood up and turned to face Callisto. It was a credit to the woman's technique and mutant abilities that he hadn't known she was there until she wanted to be acknowledged. Her face, as always, was impassive, never betraying any emotion. "Just needed a lil' courage." He told her. He downed the rest of the glass.

"Well, hurry it up before the pups get anxious."

Sean retrieved his pipe and some tobacco; he anticipated it was going to be a long day. "Are you ready for this?"

Callisto shrugged and walked out the room. "Yeah. I want to be there when they fall on their asses."

V: Unexpected Change in the Terrain

The W.H.O. contingent had driven out before light of dawn to set up emplacements and ambushes. O'Brien had made it very clear—as grateful as Her Majesty's Government was to the X-Men for the rare opportunity to field test their Abnormal Power Containment Systems in a controlled environment, there was an element of pride involved.

In other words, W.H.O. would not be beaten by a bunch of amateur civilians. Ever.

Even before the sky had begun to redden, troop transports emptied out their cargo, trenches were being dug and equipment being situated for maximum coverage. Surveyors were taking a last, final look at the landscape to determine most effective use of resources.

When the sun was in the process of rising, O'Brien was called away by one surveyor, who had a map of the area.

"This had best be good," O'Brien said tersely. He had not cracked a smile, or shown any emotion once since getting on the troop transport in the dead of night.

"There seems to be a discrepancy in the terrain, sir."

"Pardon?"

"Well, have a look for yourself."

The Surveyor led O'Brien to the hill W.H.O. was to protect, and that the X-Men were to take.

There was a discrepancy. A large rectangular cairn of dark gray stone jutted from the near side. In the increasing light, O'Brien could just make out that some form of hieroglyphics covered its aged surface.

Carefully, the two men made their way to the spot. A chill ran through them at the same time, the sort of deep-down cold that cuts straight to the marrow. O'Brien looked the object up and down.

"Any idea what language this is?" O'Brien asked the surveyor.

"No idea, sir."

Tentatively, O'Brien reached out to touch the object's surface. The stone was unnaturally frigid to the touch. He brought his hand back quickly, as if bit.

O'Brien was going to tell the surveyor to get Muir Island on the phone and cancel the maneuvers pending a closer examination of the anomaly.

But other forces had plans for the day, and descended upon W.H.O. They struck quickly, and deadly and decisive force.

And as the smell of death rose into the morning air, the pictographs on the cairn glowed faintly.

VI: Alex Summers

Alex took his time getting to the muster room. He suspected he would have all day to let Sean down; there was no need to rush. In his head, he was making plans for finding Lorna once he went stateside.

He passed the others' quarters. Some had already for the final meeting before being taken to the mainland. Alex smiled as he passed Longshot's room; the door was wide open. The team would need that sort of enthusiasm—and more than a bit of the kid's wild talent.

Alex turned the corner. There, locking up her room, was Betsy. She was dressed in her combat "uniform," a practical outfit made overly pretty with the addition of off-the-shoulder, billowing sleeves and a set of streamers emanating from each forearm. Its pink color clashed with her purple hair. *If only the thing was gray or black,* Alex thought to himself, *it wouldn't be half-bad.*

As he got closer, Alex's smile disappeared. Betsy had her head against the door, eyes half-closed. Her face was paler than usual, and she seemed unsteady on her feet.

"Betsy, you okay?" Alex asked gently.

Betsy straightened up immediately and pasted on a smile that wasn't convincing anyone. "I'm fine, Summers."

"Well you look like a couple of miles of unpaved road. You sure?"

Betsy gritted her teeth. "I'm fine," she repeated. "It's just that sometimes, particularly when I'm around a particularly nervous bunch, the thoughts of my comrades overwhelm my natural blocks. I just didn't sleep well."

Alex backed off. The explanation rang false, but he was reluctant to push further. "Okay, okay . . . but maybe you should sit out the operation."

"I think I'd be best qualified to make that decision, don't you?" she shot back, turning away from her door. "We should get to the muster room, don't you think?"

"Yeah," Alex finally said. There was no point in pushing things. *But I'll be keeping an eye on you, Betsy,* he promised himself silently, hoping she'd pick that stray thought up.

The final address was mercifully brief.

"Alex is acting field leader during the exercise," Sean told them tersely. "Any concerns and suggestions are to go to him. Callisto will be on hand to advise Alex, but she is not there to win the game for you. Betsy, you take networking, and Rogue I need you to serve as the advance scout.

I want you to secure that hill quickly and cleanly. The neater our success, the happier I'll be. If you win but leave a path of wreckage and bruises, I will hand over training to Callisto on a permanent basis."

There was a smattering of moans. Callisto grinned wolfishly. "Oh, I'd love that."

"I shall be in constant touch with Alex, but I won't shower him with advice. I want to see you succeed on your own. As a team."

Sean looked over the gathered mutants. "Are you ready to show up that lot at W.H.O.?"

The cheers were mixed. Alex got the impression that some— Betsy in particular—weren't convinced they were entirely ready.

* * *

On the barge, Alex turned to his "troops." "Okay, I think Sean had a good idea. Rogue, you're our only flyer, so it'd be a good idea to do a recon."

"I could do that now if you'd like, sugah," the southerner suggested with a slight smile.

Alex paused. "If she's okay with it, I'd like you to absorb Callisto's abilities. The heightened senses could allow you to get a good picture without being found out right away."

Callisto shook her head. The mini-video unit Cassidy had fitted over her eyepatch gave her the appearance of some form of cyberpirate. "Oh no you don't, puppy dog. I thought Irish and I made it clear I'm here to advise, not contribute."

Alex massaged his forehead then straightened up. Grabbing a headset from the forward locker and handing it to the young southerner, he said, "Okay. Rogue, just give us a look around. Don't get too close."

Rogue adjusted the headset and smiled sweetly. She rose from the launch like something out of a fairy tale. The sea breezes tousled her hair gently. She threw Alex a smart salute and said, "Ah'll be right back."

"As long as the soldiers aren't too cute," Alison muttered under her breath. Alex elbowed her in the ribs when no one was looking. She yelped, but otherwise kept silent.

Alex watched Rogue rise higher in the air and fly off to the mainland. She really did have a gracefulness he hadn't considered.

The barge was silent save for the motor churning the water. The others shifted nervously in their seat. He turned up the volume on the headset and asked, "Can you read me, Rogue?"

"Clear as crystal and pretty as china," Rogue replied.

"Will we each get a headset to play with?" Longshot asked.

Alex looked over his shoulder. "No. Rogue's abilities make it difficult for Betsy to patch her into her telepathic network. So she needs a headset."

The headset came alive in a burst of static. "I got the target in sight, Havok. I'm moving in for a closer look."

"Be careful, Rogue."

The others moved closer to Alex, anxious to hear the first report on the opposition. Alex kept his eyes on the approaching shore.

"I see some trenches, Havok. . . . Maybe a dozen people that I can see, four above ground."

"Any idea what they're packing?"

"I'm just a simple girl, sugah—I don't recognize some of the hardware they've got in their hand—"

There was another burst of static, and what sounded like a deep *thump*. "Rogue! You okay?"

"They're not suppose to be using live ammo! Sean told us they were non-lethal."

"What are you talking about?"

"I'm talking about a shellburst that almost singed mah tail-feathers!" The headset broke down into static again, followed by a sizzling noise. Alex heard Rogue cry out—whether in surprise or pain he couldn't tell.

"ROGUE!"

"This *ain't* what we signed on for!"

"Pull back! Pull back!" Alex barked.

"What in the world is going on?" Betsy asked. There was a confused, lost look on her face. She seemed flushed, as if straining to keep something under control.

Alex pushed past Betsy and Longshot to Callisto; Alison wisely sidestepped out of his way. "Did you know about this?"

Callisto remained stone-faced. She shook her head. "News to me, pretty boy."

Alex turned. "Does *anyone* know what the Hell is going on?"

VII: Sean Cassidy

Sean sat forward in the command chair, the same question in his mind. Alex's face filled the monitor. Sean's fingers fumbled across the keyboard, dialing Alistair Stuart's private line with more speed than grace. His heart was slamming against his ribcage like some demented, drug-addled dancer. He tapped his throat mike, opening the radio channel to Havok's headset. "I'm trying t' find out myself, Havok."

Sean heard Betsy call out, "We're making landfall" from somewhere behind Alex.

Stuart's phone was ringing. "I'm aborting," Sean said hurriedly.

"Abort? But what if something's gone wrong on their end? We should at least investigate."

Sean felt a little twinge of satisfaction at Alex's response, but tamped it down. The phone continued ringing. "Investigate, but don't engage, Alex. Until we get a clearer picture from Stuart, my concern is that you lot come out safe."

Alex's face twisted into a rueful grin. "We're supposed to be X-Men, Sean. Safety's a long lost concept."

VIII: Alex Summers

Alex turned away from Callisto. "Alright—we stay close. Until I hear otherwise, we're assuming this is not part of the exercise."

The others were climbing out of the launch. "What do you have in mind?" Alison asked. She swiveled her head from side to side. The silence was oppressive.

"I want a wedge here. Longshot at point—"

"Longshot?" Betsy asked. She seemed taken aback by the choice.

"He's the fastest and most agile of us, Betsy, and he's got that weird wild luck thing going for him. It may keep him alive upon first contact. Ali, you and I form the point of the wing to provide sniping potential. Rogue, you'll be air support. Betsy, you and Callisto are in the back."

Betsy put her hands on her hips. "Well that's not very wise is it? My psychoblasting effect is equally as effective as the Dazzler's, maybe more so since it is not dependent on outside stimuli."

Alex shot her a stern look. "Yeah, I want you questioning everything I say, Psylocke. You keep talking about being such a pro at this game, start acting it."

"But—"

"You're our network, Betsy. I need you to keep communication flowing. And if what we're up against cuts through us, I want you there to blow the brains out of anything that tries to get at Callisto."

"I can handle myself," the Morlock replied sharply.

"I don't doubt it. But if we fall, I want to know the last woman standing can track these bastards back to where they live and rip them open."

Callisto shifted her stance and grinned wolfishly. "There is that."

Alex looked at each member of the team in turn. "Are we ready?"

The answers he got were varied but meant the same thing: yes.

Except for Callisto's response. She met Alex's gaze and asked, "Are you?"

They headed inland. Alex was hyperaware of his own breath reverberating in his skull, and the thumping of his heart. He could see at the furthest periphery of his vision Betsy and Callisto keeping pace. A quick glance down at the regulator badge on his uniform showed that the cosmic energies were building slowly, concentric circles moving outward like ripples.

The map Sean had drawn was in Alex's head. It was a good mile before they hit the first emplacements, according to Rogue. And from there, it was another seventy-five yards to the hill.

Three quarters of a football field of who knows what, Alex thought.

He wasn't worried about the run tiring out the group. Alex was more worried about "runner's rapture." If the team became hypnotized by the rhythm of their progress, hit that physical high that whited out the mind in a sheer gush of adrenaline, they could be taken off guard.

If the map was correct, the clearing was up ahead. *On your toes, people! It's showtime!* Alex telepathically told his crew through Betsy.

I would think so, Longshot replied. *I am in the field and these men are shooting at me.*

Even without that declaration, Alex could hear the gunfire.

IX: Sean Cassidy

The distant crack of gunfire came over the monitor. Sean felt his stomach knot. This was going sour far more rapidly than his nightmares had predicted. He dialed Stuart again quickly and cursed under his breath with each ring.

The sound of the connection being made was like a soft kiss. "Stuart."

"Are your people daft, Stuart? I'm getting reports you lot are using live ammo!"

"You know more than I do, Cassidy! We lost contact with our group ages ago, and there's been something mucking up our lines. I've only just gotten full service back."

Cassidy leaned forward in his seat. He looked from Callisto's monitor to the phone line. "What do you mean, 'mucking up your lines'?"

"I mean someone's been jamming our signals, Cassidy," Stuart barked back. "Whoever is out there is not ours . . . and judging from how they've been preventing us from contacting you, it's a damn sight large possibility that they don't want to share holiday snaps with your lot."

X: Alex Summers

Alex's headset came alive with another burst of static. "Did you get that, lad? The group you're facing is not W.H.O. This is *not* a game."

"Nothing personal, Sean," Alex snapped as he hit the ground and let loose with a beam of wild concussive force, "But we figured that out already."

The scene was chaotic. The troops had opened fire the moment the X-Men broke cover. The opposition looked nothing like W.H.O. field personnel; their uniforms were gray with black armor panels and yellow symbol in the form of a stylized sun on their chests. And, as Rogue pointed out when she played scout, their weapons were unlike any Alex had seen before; metallic monstrosities with a smooth, curving design that made them look more like alien organs than weaponry.

Alex kept trading fire, taking the moment between blasts to survey the enemy. The one thing he could be thankful for was that these men in black didn't seem to be as used to engaging in firefights with superhumans as the W.H.O. troops would have been; their blasts tended to be scattershot and their formation quickly degenerated. Alison, now being charged by the whizzing of bullets around her, was able to create a weak laser barrage that kept them contained. Rogue was doing her best to keep the sun behind her, diving out of its blinding brilliance to snipe at her opponents.

Longshot, to Alex's surprise, was perhaps the most effective of the lot. He was cartwheeling and gamboling in the thick of these troops, drawing fire that never *quite* hit him, and throwing his knives in such a way that they always got stuck in the troops' barrels.

The strangest elements in the battle were the three figures Alex could detect flitting in and out of his view. One of them was dark and decidedly young looking; another was bald and had a grayish complexion that did nothing for the yellow sun symbol tattooed on his forehead. The third, who seemed to stay the closest to the large stone that jutted out of side of the hill, was a hulking brute who looked more simian that human. All three dressed in black suits and ties with varying degrees of incongruity.

Alex kept alternating between firing and commando crawling

closer to the hill. *Longshot,* he telepathically said through Betsy, *there are three guys I think may be in charge here. See if you can take down one.*

Cert%nly, c&*pt

What the?

Alex fired again, then addressed Betsy. *Betts, what's going on?*

It took a moment that seemed like an eternity before Betsy replied, obviously disoriented, *I'm sorry, Alex. There's . . . something is interfering with my telepathy. He's . . . they . . . my God . . .*

The headset came alive again. "You'd better get back here, pretty boy. Princess collapsed."

"Dammit," he hissed through gritted teeth. Alex scrambled to his feet and laid down a wide swath of energy to keep the troops pinned in near the hill. He headed for where Betsy and Callisto were, praying all the while that he wasn't inviting a bullet in the back.

Callisto was holding Betsy awkwardly in her arms when he found her. The British telepath was limp but conscious—barely— her limbs flailing weakly in an attempt to gain purchase. Alex looked to the Morlock and asked, "What happened?"

"You tell me, pretty boy. One minute she's doing that spooky telepath zone-out, the next she's a heap of bones."

Alex patted her cheek. "Betsy, can you hear me?"

Psylocke's head lolled on her shoulders before her eyes flickered open. "A-alex . . . there's . . . there's something out there. . . . I should have . . . known from the interference . . . I was picking up on this morning."

"You told me you were being overwhelmed by our nerves—"

"I . . . lied. Didn't want you thinking . . . I was unfit for . . . duty." She found her footing and stood up. She stumbled a few steps away from Callisto. "I-it's what I've . . . been feeling all . . . all day, inhibiting me . . . *infecting* me. I can't get a . . . full fix on them . . . but they're alien, fundamentally wrong. . . ."

"We gotta deal with Martians now?" Callisto sneered.

Betsy shook her head. "No . . . whatever it is . . . it's from . . . outside our reality, and . . . and whatever it's horribly, unspeakably corrupt."

"I don't like the sound of that."

"Join the club, pretty boy."

Alex tapped the headset. "Rogue, I need you back here to watch over Psylocke for a moment."

Betsy weakly put up her hands in protest. Alex reached out to steady her. "No, no . . . I . . . I will be fine."

"No. You're my only link to the team and I need you safe." Alex glanced at Callisto. "Come with me."

The Morlock spat at the ground. "Uh-uh, pretty boy. You know the rules."

"I don't want to violate them. You're the one with the camera. I want Sean to see what's going down."

"What are you going to do?" Betsy asked.

"There are three guys out there who don't look like they belong. I'm willing to bet they're overseeing the thugs in black, and they may be connected to what you're plugged into. So I'm going to grab one."

Alex ran out on the field, his energies cycling on high. The field had taken on the smell of a battleground—that strange mix of roast pork, copper, and overheated metal that grabbed a person by the throat. He fought against the urge to gag and opened fire whenever the enemy was closing in.

"Sean, are you getting the pictures from Callisto's comm unit?"

"I am."

The hill was coming up fast, filling Alex's view. He kept an eye on Callisto, taking cues from her movement around the field. Her reflexes and senses being what they were, she moved with a wraith-like fluidity. She would duck under blows a full second before they were launched, then strike out at just the right point to send the charging opposition flying backwards. It made her something close to beautiful in a way, and Alex had to concentrate to keep from watching her too closely.

Callisto turned her head and shouted, "Mind yourself!"

For a split second, Alex thought the Morlock was being self-conscious. Then something slammed into the small of his back, driving him to the burnt grass hard. His body skidded over the ground, his assailant pressing his full weight on him. Alex launched an elbow backwards and felt his blow connect. His attacker grunted in surprise, his grip loosened. Alex twisted his body and found himself face to face with the dark-haired Suit. Both man and suit were a little worse for wear; portions of the fabric was torn, and the man sported a swollen cheek just turning purple and blood flecked teeth. The man punched Alex in the face before grabbing his throat. He pulled his other arm back.

"Tag, mate," he muttered in a thick northern English accent. The fingers on the suit's free hand started glowing an angry red and elongated into spikes. Alex had both of his hands around the suit's arm, trying to tear it away from his neck. He felt dizziness overtake him.

XI: Sean Cassidy

Sean struggled to take in the pictures Callisto's unit was broadcasting. Since heading out onto the field, the Morlock had been running at a fast clip, so the information came at him in near-subliminal blips, the next image already up on the screen before he could retain it.

He head Alex starting to choke, heard the wisecrack from the opponent. "Callisto, lass! You've got to—"

And then he saw the cairn sticking out of the hill.

That registered. Two years previous, when Sean had been a member of the X-Men, they found a similar cairn standing in the middle of the Westchester wilderness. Something had come out of it from another dimension and almost annihilated them, something called. . . .

"N'gari . . ."

Sean slammed his hand down on the commlink button, opening all the channels available. "Retreat, X-Men! Retreat! The environs are hostile, potentially terminal. Disengage immediately."

"What?" Alex said through a crackle of static.

"Move yourselves out, Summers! This is serious!"

And then for a moment, Callisto's videocam caught a glimpse of a simian-looking gentleman in the black suit stepping in front of the cairn. Memories of the nightmares Sean had for weeks after the X-Men encountered a similar cairn flitted through his head . . .

Just as gray, spindly arms reached out to grab the man before it.

No, not reached out, Sean realized after a second. Reached *through*.

XII: Alex Summers

Things started to speed up in Alex's mind as his vision began to dim.

As his opponent kept the pressure on his throat, survival instincts kicked in. It looked like the dark-haired man was going to drive the red spikes that had become his fingers into Alex's face. Before the blow could connect, Alex brought his knee up into the man's crotch. His opponent gasped, his hand falling to the right of its intended target.

"Stupid suit," Alex choked out.

Before either man could respond further, Callisto closed the distance between herself and Alex's attacker. Securing an arm around the man's neck, she pulled him off Alex. "If anyone kills the pretty boy, it'll be me," she whispered in his ear.

Alex half believed her.

Suddenly, Alex's headset exploded in a flurry of static. Sean's voice, much louder than before, said, "Retreat, X-Men! Retreat! The environs are hostile, potentially terminal. Disengage immediately."

"What?"

"Move yourselves out, Summers! This is serious!"

To the side, Alex saw Callisto stop struggling with her dark-haired, dark-suited opponent. He felt a chill run through his body as he sat up. There was something on the former leader of the Morlock's face he'd never seen in the time he'd known her.

He saw her taken by surprise.

The catalyst for this reaction was accompanied by the loud sound of flesh and bone being punched out of place with the force of a die-cut drill bit. Alex looked behind him to see the big monkey man run through by two gray, scaly arms that ended in long claws. The arms moved away from each other slowly, enlarging the wound. The monkey man screamed and thrashed violently before the life oozed out of him. His body tore apart like warm bread; the cracking of his bones popped like pistol shots in the cool morning air. Around Alex, troops and X-Men alike stopped dead in their tracks, their eyes suddenly glued to the hideous sight.

"It's happening again. . . ." Callisto murmured in a stunned, dream-like voice.

The screams from the enemy troops started when the rest of the monstrosity had climbed out of the now-dead agent's gaping wound.

It was the uniform blackish-gray of advanced rot, its hide mottled and pitted. The head was mostly mouth and horns, vaguely triangular but distorted by the mismatched rows of teeth and the curvature of the protrusions that grew from its brow to sweep back over its neck. Even from a distance, Alex could see the interplay of otherworldly muscles barely held together on a spindly skeleton.

The monstrosity stepped through the corpse of the Suit and swiveled its head from side to side. The ravaged body dropped to the ground like a crimson sack of meat. Some of the troops that, moments before, were attacking Alex and his fellows, managed to shake themselves out of their stunned stupor and raise their weapons to the creature. The creature continued surveying the landscape, its claws clacking open and closed reflexively.

"Sean—do you have any idea what thing is?" Alex called into the headset.

"Aye," the Irishman responded. "That's a N'gari. I faced them with the other X-Men shortly after you and the original members left. They're extradimensional demons, walking slaughterhouses. There's no point in your engaging it with the training your team has."

The first of the troops fired at the nightmare standing in front of them. The creature took two steps back on its hind legs, a bellow of surprise piercing the air.

"But, Sean, this thing is going to run loose in the countryside."

The other troopers joined in laying down a barrage of weapon fire. Only instead of driving it back, the creature charged and swiped at the nearest soldier. Its claws neatly bisected the man, prompting a shower of organs to cascade to the ground. The man's fellows began screaming, but the N'gari had waded into a clump of them, its claws slashing through them like wheat.

And a second of these monsters were climbing through the cairn.

And a third.

Alex fired off a rapid burst of cosmic energy at the new arrivals. With complaining roars, they stepped away from the troops. His mind raced, desperate for a plan.

"Retreat!" Alex called out at the top of his lungs. He pointed to the black-haired man, now secured by Callisto in a full nelson. "He's coming with us."

Longshot, who had been close to the spot of the N'gari's entrance, took a running jump and bounced on top of the head of the creature emerging. He stepped from N'gari head to N'gari head, leaping off the last one and narrowly avoiding the claws of the demons' lead. The three-fingered mutant grabbed hold of a tree branch and pulled himself up into the protective foliage.

Callisto followed behind Alex, dragging the dark-haired man with her like a sack of potatoes. Alex looked over his shoulder and let go with a series of cosmic energy bolts, throwing dirt and sod into the air to mask their retreat. Alison gathered up the ambient sound and let fire with a dazzle-burst of incredible intensity, briefly overwhelming the landscape with a wash of photonic color.

Alex feared it was going to be a long time before the team was safe.

XIII: Sean Cassidy

"How's the exercise going, luv?"

Sean felt Moira MacTaggert come up behind him and slip her arms around his waist. Second only to Charles Xavier in the field of mutant genetics, she was Sean's lover, and a source of support during the period when he had to adjust to losing his sonic abilities. Sean stood, his seat long abandoned, looking closely at the screen for any indication that a N'gari was closing in on the team. He slipped his hand over hers and squeezed gently. "Moira, it's not an exercise by half."

Moira looked over his shoulder. "Och, looks like a war zone."

"Aye," Sean answered. With a sinking feeling in his stomach, he added, "I think you'd best set up triage. There may be a need."

XIV: Alex Summers

The second they hit the heavy brush surrounding the fields, Alex grabbed the man in the black suit by his shirtfront. He practically tore the man from Callisto's grasp. The adrenaline from the hurried retreat still rushed through Alex's veins, and he felt dizzy from the tension. "All right, what's going on?"

The man smiled shakily. "A bit hard on the coffee today, were we?"

Alex slammed the man against a nearby tree. "There isn't time! Who are you, and what's going on?"

The man's face softened. He held up his hands. "Alright, sunshine. Just be careful with the neck, aight?"

Alex released the man and stepped away. There was a rustling in the trees to the right, and Longshot dropped down to the ground. He glanced over his shoulder. Alison was at his side instantly and checked him for scratches tenderly. "The monsters are preoccupied with the gunmen. It's not pretty," Longshot told them.

"Couldn't have eviscerated that toerag Scratch, could they?" the dark haired man muttered. Before he could say anything else, Rogue's arm shot out, pinning him against the tree by his neck.

"Those are your men out there being slaughtered, sugah," she told the dark-haired man tersely. "It's in poor taste to be joking now, don't y'all think?"

The dark-haired man choked and sputtered before motioning to his jacket pocket. "Take a look there, sunshine! I'm Black Air! Her Majesty's Government!"

"Never heard of them," Alison mentioned as she and Longshot rejoined the group. She reached into the man's jacket, prompting a flicker of a grateful smile from him.

Betsy had propped herself up against a gnarled tree. She looked like death warmed over, paler than Alex imagined possible. Mopping her forehead, she murmured weakly, "They're a bit of a joke at STRIKE . . . some people there think they're made up."

"Then our PR is working, innit? Jesus wept, the whole point of a secret service is to be secret."

Alex looked to Rogue. "See if you can go out there and help the troops. Stay to the air, and pick-and-move. Those things get too close, run back here."

The southern woman nodded and took off. The dark-haired man took two unsteady steps away from the tree where he had been pinned. He mumbled a "ta," before Alex elbowed him in the stomach without looking. The agent fell to his knees, coughing.

"Peter Wisdom," Alison read off the ID and handed it to Alex. He glanced at it briefly, then tossed it aside. Alex took a deep breath, looked down at the ground before planting his foot into the agent's chest and pushing him to the ground.

"I figure we have only a few minutes before those three monsters find us and cut us into ribbons," Alex hissed at Wisdom. "You better spill everything you know now or I'll save them the trouble of shredding you!"

"Leave some for me," Alison commented dryly. She was giving off a slight glow from absorbing the sounds of the carnage. In Alex's headset, the sounds were closer, more magnified, as Rogue was weaving between the demons and the hapless troops, trying to buy them some time.

"Aight! It's not as if I'm anxious to die with you lot, now is it?" Wisdom shot back. Alex removed his foot. The agent got to his feet and straightened his suit, all the while staring intently at the X-Men. "Right. Black Air is charged with dealing with this sort of thing when it's too nasty for W.H.O. to deal with, aight? A great deal of our mission statement concerns the securing and mastering of objects of a mystical nature in case you poncy spandex types go renegade. We've heard rumors that the 'fairy mound' you folks were going to have fun and games with was a gateway into another dimension—"

"Populated by big things with teeth that can kill us," Betsy suggested.

"Yes, populated by big things with teeth that can kill us. Our higher-ups ordered us to monitor the mound for activity . . . and when you and that spotty-bottomed W.H.O. team decided to have your reindeer games here, well, that changed things, didn't it?"

Longshot tilted his head to one side. "If you are not our opponents, where are they now?"

Wisdom glanced sideways at the other-dimensional mutant. "Our orders were to secure the location with ultimate deniability. To Scratch, that meant we had to take care of them."

Rogue lowered herself to the ground just as Alex pushed Wisdom back against the tree, putting his entire weight on the secret agent. "Take care of them *how*?"

"I would assume that would be obvious," came a voice from behind Alex. He looked over his shoulder to see the remaining (tattered) black suit, the gray-skinned man with the sun tattooed on his forehead. He was carrying a gun almost as large as his arm, and was decidedly worse for wear.

"Ask Desperate Dan over there," Wisdom mumbled.

The pieces were falling together in Alex's head—as well as, he assumed, the others. Rogue came up beside Alex and told her, "It's a horror show, boss. There's not much left outside of the beasties."

"Yes," the new arrival said dryly. "My gratitude for sparing me from that fate."

It was Betsy, surprisingly enough, who made the accusation. She pulled herself off the tree and half-stumbled toward the tattooed man. "You killed them, you pratt."

Wisdom smirked. "Rather . . . Scratch over there has a talent for that sort of thing. I'm not too flash on it myself."

Alex raised a hand to stay her. "Betsy . . ."

The telepath turned. "I'm half inside these creatures' head, Alex. I can *feel* what's going on. This . . . bastard . . . ordered the W.H.O. troops murdered."

"This isn't a game, miss," the man Wisdom called Scratch said tersely. "Our mission statement was to use terminal force on anyone interfering with the operation. That meant the W.H.O. troops. But that's in the past; I would think we should concentrate on getting out alive."

Betsy's energy signature flared; suddenly, her face was covered with a purplish glow in the shape of a butterfly. "You thorough idiot. You don't understand. These things are death gods where they come from. They feed on the cessation of biological activity. When you slaughtered those poor men, you *called them here!*"

The butterfly flared. The tattooed man's head snapped back as if shot, and he fell to his knees. Longshot and Dazzler made to go to the man's side, but Alex held them off.

It was the first time Alex had seen Betsy's psychoblasting abilities up close. He began to sympathize with her complaints during training.

Betsy straightened herself. She murmured, "Well, that was . . . refreshing."

"Would you marry me?" Wisdom said with frank admiration.

Before anyone could respond, there was a tremendous crash, as several of the trees splintered and fell. A stench of blood and torn flesh filled the air.

One of the N'gari burst through and roared.

XV: Sean Cassidy

Sean felt his heart stop. He brought the microphone to his mouth. "Scatter, lad! That thing will kill you!"

The screen was filled with the N'gari bearing down, its mouth open in a shuddering, high-pitched howl. Sean shivered involuntarily; he forgot how many teeth the demons had. . . .

The view was shaky, as he imagined Callisto was already moving, trying to avoid the creature's reach. He caught a fast glimpse of Longshot launching himself at the thing, his heels smashing into the spot just above the thing's eyes. As Longshot rebounded, Sean saw a photon stream slam into the thing's chest. The N'gari was driven back all of two steps.

That, to Sean, was the biggest source of despair; he had faced the demons before, and Storm, the one person who repelled the N'Gari in that long-ago time, was in the states. . . .

Sean watched a green-and-yellow blur—Rogue, he assumed—fly into the picture and land a blow on the creature's back that sent it stumbling to its knees. From off screen, three throwing blades found their marks in vital joints thanks, he assumed, to Longshot's unconscious probability field. For a moment, Sean thought his team might actually have the power to repulse the N'gari invaders.

That moment evaporated into air as he realized it took exactly three seconds for the creature to recover and continue its charge toward Callisto and the video camera.

There was a discharge that briefly blinded the screen as lightning arced across the demon's spine. It reared up and howled, unwittingly exposing its belly—

And the picture sputtered, a white-hot radiance blotting out the scene. Undulating concentric circles of coruscating energy that hit the N'gari dead center, propelling it backwards and back into the field. It was hard to tell from the now-washed out video picture, but it seemed that the demon was temporarily incapacitated.

Havok's voice came through clean and clear. "Okay, we have a moment's time. We need a plan."

"Lad, these things are lethal. You're risking everyone's life there—"

"I said we need a plan," Havok reiterated. He stepped in front of Callisto's camera. "If we don't do this, people will die. I don't care about these idiots who tried to kill us, but I'm thinking these things could find their way to the nearest town easily. I will *not* have innocents slaughtered because I wanted to retreat. That's all there is to it."

XVI: Alex Summers

Alex turned to face his fellow X-Men. "Rogue, quick . . . see if you can cobble together a barrier from the wreckage. There are two others out there and I'd rather they not see us right away."

"Gotcha, boss," Rogue replied and set to rearranging the smashed foliage.

Alex faced Callisto. "Sean, you've faced these things before. How did you stop them?"

"Storm used her power t' seal off the cairn . . . she nearly killed herself doing so, though."

Alex pointed to Scratch. "You—you set off an electrical discharge just then."

"It's his mutant gene," Wisdom suggested with a laugh. "All the S-Branch types have one."

"Shut your gob," Scratch shot back at his fellow agent with a voice like a knife.

"We should shut both your holes for you," Betsy spat out.

"Shut up everyone!" Alex shouted.

The quiet amongst the X-Men was amazing. Alex, for the first time, felt all eyes on him.

Better take advantage while it's in operation, he thought.

He tried to meet everyone's eyes. "We don't have a chance against these things if we're separated. If we continue stick-n-move tactics, we can keep them off balance. *Don't* bunch up, but keep everyone in sight. Our goal is to stuff them back into that rock and blow the rock to kingdom come."

"Rather," Wisdom drawled. Alex glared at him.

"Rogue, I want Mr. Scratch to go aerial. He's got the closest thing to Storm's power. Longshot, you, Dazzler and I will work on three sides, try to contain them. Betts, we'll need networking." He turned to enter the field, expecting his team to follow behind him.

Instead, he heard a cough. Turning, Alex saw Betsy, still unsteady but standing with arms folded and a look of regal entitlement on her face.

Beyond, the field sounded deathly quiet. Alex could imagine these creatures positioning themselves, biding their time until it was suppertime.

He allowed himself a half smile. "Oh, and keep a short leash on our two guests from Black Air. If they try to bolt, fry their brains from the inside."

Psylocke nodded slightly.

Alex wondered if his compatriots wanted to run as much as he did.

He had seen what these things could do. He had spent part of that impromptu conference *hearing* what those three demons were doing to the Black Air troops. And the Black Air troops were men in armor utilizing heavy weapons. The X-Men, on the other hand, may have a variety of special abilities but they were also wearing spandex and leather—if one of the N'Gari got ahold of one of them, it would be little protection.

He made his way carefully out into the main field, his senses open. The sounds of carnage had quieted during the period they were hidden away in the woods. During the period where he worked through some sort of plan with the others, thoughts of what had happened in the area surrounding the cairn gamboled through his head at a rapid pace . . . and always returned to a flash of the demon tearing their way through himself, or one of his team.

The smell hit him first like a punch in the face, a ripe offensive stench that was equal parts decay, blood, fear and adrenaline. To his right, at a distance, he heard Alison gasp involuntarily.

Alex tried to summon up memories of the field before they were attacked—memories he only had from the photos and film footage Sean had shown them in preparation. It looked nothing like what he was looking at now. The grass was stained crimson and brown; bodies were strewn about the ground, ripped open like a bunch of carelessly used toys. The weapons the soldiers had hoped would protect them now lay useless, marked liberally with tooth and claw marks.

Longshot, he telepathically called out through Psylocke's network, taking a step onto the killing field, *if you get the chance, grab one of these weapons.*

Almost immediately, Alex saw a flash of black tumbling onto the ground, cartwheeling through one of the rare clear strips of land. When the blur of movement stopped, Longshot stood at the foot of one of the trenches W.H.O had prepared with one of the Black Air rifles in hand.

"Is this what you wanted?" the extradimensional X-man asked. He grinned expectantly.

Alex nodded. Longshot straightened up, the pride in his accomplishment plain.

And that was when a N'Gari threw off the corpses it was hiding under and rose from the trench with a roar. Longshot pivoted, his newly acquired rifle aimed for the monster's throat. Alison stepped forward, a nimbus of light flaring around her.

"I need an electrical charge *now*!" Alex barked, running toward Longshot.

He saw Rogue, her unwilling passenger dangling from one arm. Scratch seemed more intent on twisting out of her grasp until a familiar energy discharge resembling a longtail butterfly manifested over his eyes. He convulsed, then motioned toward the N'gari bearing down on Longshot.

The monster swiped at Longshot. The boy was already spinning in the air like a champion ice skater, gun firing, long hair whipping about his face. At the same time, the creature reared up, something green and viscous spattering from its throat. There was a flash of gray, and Longshot tumbled head over heels and landed roughly on one of the tattered corpses. Alison fired a photon beam, driving the creature back against the far trench wall as she headed toward her teammate.

"Dazzler! Remember the plan!" Alex shouted. He took off at a run, acting on instinct and an overwhelming desire to keep his friends from dying.

Suddenly, Alex felt all the hairs on his body stand on end as a massive electrical charge arced from Scratch's outstretched arm to the N'gari. The creature screamed and convulsed.

Betsy's voice appeared in his head. *Sorry it took a moment, but Mr. Scratch was resistant.*

Resistant to what?

He could almost see the smile bloom on Betsy's face. *Why Mr. Summers, you have seen me take over a person's motor facilities before, have you not?*

Alex came at the monster at an angle. He aimed and fired, hitting the creature full force with his concussive power. *Just keep in up, Betts*

There was a second discharge from Scratch's airborne form. A smell like singed hair pervaded the air.

As if you had cause to doubt, Betsy replied.

Alison had gotten to Longshot's side. She cradled him with one arm, her whole form giving off sparks borne of the creature's roaring. One of the extradimensional mutant's sleeves was ripped open, and a gash ran from shoulder to wrist. Alex's heart was pumping as he moved closer to the two of them, his thoughts filled with ways to get them out of the N'gari's reach.

And then he was flying through the air, his side numb with the impact. As his body tumbled through space, he caught a glimpse of a second N'gari keeping pace with his trajectory. His headset came alive with Rogue's southern drawl, screaming in his head, "go limp, boss!"

The only flying X-Man grabbed him in her free arm. Her flight path wobbled to adjust to the added weight. She headed for a higher elevation as her other passenger—still possessed by Psylocke—gave the second monster an electrical shock.

Alex muttered, "Good catch."

"Ah thought so," Rogue responded. Alex couldn't help noticing she was grinning.

Rogue and Alex looked down on the field. With its intended prey out of reach, the second N'gari was closing in on the wounded Longshot and his protector, Dazzler.

"Drop me," Alex said.

"From this height? You'll break your neck!"

"*Drop me!*"

Rogue did as she was ordered. Alex was once more in freefall. *Man, this better work like it used to in the Danger Room,* he thought to himself. He extended his arms toward the ground and began firing a series of short bursts of energy. The first blast hit the ground, and the concussive shockwave moved back up the line of the blast, causing his body to shudder unpleasantly. But Alex focused beyond the sudden pain and continued launching short pulses.

By the time he was almost to the ground, he was feeling his momentum bleeding off noticeably. It was still going to hurt, but at least nothing would be broken.

He curled himself up to prepare for impact. When he hit the ground, Alex skidded along the ground for several feet. He landed with a sickening *thud* against one of the discarded, tattered bodies. There wasn't an inch of him that didn't ache.

"Any landing you walk away from," he muttered under his breath.

He looked up. A N'gari filled his view, one clawed talon raised. Alex twisted left just in time to keep the creature from connecting with—and severing—his head.

Alex scuttled to his feet, backpedaling from the monster. His body was screaming with pain from the punishment it had taken so far. Dazzler had gotten Longshot to his feet and was trying her best to guide him away from the demons, dazzle bursts coming off of her at an accelerated page. Betsy and Rogue were still providing air support, but Scratch's electrical discharges were coming further and further apart. Despite Dazzler's effort, the two N'gari were closing in slowly. And Longshot—Longshot hobbled along as fast as he could, but his injured arm hung dead at his side, and he displayed a stiffness Alex had never seen in the man before.

Alex let loose with another concussive blast, carving a wide swath to drive both of the N'gari away from Longshot. *Betsy, we need Scratch to project more!* he telepathically communicated. Behind him, an electrical discharge slowed the N'gari on Alex's trail.

I am trying my best, luv, Betsy responded, *but his body can only generate so much energy at a time.*

There was a roar at Alex's back. He made to turn, but a cold pain exploded across his shoulders. He suddenly felt himself falling to his knees.

Turning, he saw the third N'gari gaining on him. Tatters of black cloth hung from its talons. Alex cursed and prepared for the worse. . . .

But then there was a whistling noise, accompanied by some red streaks of fire. The fire found its mark on the N'gari's back. The creature howled in pain and spun around to face its tormentor.

Beyond the creature, at the edge of the woods, stood Wisdom

and Callisto. Callisto carried what seemed to be a branch that had been ripped off a tree at the roots. She took off towards the third monster at a run. She ran past the creature, thumping it hard in the spot it had been burned. The creature howled anew.

Alex got to his feet just as Callisto came up besides him. "I thought you were just here to observe."

"Screw observation. I want to live."

The N'gari galloped towards the two of them. Callisto shoved Alex out of the way and waited, the branch thrust outwards like a lance. Alex turned as he hit the ground and fired at the two N'gari who were menacing Dazzler and Longshot. The extradimensional X-Man was now able to move at an unsteady run, but the way his wounded arm hung limply at his side worried Alex.

Just as the third N'gari was upon Callisto, she hooked the branch under the creature's chin and tumbled backwards. The demon was lifted off its feet and went flying into one of its fellows, who fell into Alex's blast.

They had won a few seconds of time.

And in those seconds, Alex figured out what they could do to stop them.

XVII: Sean Cassidy

Watching from the Institute was maddening. The battle was coming to Sean in snatches of impressionistic tableaus, visuals of carnage punctuated with the kind of noises that made him assume the worst. He felt sick with worry.

He had been entrusted with the training of a group of X-Men. He pushed Alex into being a leader. And thanks to his efforts, Sean would be responsible for their demise.

The tide seemed to have turned briefly in the X-Men's favor, with the N'gari scattered and disoriented. Sean knew that both Alex and Longshot had been injured. He feared that this moment would be too brief.

And then he heard Alex say, in amazement, "I have it."

"Give us some good news, lad," Sean replied through the commlink. "I'm inclined to call STRIKE and have them raze the place."

And then Alex told him the plan in a breathless series of phrases.

And as Sean worked it over in his head, he realized it just might work.

XVIII: Alex Summers

Alex gave Rogue her orders hurriedly, keeping in touch with Betsy to make sure it would work. The N'gari were already coming out of their stupor, and he busily spread the word.

The ground-based X-Men scattered, giving the creatures a wide berth. As Wisdom let loose with those thermal discharges he called "hot knives" to distract the demons, Longshot ran for the woods, quickly becoming lost in the foliage. Rogue, with the Psylocke-controlled Scratch in tow, still kept an aerial position.

There were only a handful of yards between them and the cairn. The three demons were fully recovered and seemed to be ready to give chase.

Alex, Alison and Wisdom ran toward the hill, taking turns to harrow the creatures. Their intention was to slow the N'gari's advance; stopping them dead would take too much effort.

The hill was getting closer. In response to the mutants' proximity, the cairn seemed to glow with a malignant energy.

Oh, God, please don't let the gateway vomit up a new batch of these monsters, Alex said to himself.

He could feel the creatures gaining on him. His shoulders still ached with the frigid numbness of a N'gari's glancing blow; he knew if the timing wasn't perfect, one of the nightmares chasing him would tear him apart. He'd never see Lorna again.

The crew was fifty yards away from the foot of the hill.

Thirty.

Twenty.

"Now!" Alex called into the headset.

Three things happened.

The first thing was that Rogue touched her unwilling flying partner, Scratch, with her bare flesh. Instantly, the memories and mutant abilities of the Black Air agent flowed from his person to hers, and he became temporarily an empty vessel, incapable of independent movement.

The second thing that happened was that Psylocke moved into that empty vessel, taking control of the body and forcing it to resume the function it was needed to fulfill in the plan.

The third thing that happened was that a W.H.O. troop transport, its back wide-open, roared out of the woods and slammed into the pack of N'gari. One of the demons fell under the massive armored truck, lifting its back wheels off the ground. A second found itself flipped into the hollow back end itself. The third, sensing the presence of the driver, climbed over its fellows and onto the roof.

The door of the transport flung open, and Longshot leapt out. Even with his injured arm, he was able to land on his feet. With a grin wider than Alex thought possible considering the situation, he flipped up onto the roof, dove under the confused N'gari and tumbled off the vehicle and toward the hill. The creature turned as its fellows struggled to extricate themselves from their situation.

Longshot bowed, launching several throwing knives with this good arm as he rose. "Imagine the difficulty of that!" he called out gleefully. The metal knives buried themselves deep in the creature's hide.

Rogue landed near the transport. She dropped the possessed Scratch, Psylocke's longtail butterfly energy signature still over his face, at her side. The southern mutant's hair stood on end, her body fully charged with the electrical energy she copied from the Black Air agent

"Time to fry, sugah," Rogue said with a tight smile before both she and Scratch opened fire.

The massive electrical discharge ran along the length of the truck like wildfire, catching the N'gari in a cage of primordial energy. Some energy arced and found the metal blades in the body of the N'gari on top. They shrieked as one and writhed in pain, trying desperately to escape from the energy discharge. The air became thick with a heavy, greasy smell as their flesh was seared. The two combatants continued firing for as long as they could. The unholy symphony of the demon's agony drowning out the *whoomph* as one too many sparks found their way to the transport's gas tanks.

The explosion knocked everyone off their feet, scattering them like tenpins. Alex fought against unconsciousness just long enough to see a rain of rotten, burnt meat surrounding him.

The cairn, solid stone for all this time, suddenly gained a fluidity as it flickered and distended. Its whole form roiled like boiling water. For a moment, Alex feared that this was a prelude to another apeture opening. But that fear dissipated as there was a rumbling noise that sounded like God clearing his throat, a flash of light, and the cairn was gone.

Damn, I'm getting too old for these Hail Mary passes, was his last thought before he succumbed.

XIX: Sean Cassidy

In reviewing the events of their "war game," Sean had to admit the results were mixed.

Wisdom and his superior had slipped away in the confusion surrounding the explosion. More frustrating to Sean, Alex, and Alistair was how Black Air took advantage of the confusion and erased evidence of their team being there in a matter of hours; all W.H.O. found were a mess of naked bodies stripped of any identification. Sean also had to contend with an X-Team that was seriously worse for wear; five individuals—and their trainer—who needed some recuperative time in the infirmary.

On the other hand, they'd succeeded. And they'd succeeded thanks to Alex.

He sat in Moira's office across from the young man, his pipe clenched between his teeth. They were discussing the experience, and where they would go from here.

"I'm not perfect at it."

"And Scott was first time out? Or the Professor?"

Alex had flinched at the mention of his brother. There seemed to still be a kernel of doubt in the man's mind concerning Sean's motivations. But the doubt was much smaller now, something Sean could manage to work and eliminate entirely.

"I know I can do this."

Sean laughed. "Lad, you already know the first rule, aye?"

"What's that?"

Sean paused, puffed on his pipe. "You do what's right for your people, and for the world. You do that, and most everything else will fall into place."

Alex nodded. "I hope so. I'll see you tomorrow."

Sean watched the younger Summers leave. He smiled to himself. In his head, he was already planning what he was going to say to Ororo and Wolverine. And how much he was going to have to pay in drink costs once everyone was on their feet.

He may have had to lead Alex Summers up the hill backwards to get him to see the breadth of his abilities but the view from where the young man was standing had the potential to be spectacular.

1990s

THE CAUSE

by Glenn Greenberg

NICKY IACONA had just finished performing his Saturday evening magic show at the Pavilion Community Theater, in the upstate New York town of Salem Center. He was sitting in his tiny, dimly lit dressing room, toweling off the sheet of sweat that covered him, and reflecting on his slowly burgeoning career. With only 300 seats, the Pavilion was hardly a "big-time" gig. But then again, Nicky Iacona was hardly a "big-time" magician. Yet.

The 22-year-old Nicky had been working as a street magician in Manhattan for nine years, making a living—or what passed for one—by performing his unique tricks to the momentary delight of passersby on the busy sidewalks of the sprawling metropolis. Within the last few months, though, his reputation began to grow, and he started getting offers to perform in other venues. Not the most prestigious ones, to be sure, but ones with actual roofs on top of them. Maybe, he thought, this was just the start of his journey to fame and fortune. Someday, he was determined, he'd be remembered in the same breath as Houdini, Blackstone, David Copperfield—well, maybe not Copperfield. As far as Nicky was concerned, all *that* guy ever really did was make his supermodel girlfriend disappear.

So, for the last 90 minutes, Nicky had stood on the stage of the Pavilion, apparently generating breathtaking bursts of light-energy from the palms of his hands, and doing amazing things with them. Such as creating balls of light and juggling them. Or seemingly sculpting giant, three-dimensional light-images of George Washington, Abraham Lincoln, Pamela Anderson, and, for the big finale, an enormous, animated Godzilla, that actually lunged at the audience before disappearing into nothingness.

The crowd absolutely loved it. They had never seen such effective, realistic illusions before. But then again, what they saw had not really been illusions. Just as Nicky Iacona was not really a magician. In truth, Nicky was a mutant. The light-energy he generated from within himself was very real, an amazing power that had manifested itself when he reached puberty. But with the widespread anti-mutant sentiments in America—and around the world, for that matter—Nicky had to keep his newfound abilities a secret. After familiarizing himself with these abilities, after teaching himself how to harness and wield them, he soon found a way to use them to his advantage, without revealing their true nature. With this gig at the Pavilion, and more shows booked at other community theaters around New York State, it was looking like Nicky's strategy was finally starting to pay off.

Suddenly, Nicky was interrupted from his musings by a knock on the door. He opened it, and was greeted with two big smiles, coming from a handsome young man with sandy-brown hair, around Nicky's age, dressed in a plain dark suit, and an attractive, dark-haired young lady in a conservative black dress, who couldn't have been more than 18 years old.

"Mr. Iacona," the smiling young man began. "I'm Bill North, and this is Annette Butler. We're really big fans. We just wanted to meet you and tell you how much we enjoyed the show. Hope you don't mind."

"Not at all," Nicky replied, and invited the pair into his dressing room. He was thrilled to be getting such a response, to actually have people wanting to visit him backstage and heap praise upon him. After years of toiling away as an anonymous street performer, it was great to be getting such recognition. He wondered if, someday, he would be so big and famous and surrounded with staffers and handlers that it would be impossible for enthusiastic fans like these to have direct access to him. He sincerely hoped not.

Nicky sat back down in his chair, and was about to invite Bill and Annette to do the same, when he noticed that Annette had closed the door to the dressing room and had taken a position in front of it. Bill was standing further into the room, his body noticeably rigid. Neither of them was smiling anymore. Nicky immediately realized that something was wrong.

"Uh . . . what can I do for you?" he asked, trying not to sound as nervous as he felt.

"Nothing," replied Bill, who was suddenly seething with contempt. "Nothing except serve as a message."

"Wh-what message?" Nicky asked, the fear now rising within him.

This time Annette responded. "That the days of your kind are numbered. Humanity is taking back this world, and we'll soon be free of the threat of mutants."

They know, Nicky thought. *I don't know how, but they know.*

"Get out of here," Nicky told them, trying to sound defiant instead of frightened. "Get out of here before I call the cops."

Bill laughed out loud. "You've got to be kidding me," he said.

Suddenly, Bill and Annette were holding pistols—equipped with silencers—in their hands, and pointing them directly at Nicky. He could feel his heart pounding like a jackhammer, could feel his pulse racing, could feel the sweat rolling down his forehead. He knew he had no choice. He had never used his powers against anybody else before. He'd never had to. He'd only ever used them to entertain people, to make them happy. But now, to defend himself against these hate-mongers, he would have to use his wonderful abilities as a weapon. A tear formed in his eye.

He began to generate a burst of energy that would take the

form of solid projectile, and blast Bill and Annette through the door and into the hallway beyond. Maybe they'd survive, maybe they wouldn't. It was either them or him.

But Bill and Annette were too fast. Before Nicky could complete the burst, they both opened fire on him. Repeatedly. Nicky couldn't keep track of how many times he'd been hit. He collapsed to the floor in shock.

Bill walked over to Nicky's collapsed body and kicked him in the gut.

"Mutie," Bill said with disgust.

Nicky heard Annette giggling, like a mischievous schoolgirl. She was *enjoying* this, enjoying seeing him writhing on the floor in pain and horror. How could anyone take such perverse, naked pleasure in another person's suffering?

The young magician felt himself fading rapidly. As his vision began to blur, he watched Bill pull out a tiny cellular phone and make a call.

"It's me, sir," Nicky heard Bill say into the phone. "It's done."

As Bill closed the cell phone and put it back in his pocket, Annette anxiously asked, "What did Mr. Merritt say?"

Bill's voice was becoming more distant, the words becoming harder for Nicky to understand, but he thought he heard Bill say, "He said we should get back to headquarters right away. That we've served the Crusade well. And that the leader himself will express his own personal gratitude when he finally returns to us."

"All in all, a very successful day," Nicky thought he heard Annette reply, with a satisfied confidence in her voice.

Nicky couldn't be sure if what he was seeing was real or hallucination, but it seemed to him that Annette then stuck her hand into the pool of his blood that was spreading on the floor of the dressing room. But . . . why?

As darkness closed in around him, Nicky Iacona heard what sounded like the door to his dressing room opening, then closing.

And that was the last thing he ever heard.

* * *

It was early morning at Professor Xavier's School for Gifted Youngsters, situated on the outskirts of Salem Center, New York, when the man known as both Logan and Wolverine walked into the stately mansion's screening room. The huge, flat-paneled television screen, built into the wall beyond the chamber's fireplace, was broadcasting a Sunday morning news show, anchored by a local female reporter named Lisa Tang. Several of Logan's X-Men comrades were seated on the couch, watching intently: Scott Summers, code named Cyclops; his fiancée, Jean Grey, formerly known as Marvel Girl and currently operating without an official code name; and Ororo Munroe, also known as Storm. Their mentor, Professor Charles Xavier, was seated nearby in his motorized wheelchair.

"Where are the others?" Logan asked, wondering why there were so few other X-Men around.

"Still asleep, or away for the weekend," Ororo Munroe replied. "Now shush, we're trying to watch this."

". . . The young magician's body, found in his dressing room at the Salem Center's Pavilion Community Theater, was riddled with bullets," Lisa Tang was reporting. "Anti-mutant sentiments were found on the dressing room door."

On the TV screen, Logan watched as the face of the reporter was replaced by footage of the dressing room door at the Pavilion, with the words "Mutant scum" scrawled in red paint—or was it blood?

Tang continued. "Police are investigating, but so far, there are no suspects."

Logan took a seat in one of the screening room's comfortable easy chairs. "Right in our own backyard," he muttered. "And we couldn't do squat to prevent it."

"It's like a sudden epidemic," Scott Summers replied. "An all-new wave of brutal, vicious hate crimes against mutants over the last couple of weeks. This magician is only the latest. Just when we thought the hysteria was starting to die down a little bit."

Logan grunted, eyes fixed on the TV screen. "Yeah, well, we know what lit the fuse, don't we?" he said.

Then, as if on cue, Lisa Tang shifted to a related news story, and the photo of a well-dressed, middle-aged, white-haired man appeared on the screen beside her.

"It is now only a matter of days until the parole of the Reverend William Stryker, founder of the Stryker Crusade. Just a few years ago, the Stryker Crusade was one of the foremost—and most influential—television evangelical ministries. But its power and influence have been greatly diminished, ever since Reverend Stryker was sentenced to prison for manslaughter, conspiracy to commit murder, and his connection to a group of his supporters calling themselves 'The Purifiers.' This group is known to have been responsible for the deaths of several people, including children, who were believed to have been mutants."

The news program shifted to video file footage from several years earlier, of a rally at New York City's famed Madison Square Garden. Reverend Stryker could be seen at a high podium, shoving a woman clad in a skin-tight jumpsuit off the stage and shouting, "Mutant hellspawn—I deny you!" Lisa Tang then spoke over the footage: "Stryker's downfall was caught on tape, at an anti-mutant rally he was presiding over at Madison Square Garden. The woman being shoved off the stage by Stryker was allegedly one of his own 'Purifier' agents. The reverend had apparently just learned that she was actually a latent mutant. The woman broke her neck in the fall and died instantly. Reverend Stryker later referred to the shove as 'an act of self-defense.'"

The video footage then cut to a shot of Stryker being confronted on the stage by the X-Men of that era. Back then, the team consisted of Cyclops, Wolverine, and Storm, along with three other young mutants who had since moved on. There was Peter Rasputin—Colossus—who could turn his skin into super-strong organic steel; Kurt Wagner, the teleporter known as Nightcrawler; and young Kitty Pryde, who could phase her body through solid objects and was at that time operating under the code name of Ariel. In the video footage, Stryker could be seen pulling out a gun and pointing it directly at Ariel, preparing to fire. Suddenly, Stryker himself was hit by a bullet in his side, and then quickly apprehended by police officers. Lisa Tang's narration continued: "Stryker was ultimately brought down by the outlaw band of mutants known as the X-Men, who confronted him at the rally. When he pulled a gun on the young mutant girl in costume that you see on your television screen—we're not sure of her identity—he was shot by a New York City police officer."

The video footage then shifted to a brief shot of the police officer, who murmured into a reporter's microphone, "He was gonna shoot an unarmed little girl. I don't care if she's mutant or not. Someone had to stop him."

The video footage ended and the image of Lisa Tang reappeared. "Reverend Stryker has been described as a model prisoner, and has reportedly provided counsel and spiritual guidance to many of his fellow inmates over the years. He has not announced any plans for his life outside of prison," she said, "but it is speculated that he will write his memoirs—"

"Too bad for him the title *Mein Kampf* is already taken," a sneering Logan interjected.

Tang continued. "—Or that he will return to what's left of his ministry and attempt to rebuild it. One thing is certain: the reverend himself is remaining extremely tight-lipped on the subject."

The news report continued with footage of a crowd of pro-mutant demonstrators, protesting Stryker's upcoming parole. "Mutants are people too!" shouted one protestor, wearing dark sunglasses and an oversized baseball cap. "We ought to be embracing them, making them feel like part of our society! Isn't there enough hatred and prejudice and violence in the world? Stryker and his followers are the ones who ought to be exterminated—wiped off the face of the *bleep*ing Earth!"

This was followed by a clip of an interview with someone who described himself as a "freedom fighter for the human race," his face obscured and his voice electronically altered at his request, to protect his identity.

"Mutants represent a clear and present danger to the survival of normal humankind," he proclaimed. "With every passing day, they get closer and closer to finally using their powers to strike out against us and take control of the world. They could enslave us—or cause our very extinction. We can't let that happen. Reverend Stryker's parole couldn't have happened at a better time."

Scott Summers shook his head in dismay. "The extremists on both sides of the issue are now getting all the media exposure they could possibly want," he commented. "They've been on the news day and night, ever since Stryker's parole was first announced. Leave it to the press to fan the flames."

Charles Xavier picked up the remote control and turned off the television. The group sat in silence for a long moment, until Logan finally turned to Xavier and spoke up.

"I'm surprised they didn't ask *you* to weigh in on this topic, Charley."

"They did," Xavier responded. "I declined the opportunity. I have learned from past experience that I do not have a screen presence or demeanor that could be considered . . . *inviting* to the mass television-viewing public. I'm afraid that would only serve to undermine anything I had to say."

Xavier sighed and continued. "And I fear you're quite right, Logan. The announcement of Stryker's release from prison does indeed seem to have been the catalyst for this new wave of violence against mutantkind. His supporters and allies, forced underground after his arrest, are now resurfacing and taking more overt action."

Ororo frowned. "They've become emboldened by the promise of his return. Releasing him like this . . . it's like his anti-mutant ravings are being given official legitimacy. It's open season on our kind all over again."

Jean Grey turned to Scott Summers, seated beside her on the couch. "You guys faced Stryker when I was still missing and presumed dead." She was referring to a chunk of time in the history of the X-Men when she had been in a state of deep suspended animation, encased in a strange healing pod, underneath the waters of Jamaica Bay in Queens, New York. Since her "resurrection," Jean had made it a point to catch up on what she had missed during her long absence, but reading a data file about a particular incident was not the same as actually being there. "Was he really *that* dangerous?"

Scott nodded without hesitation. "He and his 'Purifiers' were able to take us down, capture us—including the Professor. He had equipment that neutralized our powers. He very nearly succeeded in brainwashing the Professor into using his telepathic powers to kill us—and every other mutant on Earth. I think that qualifies him as dangerous."

"But do we really know that Stryker himself is involved with any of this?" Jean wondered. "I mean, he's been locked away all this time. And even with all the media attention focused on him right now, he hasn't made any anti-mutant statements, or expressed any support for what's been going on lately. I just wonder, is there *any* chance that his time in prison could have reformed him? Changed his outlook on things?"

"Oh, sure, darlin'," Logan replied, sarcasm oozing from his voice. "Prisons are *known* for instillin' a sense of peace, love, an' compassion for all life in their inmates."

"What he's trying to say," Scott told Jean dryly, "is that where William Stryker is concerned, we should be prepared for the *worst* possible scenario, not the best."

"On that assessment," Xavier added gravely, "I must wholeheartedly concur."

An hour's drive south of Salem Center stood New York City. It hours after the sun had set, a clear and warm Sunday night in September, when Gabriel Merritt arrived at his cramped, dingy little office on Broadway in downtown Manhattan, two blocks south of Canal Street. Once the workweek began on Monday morning, this would be a bustling area, packed with thousands of people going about their jobs and their lives. But at this hour, it was fairly deserted. Which is just how Merritt wanted it.

The office, ostensibly a media company called International Advertising Group, was on the first floor of an 80-year-old, twelve-story office building that had long ago started showing signs of becoming decrepit. It was dimly lit and musty, and there was litter scattered all along the hallways. Merritt tried not to notice. This office was merely a means to an end, a place to plan and organize, nothing more. But somewhere deep within him, he could not deny the fact that these current surroundings were a major comedown for him. Just a few years ago, he was working out of a beautiful, modern, sleek, midtown skyscraper with spacious, luxurious offices. But that was a different time. For one thing, he wasn't calling the shots back then, his mentor was. For another, Merritt decided that it was best these days for people in his line of work to keep very low profiles, to not call attention to themselves, and this cover operation was well suited for that. As long as Merritt was able to keep paying the rent, it didn't matter that International Advertising Group had absolutely no clients, and conducted no real business. And he was indeed able to make the rent each month, even without financial support from the nearly dismantled Stryker Crusade.

Entering the small, barely-furnished office, Merritt saw that all five of his senior operatives—three men, two women—were already there, waiting for him. That was good. He valued punctuality. And two of the group's most recent recruits were present, as well. Those two young, ever-eager operatives rushed over to greet him.

"Bill, Annette." Merritt said in acknowledgment. "Again, good work last night. It got plenty of media coverage this morning."

"Thank you, sir," Bill North replied proudly.

"It's an honor to serve you, sir," Annette Butler said with a fierce intensity.

Merritt had no doubts about Bill's unswerving loyalty to the cause, but he suspected that Annette's devotion was fueled by something other than a genuine desire to save humanity from the threat of mutantkind. He'd seen the way she looked at him, how her focus always seemed to be more on him than their mission. He had gotten somewhat used to this kind of attention from members of the opposite sex. His athletic build, his curly blond hair and piercing blue eyes, had won him the attention of many a young lady. He appreciated the attention, but there was a time and place for it. But he had to admit that Annette was quite lovely. Perhaps, when the mission was done, he could think about returning such attention.

Annette stepped in closer to Merritt—a little *too* close, as far as Merritt was concerned. "Did you see on the news what I wrote on the mutant's door, Mr. Merritt?" she asked with an eager smile.

Merritt stepped back, away from her. Her behavior towards him was bordering on being downright inappropriate. He gently patted her on the shoulder and mustered a slight, unenthusiastic grin. "Uh, yes, Annette. A very dramatic touch."

"I was *hoping* you'd like it, sir," she replied with barely contained glee as he walked to the rear of the office.

I'm going to have to have a long talk with her one of these days, he thought to himself. And he sincerely hoped that he would not lose a very promising operative as a result of that talk. But that was for another time. He shifted his attention to far more immediate concerns.

Walking over to his desk and logging on to his computer, Merritt did a status check of the widespread activities of his own group, the reorganized Purifiers, and those of other "human supremacist" organizations with which he shared information. He nodded approvingly. One of those other organizations had reported in.

"The Saviors of Humanity have located a building on the Upper East Side that's secretly being used as a shelter for mutants," he announced aloud. "They've given us a heads-up that they're hitting it tonight. They're inviting us to join them in the operation."

Merritt turned to face his Purifiers. "This is a somewhat larger-scale assignment than you're used to, but I want us to start moving in this direction. So it's a good idea that you get some experience taking part in operations like this." He turned back to the computer and began typing on the keyboard. "I'm informing them that I'm going to send some Purifiers to provide assistance."

After sending the electronic response, Merritt again turned his attention to the Purifiers. "Brent, Jerry, Colleen, Bill, and Annette. I want you to head up there. Arm yourselves heavily—we're not sure yet what powers these muties possess. But they're all teen-agers, runaways. Probably have no training in using their powers. That should work in our favor."

As five of the Purifiers began suiting up and gathering their weapons and ammunition, Merritt sat down in his chair and mused on how long he had been waiting for the time when the anti-mutant cause would once again gather swift and steady momentum. Thanks to all the controversy and media coverage surrounding Reverend William Stryker's imminent release from prison, that time had finally come. Merritt had been leading the Purifiers ever since Stryker, his mentor, had been put away, and he'd long wanted to lead his people out of the underground they were forced into after the Stryker Crusade ministry got caught up in scandal. Merritt spent that time establishing contact with the leaders of other, similar-minded groups, forming a loose coalition, and working with them on ways to stir up hysteria and public demand for the extermination of mutants. All the pieces were now falling into place, and the future seemed hopeful. But there was one question for which Merritt did not yet have an answer: what was Stryker's upcoming freedom going to mean for the Purifiers, and for Merritt's authority over them? Merritt took a deep breath, brushed away the thought, at least for that moment, and told himself, "One thing at a time."

Forty-five minutes later, on East 96th Street and First Avenue, the five Purifiers were in the back of a van that was parked in front of a four-story residential building, situated in the middle of the block. It was very quiet on the street—this was, after all, a residential area, and it was late on a Sunday night. In the van, the Purifiers were meeting up with twelve members of the Saviors of Humanity, a human supremacist group that had formed two years earlier. With a vastly wealthy sponsor backing them (whose identity understandably had to remain a secret), and with connections to both the criminal world and the shadier branches of the United States government, the Saviors had access to both conventional weapons and the latest high-tech hardware. The Purifiers were especially impressed with the somewhat-bulky-but-amazingly-lightweight energy rifles that the Saviors were toting. Easy to carry, easy to aim and fire, and, according to the Saviors, guaranteed to cause serious harm to even the hardiest of mutants. All five Purifiers silently thought that they simply *had* to convince Gabriel Merritt to do whatever he could to get some of these incredible weapons for the Crusade.

There was then a sudden knocking on the rear door of the van. One of the Saviors opened the door, and allowed in a dark-haired, grim-looking man, about 40 years old, who was projecting an aura of confidence and sheer determination that bordered on plain arrogance. He had a small tattoo on his neck, of a globe of the Earth with the letters S.O.H. stretching across. This man was introduced to the Purifiers as the Saviors' field commander for this assignment. They greeted him, and began to introduce themselves.

"Don't tell me your names," he said to them abruptly. The five Purifiers were a bit taken aback by the Savior officer's brusque attitude. After all, hadn't he invited them here? He continued, "You can call me Sharkey. That's not my real name, nor is it a regular nickname of mine, but it's one I'll recognize if you need to communicate with me. I think it's best that we not know too much about each other. That way, if any of us get caught and interrogated, we can't rat on each other or reveal any vital information about each other's organizations. We may be in different groups, but we're essentially on the same team, know what I mean?"

The Purifiers all nodded, understanding Sharkey's reasoning if not particularly caring for his personality.

Sharkey went on. "Okay. I already set these terms via e-mail with your leader, but let me run them by you. My team takes point, since this is really our mission and you're only here as guests. That means the Saviors go in first, we see the majority of the action, and we take full credit for the mission when the newsletter about it goes out to the other pro-human groups. You'll function as backup. We'll call you in if we need you. But regardless of whether you actually take part in the action, you will have the satisfaction of seeing the world lose a few more mutants, and in the end, that's what it's really all about. Any questions?"

There were none.

Sharkey's lips curled up in a slight smile as he thought about what lay ahead. "Then let's do it. These kids don't know how to use their powers, and we're going to take them totally by surprise. It's going to be like shooting fish in a barrel."

Bobby Drake, also known as the mutant Iceman, was in over his head, and he knew it. East 96th Street and First Avenue in Manhattan had become a war zone, and a residential building—a nondescript, four-story walk-up in the center of the block—was at the heart of the storm. Bobby had been on a date in a nearby restaurant, enjoying a late Sunday night dinner, when he heard what sounded like a massive explosion outside. Rushing to the scene, he saw men and women dressed in protective body armor and armed with both conventional guns and new, high-tech energy rifles he'd never seen before. They were launching an assault on the four-story building, which, from what Drake could tell, was harboring about fifteen teenagers, of all races, shapes, and sizes. Terrified teenagers, who happened to possess mutant powers. A wide variety of mutant powers.

Bobby saw that some of the teens were standing at the front of the building, and others were stationed at the windows on all four floors. All of them were trying to defend the building from the assault team. It was clear that these scared kids had little to no training in using their powers, but they were mustering whatever control they had over their abilities to fight back. One girl, a redhead of about 16, was generating crystalline projectiles and firing them wildly from her hands in desperation. An Asian boy, about 15, was creating powerful winds, just by blowing hard, that were knocking some of the attackers back into the street. Another boy, who couldn't have been older than 14, was causing more and more pieces of rubble to fling themselves in the general direction of the attackers—clearly this kid was a nascent telekinetic. But the assault force pressed on, mercilessly firing their weapons at the kids. And some of the kids were falling.

Bobby didn't need to be Sherlock Holmes to figure out what was going on here. He'd seen it all before, stretching back to the days when he was the youngest of Charles Xavier's original group of X-Men. Obviously the assault force was a militant, anti-mutant group of humans, out to exterminate those teens. They clearly invaded the building, striking in the middle of the night to ensure the element of surprise, and started firing away at the kids with extreme prejudice. Bobby couldn't know for sure which hate organization the humans were from—there were so many possibilities, after all. In the end, it didn't really matter. Running to a nearby pay phone, he placed a call in which he identified himself, gave his location, and a very brief description of what was going on. The call lasted precisely twelve seconds, and ended with Bobby hanging up abruptly. Then, switching to his Iceman identity, which essentially entailed transforming his body into a large block of ice in humanoid form, Bobby Drake went into action.

Using the organic ice he generated from his hands, Bobby formed an ice-bridge that carried him above the battle. He saw that the kids had managed to hold off most of the assault team, who were still out on the sidewalk in front of the building. But he could also see that some of the attackers had made it inside, and were stalking the halls as if they were hunting deer. Iceman began to build a wall of ice in front of the building, to separate the besieged teenagers from at least the majority of their human attackers, hoping it would give him a chance to talk some reason into both sides. But the ice-wall was suddenly shattered, by a searing stream of heat and flame that seemingly came from nowhere. Iceman turned from the rapidly melting ice-wall to locate the source of the fire-blast. He quickly found it.

"Pyro," Iceman said in recognition of the unexpected new player on the scene.

The mutant criminal, who had tangled with Iceman and his X-Men teammates in the past, stood on the street across from Iceman's ice-bridge and gave out a hearty laugh.

"Don't break up the fun, popsicle," Pyro called out. "I want to see how these tykes do against the human slugs!"

Iceman fired a massive blast of ice from his hands at Pyro, but Pyro immediately retaliated by powering up the flame-thrower on his back. Possessing the ability to control open flames, Pyro harnessed the stream of fire from the flame-thrower, and used it to create a huge fire-monster that literally swallowed up the blast of ice.

"What're you shooting at me for?" Pyro exclaimed. "We ought to be on the same side! Haven't you been watching the news lately? They're releasing that Reverend Stryker guy from jail! You know what that means? America's declared war on our kind! Let these kids defend themselves—let them show the humans that we aren't gonna take this crud lying down!"

Standing atop his ice-bridge, which extended up nearly two stories from the street, Iceman scowled at Pyro. "I had no idea you were so idealistic," Bobby replied. "Especially since you used to work for the government and help them hunt down 'our kind!' Give me a break, pal!"

Pyro scowled back, and seemed to Bobby to become very defensive. "What can I say? Desperate times, desperate measures. It was a paying gig, steady work, and great benefits. But you don't think I *really* threw in with those powerless goons, do you? Hey, if it's all heading to a war between humans and mutants, I know what side *I'm* going to be on! And I want to see if these kids can be counted on to do what'll be needed!"

Iceman shook his head in dismay. Due to the fighting that was continuing below, the damage to the building was becoming worse, and the chaos was beginning to spread to the rest of the block. The human assault team was still firing their weapons at the teens, who, in their terror, were using their powers more and more wildly. Iceman was desperate to stop the violence, but first he had to deal with Pyro, who was intent on standing in his way.

"Nutcase," Iceman said to Pyro. "What are you even doing here?"

Pyro smiled wickedly. "Who do you think tipped off the humans to where these kids were holed up?" he replied. "See, I found out about this little shelter, and figured I'd recruit some of the kids for a group I'm putting together—a militia force that's going to fight for our kind. After years of being a team player, I'm stepping up to be a boss!"

The mutant criminal continued. "But I only wanted the best of the bunch. And the only way to find out which ones qualified was to put them all to the test, throw them into real combat conditions, and see how they responded. Survival of the fittest and all that."

This guy is truly warped, Bobby thought. *More so than I ever imagined. And this conversation is keeping me from what I have to do.*

Iceman tried to turn his attention back to the teens and the human assault force, but every time he made a move toward them, Pyro activated his flame-thrower and created a wall of fire that blocked Bobby's path.

And that wasn't all. A huge crowd of spectators had formed, and they were getting dangerously close to the center of the action. Police cars, fire engines, and ambulances were also arriving on the scene. With all the flying debris and ice and scattered flames, it was only a matter of time before any number of civilian bystanders, cops, firemen, or emergency medical technicians got seriously get hurt or worse. He had to get everyone to move back, to keep out of harm's way, and he also had to help the people who lived in the surrounding buildings get to safety, as well. There was no telling if the battle would extend to the surrounding area, and cause serious damage to more structures. It was a lot for one person to take on, even a mutant, but Bobby Drake knew that under the circumstances, he was the best—the only—choice for this task. But his hands were full taking on Pyro, while also trying to get to the mutant teens and the human attack force and keep them from killing each other. It was at that point that Iceman came to the realization that he was in over his head.

But suddenly, a blue-and-red blur streaked past Iceman, and to the amazement of both the frozen mutant and his fire-controlling opponent, the flame-thrower that was part of Pyro's costume was now missing! Without it, Pyro had just become much less of a threat.

Not wanting to look a gift horse in the mouth, Iceman grinned devilishly at Pyro, lifted his hand, and sent a stream of ice crashing into the criminal, knocking him off his feet. Bobby then sealed Pyro's wrists and ankles into shackles made of ice.

"That ought to hold you for a while," he called out to the downed Pyro.

Looking up, Bobby saw a familiar—and most welcome—figure hovering in the night sky. A blue-skinned young man with massive, lethal-looking, metal wings on his back.

"Nice of you to drop by, Archangel," Iceman called out to his teammate, who, in his civilian identity, was known as the ultrarich playboy, Warren Worthington III. Like Iceman, Archangel was another member of the original X-Men team, although he had undergone a series of major changes in recent years—chief of which were the blue skin and the organic metal wings that replaced his original, natural ones.

Archangel was deactivating Pyro's flame-thrower as he replied, "I was in the city anyway, and heard about this commotion. Didn't know you were on the scene, too."

"Well, I appreciate the help," Iceman said. "Now, what say we clean up this mess?"

Archangel hung the now-useless flame-thrower on the high branch of a tall tree, turned his attention to the ongoing chaos below, and said, "I'm for that."

The two X-Men went to work. Iceman started moving all the bystanders back and away from the area, trying to ignore the horrified gasps and fear-filled jeers with which he was greeted. They weren't backing away from the danger as much as they were just trying to get away from him. *You think I'd be used to this kind of reaction by now,* he told himself. *So much for leading them to safety in a calm and orderly manner.*

Meanwhile, Archangel hovered over the four-story building and fired a mass of synapse-disrupting feathers from his unique wings into the battle zone, to get the attention of all the combatants and hopefully bring a quick halt to the fighting.

Archangel's plan worked all too well. He definitely got their attention of the human assault force. His feather-blades hit two of members of the team, temporarily paralyzing them. But the rest of the team managed to evade the blades. They turned their weapons towards him and fired.

On the street below, the Purifiers remained out of the battle, relegated to waiting on the sidelines and not being able to take part until they were called for. It was obvious to them that "Sharkey," or whatever his name really was, wanted all the glory for himself and his team. But the unexpected arrival of the two X-Men was a major development—one that needed to be communicated to Gabriel Merritt. Bill excitedly pulled out his cellular phone and began dialing the number of the downtown office, eager to provide a news update for the man to whom he felt an unswerving loyalty.

Elsewhere, Iceman shifted his attention to trying to evacuate the local residents from the surrounding apartment buildings. He rode an expanding ice-bridge up the side of a luxury high-rise building across the street from the main battle. His intention was to lead its tenants across another ice-bridge that extended down to the street, but a safe distance away. Bobby stuck his head in the window of a top floor apartment to see if anyone was inside. He heard some activity coming from one of the back rooms, and called out, to let whomever was inside know that he was there to help them get to safety. Bobby was answered with a gunshot that very nearly struck him across the forehead.

"Get out of here, you mutant freak!" yelled one of the apartment's occupants—a middle-aged man with graying hair, a droopy mustache, and a pot belly. The man was dressed in a long terry-cloth robe, with a white tank top and striped boxer shorts showing from underneath. He was clutching a smoking pistol in his trembling hand. His wife, dressed in a housecoat and with a head full of hair curlers, huddled behind him, terrified.

"Hey!" a perturbed Iceman snapped at the man. "You got a permit for that?"

Iceman was answered with an electric lamp to his face, the object flung at him by the hysterical wife.

"For crying out loud," Bobby shouted at them. "I'm trying to *help* you!"

"Go away!" she screamed in a very shrill voice that caused Bobby to wince. "Leave us alone! Oh, Horace," she cried to her husband, "why won't the mutant go away?!"

"Suit yourselves, you two," Iceman told them. "Horace, Mrs. Horace, a pleasure meeting you both." He removed his head from the window and wondered if he would get the same kind of reception from the other tenants of this building.

Hovering above the street, Archangel managed to dodge most of the bullets that were fired at him, and deflected the remainders with his metal wings. But several of the energy blasts hit their mark and overwhelmed him, sending him crashing to the ground.

Seconds later, the dazed, winged mutant regained enough of his senses to realize that one of the human attackers was striding over to his crumpled form. Archangel saw that the attacker, a dark-haired, grim-looking man, about 40 years old, had a small tattoo on his neck, with the initials S.O.H. spanning a globe of the planet Earth.

Saviors of Humanity, Archangel told himself. *One of the newer groups. Didn't realize . . . they were this well-equipped.*

The attacker lifted his energy rifle and aimed it right at Archangel's head. The shot would be from point blank range. His head still spinning, his vision blurred and his reflexes barely existent, there was no way Archangel would be able to avoid the blast. And there would be no way that he could survive.

On top of that, he could feel his wings begin to tremble, to act on their own, as they had done so many times in the past in order to protect him. He knew that they were preparing to fire off a mass of feather-blades at the attacker, and he was trying desperately to prevent that from happening. At such close proximity, a defensive maneuver such as that could very well kill the attacker, and as much as it would be an act of self-defense, the death of a human at his hands was not something that the X-Men needed to deal with at that time. But if he didn't do anything at all to protect himself, he was a goner for sure. Maybe, if he could maintain enough mental control over the wings to carefully fire off just a *few* feather-blades . . . .

Suddenly, the human attacker's energy rifle was disintegrated by a blast of crimson energy, coming from up the block! Casting his gaze in that direction, Archangel spotted the source of the energy blast, and he smiled in relief.

"Are you all right?" Cyclops shouted out to him. The crimson energy blast, of course, had been one of Cyclops's optic beams, which at full strength had the power to shear the top off of a mountain.

"Downed, dazed, but undaunted," Warren replied, trying to sound better than he felt and unsure if he was succeeding. He saw that Cyclops was not alone—Wolverine, Storm and Jean were with him. The human attacker, realizing that he had just come very close to losing his hand, dropped the butt of his rifle, which was all that remained of it, and fled as quickly as his feet would take him.

As the four new arrivals approached Archangel, Wolverine spoke up. "Drake called us, filled us in on the situation here. We figured against lettin' him go it alone. Didn't realize it was *your* fat we'd end up having to pull from the fire."

Archangel staggered to his feet. "Charming as always, Logan," he retorted.

"Let's cut the chatter," Cyclops said sharply, slipping naturally into the role of field commander. Looking over at the battle that was still raging around the four-story building, Cyclops asked, "What can you tell us about them, Warren?"

"It's the Saviors of Humanity," Archangel answered. "And I saw a few who were wearing different outfits—I think they might be from a different group, tagging along for the ride."

"Nice to see the hate-groups getting along so well," Jean said sarcastically.

Cyclops turned to his companions. "Jean, you disarm the members of the assault team who are still outside of the building. Archangel, cover Jean—while she's focusing on her task, she'll be vulnerable to any unexpected attacks. Wolverine, Storm and I will go deal with the ones who made it inside."

Jean Grey turned her attention to the members of the Saviors of Humanity who had taken up positions on the sidewalk. Scowling, concentrating, extending her telekinetic powers like a far-reaching, giant hand, she snatched all the guns, energy rifles, hand grenades, and smoke bombs from the Saviors, and levitated the whole batch in the air over their very startled heads. Then, with an additional burst of very precisely-focused telekinetic energy, Jean zeroed in on all the weapons simultaneously, causing the grenades to implode and the guns to shatter into tiny bits and pieces.

Jean shrugged, and with a lopsided grin, she said to the now-weaponless assault team, "It's all in the mind."

Archangel chuckled to himself. *Yeah, she really needed me covering her. Not that I've ever minded watching her back or any other part of her.*

Inside the building, Cyclops, Wolverine and Storm stumbled upon several dead bodies—four Saviors and two of the teenagers— sprawled in the hallway of the first floor. The trio agreed to split up in order to cover more ground. Cyclops took the first two floors, finding the bodies of three more Saviors on the second floor, along with two more teens, who were sticking halfway out of their apartment doorways. Cyclops grimaced in sadness and revulsion. After a thorough search, he determined that these floors were otherwise deserted.

Storm covered the third and fourth floors. Entering some of the apartments, she found the bodies of more teenagers—four in all— lying in shattered glass, under what was left of the windows where they tried to defend their little fortress. The windows themselves were filled with bullet holes. By the time Ororo reached the last apartment on the fourth floor and found the last of the teenagers' bodies, she became overcome with grief. She kneeled by the body of a young girl, who couldn't have been older than 13, closed her eyes, and said a silent prayer.

Wolverine covered the basement. The moment he opened the door to head downstairs, he knew that he was about to step into a major situation. With his keen sense of smell, he could tell that there were two people in the basement. And the scents of both sweat and fear were nearly overwhelming.

Quietly descending the stairs, Wolverine reached the bottom step and confirmed what he suspected: one of the teenagers, a dark-haired Latino boy about 16 years old, was confronting one of the so-called Saviors of Humanity, who was pointing an energy rifle right at the boy's chest. But the boy was pointing his index finger at the S.O.H. operative, as if the finger itself was a weapon. Smelling the unmistakable scent of ozone in the air, and realizing that the tip of the boy's finger was crackling with electricity generated from within, Logan realized that that was indeed the case.

He had come upon a stalemate, and each opponent was ready to shoot the other. The question was, who would fire first?

"I know who you are, man!" the boy shouted to Wolverine. "I seen you on TV! You're one of us! I got this guy covered, man! He killed my friends! Now you kill him! Quick!"

Wolverine clenched a fist. *Snikt*. Three sharp, adamantium-laced claws popped out of the back of his hand, from built-in bionic housings. He glared at the Savior, his lips curling back in a snarl that got louder and louder until, in a lightning-swift maneuver, Wolverine lunged toward the Savior and slashed out with his claws. The Savior and the teen watched in amazement as the energy rifle separated into three separate chunks and fell to the floor.

Retracting his claws, Wolverine slugged the Savior in the jaw, knocking him to the floor. He then grabbed the mutant-killer by the collar and started dragging him across the basement, back towards the stairs. "You're coming with me, bub," he told the downed Savior.

"Hey, wait a minute," the boy interrupted. "Aren't you gonna kill him?"

"Get out of here, kid," Logan responded, his voice barely above a whisper.

The boy would not be dismissed that easily. "No, man. This is bull! Do you know what this slime an' his friends did here? He deserves to die, man!"

Wolverine didn't respond to the boy. Instead, he began climbing up the steps, dragging the Savior up with him and making sure that the dazed mutant-killer's body bounced off of each and every one of the stairs. Finally he reached the first floor, and began pulling the Savior toward the front entrance to the building.

"Screw him *and* you, Wooferine," the boy shouted. "Now I can take care of him myself!"

The boy aimed his index finger back at the Savior. The finger started to crackle with electricity again, and the intensity was building up for what was going to be a huge blast that would undoubtedly fry the Savior to a crisp.

Wolverine grabbed the boy's wrist and pushed it up toward the ceiling. "Power down, kid," he said. The boy glared at him defiantly. Wolverine repeated, "I said power down. *Now.*"

The boy ultimately relented. "You a traitor, man," he said with disgust. "You a *race* traitor. You make me wanna puke." The boy then dashed out the front door of the building.

Wolverine looked down at the mutant-killer, and realized that the man had fainted. Still holding him by the collar, Wolverine dragged him across the floor and out the front door, on to the sidewalk, where he promptly dropped him. The man's head hit the pavement. Had he been conscious, it would have really hurt. For that alone, Wolverine wished he was still conscious.

He quickly found himself joined by Cyclops, Storm, Jean, and Archangel.

"Looks like you got the only one who survived after making it inside," Cyclops told him.

Storm added, "There are about six teens still unaccounted for. Either they found some very good hiding spots inside the building that we couldn't detect, or they somehow managed to escape."

"They escaped," Wolverine replied. "I would've caught their scent if they were still around."

Archangel then said, "The cops managed to grab most of the Saviors of Humanity as they tried to get away. Maybe two or three managed to slip through. And those other agents I saw, the ones who didn't seem like they were part of the group—I think they got away, too. I haven't seen them at all since the tide turned in our favor."

Suddenly, the end of an ice-bridge seemed to spring up at their feet. Looking up, they saw that Iceman was sliding down to join them. Archangel asked him, "How did the evacuations go?"

"I don't believe these people!" Iceman replied in exasperation. "Not one of them trusted me enough to come with me. I finally just gave up and came back here to see if Warren needed help." He looked across the street and saw that Pyro had been shackled to the captured mutant-hunters, and that the whole lot of them was being loaded into the back a police van.

"Guess not—at least, not from me," he said with a grin. "I'm glad you guys could make it. Thanks for coming."

"Well, we were at the mansion with nothing else to do," Jean replied with a casual shrug. She added with a smirk, "I guess we're getting old. We're the only ones on the team who don't usually have plans on a Sunday night—other than watching *The Simpsons*."

Suddenly, a voice shouted from above, "You lousy stinking mutants! This is all your damned fault!"

The X-Men looked up and saw a man sticking his head out of a window in the luxury high-rise across the street, on the sixth floor. "You heard me! This is your fault, you costumed weirdos!"

A woman living on the fifth floor stuck her out of her window and joined in. "This is a nice, peaceful neighborhood!" she yelled. "Who needs you here?" Pointing to the rubble, the debris, and the battered, crumbling four-story walk-up that had become a tomb, the woman continued, "Look what you did to our block tonight! You bring nothing but trouble, wherever you go!"

More people living in the high-rise were drawn to their windows, presumably having heard their neighbors' shouts. They immediately proceeded to add their voices to the chorus.

"Monsters!"

"Terrorists!"

"Freaks!"

Iceman shouted back, "Hey! I just busted my hump trying to *protect* you people—and got shot at by some of you for my trouble! Now you're turning around and blaming *us* for what happened here?!"

But the residents wouldn't listen. They just started shouting more loudly. As if that wasn't bad enough, people started gathering in the street again, and made it very clear that they shared the feelings of the residents. Then they started throwing things. Garbage, rocks, bricks, glass bottles, whatever they could get their hands on. They were getting bolder. Despite admonishments from the outnumbered police officers, who tried in vain to hold them back, the crowd started to close in on the gathered X-Men.

Cyclops heard Wolverine starting to growl under his breath, and it was getting louder. That was *not* a good sign.

But there was no way that Scott Summers would have expected that it would be Storm, not Wolverine, to finally spring into action.

Without a word, Ororo Munroe lifted off the ground and propelled herself up over the city. Using her mutant ability to manipulate the weather, she summoned a powerful storm that shocked even her teammates. Enormous bolts of lightning filled the late-night sky over Manhattan, making it seem as if the universe itself was short-circuiting around the Earth. A roaring thunder, sounding not unlike the bellowing of some angry, thrashing god, quickly followed. Then came the winds that nearly knocked the crowd below off their feet. Startled, frightened by this display of naked power, they scattered, practically stepping over each other to get away.

As Storm's inner rage slowly subsided, so too did the lightning, the thunder, and the winds. She finally descended back to the ground, her face betraying no emotions.

"Think they had enough?" she asked in a flat, cold voice. Finally, she let out a heavy sigh, and regret began to show on her lovely face. "Forgive me, my friends," she said. "In my frustration, I lost control of myself. It will not happen again."

Cyclops thought he heard Wolverine mutter something in response. He wasn't exactly sure what Logan had said, but it sounded like, "Maybe with *you* it won't."

"Don't worry about it, Storm," Cyclops told her. "We all feel the same way. Let's just get out of here. Let's go home."

* * *

An hour before dawn, Gabriel Merritt was pleased to see all five of his Purifiers make it back to headquarters safe and sound. He had been concerned that they would get picked up by the authorities as they were leaving the scene uptown, and would end up in the same boat as "Sharkey" and most of his assault team from the Saviors of Humanity. Merritt mused that as well equipped and well connected as the Saviors seemed to be, they were not as prepared as they thought they were, and it was going to cost them in manpower. Not so for the Crusade and its Purifiers, thankfully. Bill North had shown good judgement by calling Merritt on his cell phone when the mutants known as Iceman and Archangel had arrived. As soon as Merritt heard from Bill that the Grey woman had used her powers to confiscate everyone's weapons, he had told Bill to gather the other Purifiers and get out of there, as quickly as possible.

Merritt knew his team was good, and he recognized that they had the potential to become far better. But up until now, they had been primarily dealing with small-scale extermination operations— taking out minor mutants, such as youngsters who were entering puberty and just discovering their powers, or adults who had never learned how to use them to any great extent, such as Nicky Iacona. Merritt knew that his people were not quite ready yet to take on mutants of the caliber of the X-Men. Hell, even the original crew of Purifiers had proven themselves to be not up to that task. But with time and his leadership, Merritt was convinced that the new Purifiers would far surpass the original group. By sheer numbers alone, in fact, that goal had already been accomplished, with Purifier agents across New York, across all of America, covertly operating under his guidance, remaining in contact with him and with each other through that most wonderful of creations, the Internet. All of them working together for the same dream: a world safe for humanity, a world free of mutants.

Merritt told everyone to go home and get some rest, although he was planning to stick around the office for a while. By dawn, everyone had left the headquarters, with the exception of Annette Butler. She offered to sharpen Merritt's pencils, update the data files, make coffee anything he needed. Merritt politely declined, and encouraged her to leave. She made it clear that she was very reluctant to do so. Merritt knew that she had long been waiting for this opportunity to be alone with him. Short of physically picking her up and throwing her out, he did everything he could to remain polite but firmly discourage her from staying any longer. She apparently didn't get the hint.

Finally, he made a decision. It was time for him to have that talk with her. And he already knew what the outcome would be, for he had already decided—reluctantly—on what course of action he had to take with her.

"I'm afraid it's not working out, Annette," he began, gently but firmly, after having her take a seat across from him.

Her immediate reaction was shock. Clearly, she had not seen this coming.

"It's not due to your abilities, which are very impressive," he continued. "Nor is it because of your performance on your past assignments. The bottom line is, it's become very obvious to me that your reasons for being here are not quite the same as the rest of the group's. And as flattering as that has been for me, it's proven to be . . . a distraction. One that I can't afford. Especially not now."

Annette's response was predictable. She pleaded for a second chance. She begged, through tear-filled eyes, for him to reconsider.

"I *killed* for you," she insisted.

"No, you killed for the cause," he replied.

She declared that she had proven her loyalty to him time and again, and would do anything he asked of her. She swore her undying devotion to him.

"That's the problem, Annette," he told her. "You simply don't see things the way I need you to. Your undying devotion should be, above all else, to the *cause*. With the work that lies ahead, I can't have it any other way. I'm sorry."

"I'm as devoted to the cause as anybody else here," she said defiantly.

"Then prove it," Merritt told her. "If the cause is as important to you as you say it is, you'll do whatever's best to serve it. I think you should join another group, one whose goals are the same as ours. Think about the Saviors of Humanity. After last night, they can certainly use more people. And you'd be a great asset to them. I can contact them and make the arrangements, if you'd like."

Annette looked away from Merritt and sat in silence for a long moment. At one point, she seemed as if she was going to burst into tears. But then, an air of pure calm appeared to engulf her. Merritt guessed that what he had told her had finally sunk in. She rose from her chair, nodded, and murmured, "Sure, whatever," in a flat, emotionless voice. She walked out of the office and closed the door behind her.

Merritt let out a deep sigh of both regret and relief. Regret that he was losing someone who had shown so much potential, and relief that the matter had finally been resolved and he could now be alone with his thoughts. He banished from his mind any further consideration of Annette Butler—she was no longer a concern. He now had to focus on matters that were far more important.

One matter in particular was looming over him like a vulture poised upon fresh carrion. After all the work he had put in to reorganizing the Purifiers and doing his part to keep the Crusade alive over the years, after all the planning he'd done for the future, Merritt now had to seriously consider what the release of Reverend Stryker would mean for his own position of leadership and authority.

Stryker had become a near-mythic figure to the current members of the Crusade, who joined in the years following his arrest. He had come to be seen as a great hero who paid for his strong beliefs, his very integrity, with his own freedom. It was true that this perception—which Merritt had, in fact, encouraged—helped keep up the passions and the spirit of righteousness amongst the group.

But with the long absent Stryker now poised to return to society, there would be another side effect coming to the fore. Namely, the fact that anything Stryker would say and do following his release would be of great importance to the inheritors of his Crusade. The reverend had shared with no one, not even Merritt, his plans for the future, and what role in the cause, if any, he intended for himself once he was free again. Would he try to come back and reassert his control, expecting Merritt to take a subordinate role? Or would Stryker, after so much time behind bars, now denounce the cause that had led to his incarceration?

Merritt knew that either scenario seriously jeopardized his own plans, both for the Crusade and for himself. As much affection and gratitude and loyalty as he felt for his old mentor, he also had to think of himself and what he believed was best for the cause. Sitting alone in silence for several hours, pondering all the possibilities, Merritt conceived a plan that he felt would ensure that the great Reverend Stryker's name and spirit would live on, while Merritt himself remained firmly in place as leader.

That plan involved having Stryker join the ranks of such luminaries as Doctor Martin Luther King Jr., Mahatma Gandhi, Malcolm X, Joan of Arc, and, most appropriately, given Stryker's vocation, Jesus Christ. It involved making sure that Stryker's name would live on, that the reverend would achieve greater fame than he would have dreamed possible, and that his message would spread farther and wider than ever before. It involved turning Stryker into a tragic martyr, and making it look like mutants were responsible.

With only three days left before Stryker's release, it was a plan that had to be put in motion very quickly. Filled with determination and secure in the knowledge that he was doing the right thing for everyone, Gabriel Merritt logged on to his computer and began to make contact with the appropriate parties.

It was the night before Reverend William Stryker's release from prison, and the mood at Professor Xavier's School for Gifted

Youngsters was unrelentingly grim. For several days following the Sunday night incident on Manhattan's Upper East Side, the X-Men were required to step in and confront other brutal acts of violence that hateful humans and fed-up mutants were inflicting upon each other. A state of gang war between the two species more or less existed now. The X-Men, trying to do nothing more than stop the violence and protect lives, had been consistently greeted by both sides with the same kind of response they had gotten on Sunday night: cries of betrayal from the mutants, and unrelenting hostility from the humans. As if that wasn't bad enough, it had been reported on the television news that Pyro had escaped from police custody and was at large.

Charles Xavier was discussing this latest development with his X-Men as they were toweling off from an impromptu, particularly grueling practice session in their "Danger Room" training facility. The team members present were Cyclops, Wolverine, Storm, Archangel, and Iceman. Jean Grey had been stationed in the Danger Room's control booth with Xavier, overseeing the training sequence that she had programmed in to the computer system, but she had come down to the main chamber to join in on the conversation.

"Pyro, at least, has never represented a *major* threat in the grand scheme of things," Xavier commented. "Despite his newfound ambition to be a major player, I anticipate that he will always find himself in the role of follower. What I am actually concerned about is the possibility of a *truly* dangerous mutant, someone like Magneto, deciding to step in during this time of crisis and *really* cause trouble."

Wolverine, who had noticeably become increasingly frustrated and embittered over the last few days, replied, "Maybe that's what you've got on your mind, Charley, but not me. What I've got on my mind is how sick and tired I am of us having to be so damned even-handed in how we deal with all this crud."

Cyclops stepped in. "Look, Logan, we know how frustrated you've felt lately, so have we. But that's no reason to—"

Xavier cut him off. "Please, Scott, let Logan continue."

Wolverine erupted. "We bend over backwards, put our lives on the line every day, to protect human lives as well as mutant lives, and for what? Mutants think we're race traitors because we're not takin' their side against humans. Humans curse us and pelt us with garbage and blame us if it's too friggin' cold outside. Now that fascist Stryker's getting set free, and we're just supposed to take it on the chin an' accept it an' take the high road."

Xavier calmly responded, "As Jean pointed out several days ago, we don't know for sure what Stryker's intentions are now. As unlikely as it may seem, it is within the realm of possibility that his outlook has changed since we last encountered him. Granted, it is equally possible that he has become only *more* fervent in his appalling beliefs. We just don't know right now. I believe we must, at the very least, take a 'wait and see' attitude before we can determine how to proceed."

"You know what, Charley?" Wolverine fired back, "I'm tired of the 'wait and see' attitude. The 'wait and see attitude' is makin' me all edgy. I'm of the mind to *do* something already. Y'know, maybe the right Reverend Stryker should get a reminder of just how badly he was beaten last time."

With that, Wolverine turned and left the others behind. Cyclops shouted after him, "What does that mean, Wolverine? What's going on in that head of yours?"

Logan answered with silence as he exited the Danger Room.

"He's not gonna do anything stupid, is he?" asked Iceman.

Cyclops shrugged shook his head in dismay. "After all this time, I still don't have him figured out at all."

Jean frowned and added, "Hey, he keeps surprising me, too—and I'm a telepath."

Gabriel Merritt was behind the wheel of his black Toyota Camry, driving on the New York Thruway, headed upstate to the Attica Correctional Facility for the media event that was the release of Reverend William Stryker from prison. He had been on the road since three in the morning, with the intention of reaching the prison well before Stryker was released at nine sharp. Merritt was alone, which was exactly how he wanted it. He had made it very clear to his Purifiers that only he would be heading up to the prison, to pick up the reverend and provide transportation to wherever it was that Stryker wanted to go.

Not that his Purifiers hadn't voiced their great disappointment. All of them wanted the chance to be near the reverend in the first moments of his newfound freedom. But as Merritt explained it to them, only he had an established, publicly known connection to Stryker. Back when the reverend was still running the Crusade, appearing every weekend on his nationwide evangelical television show and being very much in the public eye, it was fairly common knowledge that his right hand man was Gabriel Merritt. But Merritt, as far as anyone knew, had no connection to, or involvement with, the scandal that brought about Stryker's downfall. Merritt's reputation was above reproach. And as an innocent, former protégé who only wanted to show support for his old mentor, to be the friendly face who would take the reverend back to the city he called home, it was only natural for Merritt to be at Attica. But the current group of Purifiers had been recruited *after* Stryker went to prison, and didn't have such a connection. As Merritt described it to them, he was concerned that their presence could arouse suspicion, and that was the last thing that the reverend needed. It was all for the good of the reverend, he had told them.

Of course, the real reason Merritt wanted them to stay behind was because they had no knowledge of what he was going to set in motion that day. He could not take the chance that, in their ignorance and eagerness to serve the cause, they would interfere with, and jeopardize, what he had planned.

Merritt knew in his heart that what was going to happen was all for the best. It was good for him, for his people, and for the cause. And, in a very real way, it was good for Stryker himself, for it would ensure that his name, and what he stood for, would live on in perpetuity. Merritt could feel anticipation growing within him, an increasing nervous energy, a flutter in his stomach, as he neared his destination.

Merritt made it to Attica Correctional Facility with some time to spare, and as he had anticipated, a media circus had already formed. Barred from setting foot on the prison grounds, the throng of reporters from TV, radio, and the newspapers had taken up positions on the side of a public roadway that passed by the prison perimeter. Along this perimeter stood a tall, barbed wire fence topped with razor ribbon, to ensure that no one got in—or out. A short distance away, a mass of protestors, standing on both sides of the mutant issue, was trying to shout each other down. Crudely made signs were being held up, and slogans such as "Stryker Will Lead the Way!" "God Loves Mankind!" and "Humanity Rules!" were being countered by such sentiments as "Mutants Are People Too!" and "We're *All* God's Children!" A number of police officers were also on the scene, handling crowd control and making sure that the conduct of the protestors did not get out of hand.

Merritt casually made his way through the throng of reporters and reached the fence. Down the road, at the prison itself, he could see the main gate opening, and someone stepping out into the morning light. Even at this distance, there was no doubt in Merritt's mind about who that person was. He could make out the pure white hair, and he recognized that walk—each step projecting an abundance of pride, purpose and determination. Several years older, to be sure, and perhaps a bit more tentative than he once was, but there was no denying that the strength within William Stryker had not at all diminished.

As Stryker walked down the path, escorted by a beefy male prison guard to the outer fence, he nodded at the reporters on the other side, and indicated through a nod and a wink that he would be willing to speak with them. Merritt was not at all surprised. The notion of William Stryker turning down an opportunity to speak in front of a television camera was unthinkable—that was something Merritt was sure that even a long prison sentence could not change about the man. At the thought of the reverend's oversized ego and his love for the spotlight, Merritt smiled inwardly. He had to admit, now that the moment of truth was approaching, that he felt more affection for the older man than he'd realized. Not that he would let those feelings get in the way of his own ambitions.

Out of the corner of his eye, Merritt could see the protestors starting to come forward, toward the fence, having realized that Stryker was finally approaching.

"STRY-KER, STRY-KER, STRY-KER" one faction shouted out in unison.

"CHERISH ALL LIFE, CHERISH ALL LIFE" another faction responded.

The fence was opened. Stryker turned to his prison guard escort, smiled, shook the man's hand one last time, and then stepped out into the world.

The reverend was greeted by a swarm of microphones, tape recorders, and video cameras thrust into his face.

"Hey, c'mon, everybody," Stryker said with a chuckle, "you'd think we hadn't seen each other in years!"

Merritt watched the reporters laugh. *There it is*, he thought. *The patented Stryker charm. He's already got them eating out of the palm of his hand.* Merritt couldn't help but be impressed.

Stryker then turned serious. "I do want to say that while I still believe my incarceration was a clear example of religious persecution, I have nothing but the utmost respect for the warden and the entire staff here at Attica. They perform their most difficult jobs with nothing less than consummate professionalism."

The reporters nodded, and some began to shout out questions, but Stryker raised a hand and indicated that he had more to say first. "As for the inmates with whom I served my time," he continued, "I will be praying for each and every one of them. Praying for their rehabilitation, praying that they will all get second chances to one day return to society—and to prove to us, and to themselves, that they can make a valuable contribution to the world. Because, my friends, that will show any and all doubters just how strong the human spirit really is. Through that spirit comes the ability to overcome our baser impulses, our flaws, the things that make us weak and corrupt. Evil can be channeled into goodness. I'll be praying for them every day."

Stryker then looked over in Merritt's direction and saw his former protégé for the first time. He grinned at Merritt, obviously pleased to see the younger man. With the reporters standing in between them, Merritt knew that Stryker wouldn't be able to hear him, so he mouthed the words, "Whenever you're ready to leave." Since Stryker nodded and mouthed, "Okay, just a few more minutes" in response, Merritt assumed that the reverend had understood him. Stryker then turned his attention back to the reporters and opened the floor to questions.

As the exchanges between Stryker and the reporters got underway, the protestors continued trying to shout each other down. Surprisingly, no violence had yet broken out between the anti-mutant and pro-mutant factions, despite the arrival of Stryker on the scene and the strong emotions his presence had stirred up, and there were no signs that situation would get out of hand. The protestors seemed to be satisfied with simply expressing their beliefs, and not letting their ideological opponents get the last word.

No one seemed to notice that one particular man, about five-foot-three, dressed in a mask and a distinctive blue-and-yellow uniform, had emerged from the crowd and was making a sudden rush toward the reverend. Long, sharp claws were attached to the backs of his hands.

Stryker finally noticed that the figure was headed right for him in a mad dash, and the claws were poised to run right through his mid-section. His eyes widened, he began to stammer, and he pointed at the approaching assassin.

The group of reporters took note of Stryker's reaction, and they turned to look at what he was pointing at.

"Hey, it's that mutant!" one of them shouted.

"One of the X-Men!" shouted another.

"I think it's the one they call Wolverine!" added yet another.

Shoving the reporters aside, the diminutive figure slashed out, the razor-sharp points rushing toward Stryker without a hint of mercy.

But suddenly, the claws were blocked by *another* set of claws, which were possessed by an additional new figure on the scene. This new figure was also five-foot-three, somewhat scruffy-looking, dressed in a cowboy hat, brown leather jacket, flannel shirt, and jeans. The new figure moved like lightning, and used his claws to completely shatter those of the assassin clad in yellow and blue.

"The uniform's a pretty good copy," the man in the cowboy hat said, with a menacing grin, to the masked assassin. "But your claws need some work."

Now it was Gabriel Merritt's turn to be shocked. What the hell was the *real* Wolverine doing there? How could he have known what Merritt had planned for Stryker? He couldn't have been tipped off, that simply wasn't possible. It had to be a coincidence. A stupid, bloody coincidence. But why in the world would he want to protect a man who had once tried to kill him and his friends?

The Wolverine impostor turned away and pushed through the reporters again, ignoring their questions about his identity and their requests for exclusive interviews. He ran toward a nearby car that had the ignition running, but this intended fast getaway was blocked by one of the police officers on the scene, who made it over to the car and stood in the impostor's way, pistol drawn.

Desperate to escape, the impostor rushed the police officer and knocked the gun out of his hand. He then waved the shattered remains of his claws at the cop, slashing at him wildly with the jagged edges. Diving on to the ground to evade the claws, the police officer managed to retrieve his pistol and ordered the imposter to freeze, but the impostor ignored him. He clearly had no intention of being caught, and seemed to have no qualms about killing the cop if he had to. But it was equally clear that the cop had no intention of letting this would-be killer get away.

The impostor was becoming even more desperate. He lunged at

the cop one more time, slashing the jagged remains of the claws at the other man's hand, the one holding the pistol. He was going to try to slice off the cop's hand at the wrist . . . which left the cop no choice but to shoot the impostor down in self-defense.

The impostor crumpled to the ground and didn't get up again.

The man in the cowboy hat, now standing near a dismayed Merritt, commented with a wry grin, to no one in particular, "I guess that settles which one of us is the real deal."

Having just watched someone get gunned down right in front of them, the protestors flew into a panic and started stepping on each other in a mad attempt to flee the scene. The small force of police officers could not contain them. A full-scale riot was breaking out. Reporters trying to cover this shocking turn of events were getting shoved around and crushed in the wild sea of people.

But the crowd was suddenly halted by a rapid shift in the morning sky's color from a cloudless blue to a dark, murky gray, and the deafening, crashing boom of a nearby thunderclap. With the protestors momentarily startled, the riot was at least temporarily paused.

Storm hovered over the crowd and shouted in her best commanding voice, "Now that I have your attention, I beseech you to stop this insanity right now and *calm down!*"

Archangel hovered near Storm, prepared to fire his featherblades into the crowd to paralyze the rioters, if necessary.

On the ground, Cyclops, Jean Grey and Iceman took up positions around the perimeter of the crowd, trying come off as firm but not threatening.

"We're not here to hurt anybody," Cyclops said. "Just take it easy. We're here to help."

Now unsure of what to do, of how to react, the protestors ultimately just settled down.

Cyclops continued, "Please go to your cars in a calm, orderly fashion, and leave this place. We want you to be safe, no matter what you may think of us."

From above, Archangel watched over the protestors to make

sure that they did as they were requested. Anyone that didn't would have to deal with him. Fortunately, they were all so anxious to get away that they caused no further trouble.

Storm and Archangel soon descended to the ground to rejoin Cyclops, Jean, and Iceman. As they did, Logan made his way over to them.

"I don't remember leaving a trail of popcorn for you to follow," he said, brimming with attitude.

Cyclops held his ground and replied, "An educated guess. It seems that we understand you better than we thought we did."

"Maybe, maybe not," Wolverine said to him. "If you think I really came here to—"

But before Logan could go any further, he and the other X-Men noticed that Reverend Stryker was gathering the reporters around him once again, to offer a statement about the incident that had just occurred.

"This I gotta hear," Wolverine murmured.

As an ambulance and additional police cars were arriving on the scene, Gabriel Merritt anxiously took Reverend Stryker by the arm and tried to usher him to his car. Merritt was tense, very much on edge. After what just happened, he very much wanted to get the hell out of there, as quickly as possible, before anything else could go wrong. But the older man extricated himself from his former protégé's grasp and called the scattered reporters over to him. The reporters happily obliged, eager to get Stryker's reaction to an incident that came very close to being his assassination.

"Ladies and gentlemen of the press," Stryker began, "let me say right off the bat that as a man of God, I stand for the sanctity and the preservation of human life. The 'mutant assassin' who tried to kill me just a few moments ago, who himself was killed while attacking a police officer just trying to do his job, was apparently a human in disguise."

Stryker looked deeply troubled as he continued. "We cannot let it come to this. If humans start killing each other over the mutant problem, then the mutants win."

A rough-sounding voice that was now familiar to both Stryker and Merritt quickly responded. "Let me remind you, Reverend, sir, that it was a *mutant* who just saved yer precious life."

Stryker turned towards the voice, to see that Wolverine was approaching, accompanied by his fellow X-Men.

A faint smile appeared briefly on Stryker's face. He then answered, with a hint of disbelief in his voice, "What do you and your friends expect from me? Gratitude? A complete reversal of my longstanding views on mutants? That's simply not possible. Saving my life was *your* choice. I didn't ask you to do it."

The reverend continued, without any real malice in his voice, but with a firmness that conveyed how much he really and truly believed in the righteousness of what he was saying, and that there was nothing he could do to change that, even if he tried. "Mutantkind is the natural enemy of the human race, the greatest threat to the future of humanity. Mutants are an abomination in the eyes of all that is holy. It's my mission, my calling in life, to stand against you and your kind, no matter the cost."

Cyclops stepped forward, defiant. "We have a mission, too, Reverend" he replied. "But ours is one of peace and hope and understanding. We'll never give up the dream that this will one day be a world for everyone, human and mutant. And when that day comes, you'll truly be defeated."

With that, Cyclops made it clear that he was finished with Stryker. He turned his back on the reverend and began walking away in a determined stride. The other X-Men fell into step behind him in a show of loyalty, unity and friendship. Not one of them looked back.

After a long moment of silence, Stryker finally allowed Merritt to lead him to his car for the long drive back to New York City.

That night, at Xavier's mansion, a frowning Bobby Drake hung up the telephone in the far corner of the screening room.

"How do you like that?" he muttered. "I just checked my voice mail—nothing. Thing is, I left three messages with Callie, my date from last Sunday night, and she hasn't returned *any* of them."

"Not a good sign, popsicle," Warren Worthington replied lightly, but with a hint of genuine sympathy. The winged mutant was perched on the back of the couch that faced the large television screen.

Drake reluctantly agreed. "I guess I shouldn't have ditched her in the middle of dinner with no explanation if I wanted to get another date with her, huh?"

"Just get over here already," Warren told him. "Dan Rather's coming back on."

Dejected, Bobby walked over to the center of the screening room, and plopped himself on a rug that was lying on the floor. He and the other X-Men who had been to Attica that morning had gathered in the screening room with their mentor, to watch the extensive news coverage of Reverend Stryker's release from prison. Of course, the main angle of the story ended up being the fact that a team of mutants—the very same group that helped bring down Stryker in the first place—had now saved the reverend from an assassination plot. A plot carried out by a human assassin, no less.

The reactions from extremists on both sides of the mutant issue were particularly subdued, almost confused. No one who was interviewed for the various news broadcasts seemed to know what to make of the incident, or what to say about it. That, as far as the X-Men were concerned, made for a pleasant change of pace.

"I suspect," Charles Xavier commented, "that this incident will have the effect of putting at least a temporary end to the human-mutant 'gang war' situation. That would be a good start."

Xavier then turned to Wolverine. "It turned out to be quite fortuitous that you were there at the prison this morning, Logan."

Wolverine, sitting in one of the easy chairs, shrugged his shoulders. "Well, what did you all think, that I was there to bump off Stryker myself? C'mon, give me some credit. I was only there to show my face, to send Stryker the message that I'm gonna be keepin' a close eye on him and his future activities."

He then turned to Scott Summers, who was seated on the couch next to Jean, and added with a sardonic grin, "*You* knew that was why I went up there, right, Cyke? I mean, you understand me so well and all."

Scott abruptly sat forward on the couch to answer, clearly trying to keep his temper in check. "Look, no matter what you might think, I gave you the benefit of the doubt, and firmly believed that when the chips were down, you would do the right thing."

"Then why'd you follow me?"

Scott faced Logan, and though his eyes were covered by the ruby quartz glasses that held back his potentially lethal optic blasts, Logan had no doubt that Summers's eyes were looking directly into his own.

"Because we wanted to send Stryker the same message, Logan. And we felt that message would be stronger if we delivered it as a *team*. A team that includes you."

Scott and Logan matched each other's gazes for a long, quiet moment. Finally, Logan nodded, and Scott briefly nodded back. Right at that point in time, the two men truly did understand each other.

Xavier broke the silence. "Well, I agree that it will be necessary to keep an eye on Reverend Stryker, since it's clear that his views have most certainly not changed."

"Can those who thrive on hate *ever* really change?" Ororo solemnly said in response.

Jean, a troubled expression crossing her beautiful face, spoke up. "I'm I'm not so sure that Stryker is going to be much of a threat in the future."

All of her teammates shot her quizzical looks. "What do you mean?" Scott finally asked her.

Jean sighed, trying to put it all into words. "Well . . . as we were walking away from Stryker, I saw his assistant, Gabriel Merritt— the one trying to usher Stryker away. What stuck in my mind was his expression. It showed . . . *disappointment*—as if he were disappointed that the assassination attempt had failed."

Xavier, clearly intrigued by this information, leaned forward in his wheelchair, placed his fist under his chin, and simply said, "Very interesting," almost to himself.

The X-Men glanced at each other, silently considering the implications.

"But I sensed there was *more* than just disappointment," Jean added. "As they were getting into the car, I saw Merritt's face show determination—a feeling of, 'If at first you don't succeed . . .'"

It was late at night in New York City. In a tiny, rented studio apartment on 27th Street and Broadway, a small, portable television ~~was sitting on~~ top of a mini-refrigerator. It was tuned to an overnight network news broadcast that was examining the events surrounding Reverend William Stryker's release from prison earlier in the day. But the apartment's occupant, Annette Butler, was paying little attention to the broadcast. She sat on the floor, crosslegged, underneath the tall wooden loft that held her mattress. She was rocking slowly, back and forth, her mind focused on nothing other than her next move.

She happened to glance at the television screen and saw footage of Reverend Stryker outside of the Attica Correctional Facility, being escorted to a car by a most familiar figure. Gabriel Merritt. She focused on Merritt's face, studied it, and felt a strong surge of emotion inside of her. She looked down at the pistol she was cradling in her lap. The same pistol she had used several days earlier to shoot that mutant would-be magician, Nicky Iacona.

She picked up the pistol and aimed it at the television screen. At Merritt's head. In her mind's eye, she saw herself pulling the trigger, and Merritt's face exploding in a mass of blood and gore. She smiled, and gently placed the gun down at her side. It felt good, this imagined scenario. It felt *right*. She knew that the path she had chosen was the correct one.

Yes, she definitely knew what she was going to do. And she definitely knew where she could find him. All she needed to decide was *when*. But she would figure that out soon enough.

She looked back on her experience with Gabriel Merritt and the

Purifiers, and heard a voice in her head telling her that she had been exploited. That she had been taken for granted. And in the end, she had been cast out, like some unruly dog that gets kicked out of a car and left on the side of the highway.

Merritt's face appeared on the television screen again. Annette lifted the pistol and aimed it at the screen one more time. She smiled, kissed the air in front of her, and whispered, *"Bang."*

2000s

GIFTS

by Madeleine E. Robins

Salem Center, New York. Midnight.

Silence is a funny thing, Elisabeth Braddock mused. There are
times when it is palpable, something you could pick up in cupped
hands and let sift through your fingers like sand. There are warning silences and the sweet silence that comes with the cessation
of prolonged noise. There are awkward silences and weighty silences. There are silences that are simply a lack of noise; there are
silences that are something more profound and more lonely.

Sitting in the midnight kitchen Elisabeth had tuned out the
hiss and rattle of the coffee maker, the hum of the refrigerator and
the pinprick ticking of the clock, even the settling creaks of the
Mansion's venerable joists. She stared into her coffee cup, sifting
through the silence that surrounded her, seeking uselessly for a
whisper, an echo, of the voices that had once swirled and eddied
around her. Since her mutant telepathic abilities had first manifested themselves Betsy had moved through a world awash in the
thoughts and emotions of other people. If she ever thought of
being lonely she had only to reach out to know what the people
around her knew, what their needs and desires were. She had only
to touch another mind to know, as certain as the sun rose, that

she was not alone. Now, in the quiet night kitchen, she would have given almost anything to move through that sea of feeling and thought again, to be connected to the world, to know in an instant what the people around her—people she loved—were feeling, wanting, hoping. In the mental hush in which she existed now, Betsy found it difficult to know how she herself felt. Without her telepathy, how could she know?

"Hey, Betts? You okay, honey?"

The words, the sweet alto drawl that gave them voice, were just more *noise*. Betsy heard them but did not immediately realize that they were meant for her. It was not until a gloved hand touched her shoulder that she woke from her reverie.

"Y'all looked like you were about to fall into that coffee cup," Rogue said. She frowned, but her eyes were sympathetic, concerned. "You tired or just thinking?"

"Brooding," Betsy said, and attempted a smile. She had the clipped, precise consonants of an educated Englishwoman, softened by the years she'd spent in the United States. She took a sip of the coffee in her mug and made a face. "Ugh. Stone cold."

"Y'all been *brooding* for a while, then," Rogue said. "Anything I can help with?"

Betsy pushed a lock of startlingly lilac-colored hair back from her forehead. "Are you asking as team leader or as a friend?"

Rogue took the mug from Betsy's hand, tossed the contents into the sink, and poured fresh coffee for both of them. She brought the cups back to the table and poured half-and-half lavishly into Betsy's mug. "I must be a friend; I know the way you like your coffee. Betts, if you don't want to talk I'll go away, but—"

"No." Betsy ducked her head apologetically. "Please don't go. I've just been—moaning to myself. Harsh fate, all that rot. I miss my telepathy, still, after all this time. It's so isolated this way, I'd forgotten. I must have been able to bear it when I was a child, back before my powers manifested. All I remember is . . . being a brat. How do you cope with the loneliness?"

Rogue laughed. "Us folk who aren't telepaths don't think much about what we're missing. But," she added more seriously, "isolation—You don't have to be a telepath to know about that. "

Betsy put her hand to her mouth, aghast. "Oh God, Rogue, I didn't mean—"

"Nah, of course you didn't, honey. You can't touch minds, I can't *touch*, period. Not unless I want to soak up someone else's memories and abilities, maybe even kill 'em." Rogue smiled lopsidedly. "Ain't we the gorgeous pair?"

"Yes, certainly you are," a new voice spoke. It was Nightcrawler, leaning against the door sill in jeans and a butter-yellow t-shirt, smiling appreciatively.

"What *you* doing up at this hour, Elf?" Rogue ran a hand through her hair, the fierce white streaks that framed her face in stark contrast to the warm auburn of the rest.

"Looking for coffee is not sufficient excuse?"

"Most people want warm milk at midnight."

"Were we 'most people,' Rogue, would we be here?" Nightcrawler poured himself a mug of coffee and sat at the table across from Betsy. "Being in seminary is really very much like being an X-Man; late hours, frequent recourse to prayer. But the coffee in the seminary kitchen is far better." A slight accent, and the formality of his grammar, betrayed his German childhood. *But formal is the last word you'd come up with for Nightcrawler*, Rogue thought.

She grinned. "You feeling homesick for the seminary, Kurt?"

He shook his head. "Not tonight. I was only taking a walk, sorting some things out, when I saw the light, and was inspired to come looking for coffee."

Betsy grimaced at her mug. "*Inspired* is not a word I'd use in the same sentence as *coffee* in this kitchen."

"You have a point. But if it's so terrible—and it surely is—then what brings the loveliest of the women of the X-Men here on a quiet night?"

"Same thing, I guess. Coffee and reflection." Rogue stirred sugar into her coffee. "Boy, that's German grammar for you: the women of the X-Men. Sounds like a photo-spread in *Playboy*."

Nightcrawler laughed delightedly, his teeth white against the cobalt blue of his sleek fur. "Perhaps so; but would the *X-People* have sounded so well? The Exes? X-Volk? X-Humans?"

"Or something more descriptive?" Betsy suggested. "Something with adjectives in it: fantastic, amazing, astounding, fabulous—"

"Gorgeous?" Nightcrawler interjected.

"Ridiculous," Betsy finished. "I think we have to trust Charles Xavier's instincts even in this."

"I 'spose—" Rogue began. What she was going to say was lost to the sudden blare of the alarm ringing through the halls of the mansion.

LaGuardia Airport, Queens, New York. Midnight

Marita Citrin did yet another head-count and came up, reassuringly, with seventeen students, all alive and kicking. Each time she took the Rossmore High School Drama Club to the American Drama Association High School Festival in Minneapolis she joked that she spent more time counting heads than worrying about scripts or sets or costumes or performances. Win a medal, great. Have a good time, fine. But get them all back home to their parents in one piece—the paramount thing. Seventeen tired students waiting at the gate in LaGuardia Airport, groaning as yet another delay was announced in the final leg of their flight back home to Boston. They sprawled against the wall, propped on their backpacks, or slouched in the hard plastic seats, playing with Gameboys, dozing, talking intently.

Every year Mrs. Citrin took the Drama Club to the ADA Festival, and every year certain things happened like clockwork. A critical prop always got left behind; the wardrobe mistress always threatened a nervous breakdown; and one of the romances that sprang up like brush fire during rehearsals always blew up on the trip. Thank God this time the kids had waited until *after* the performance to split up, Mrs. Citrin thought. Although she wished, for

Amy Langel's sake, that Joe Nadderley had been a little more adroit. In the last two days he'd paid attention to every girl in the cast and crew *except* for Amy, his co-star and girlfriend, making obvious to everyone what he wasn't willing to say directly. And poor Amy had gone from bewildered to quietly miserable without saying a word.

Joe was sitting now with Claudia Peña, his arm draped across the back of her seat, his face tilted attentively down to hers. Amy, hunched against her backpack along the wall, watched them. Her short, dark hair fell forward over her face; her lips were pressed into a small, hard circle. She had made a marvelous Viola in their production of *Twelfth Night*, spirited and inventive. Her chemistry with Joe's Duke Orsino had been electric—maybe too electric. Watching the two kids now, Marita Citrin suspected that Joe had dropped Amy because the intensity of their connection scared him. *Poor babies*, Mrs. Citrin thought. *You don't learn how to handle this relationship stuff without living through it; and you haven't a clue when you're sixteen that you* will *live through it.*

A bass rumble shook the terminal building; Mrs. Citrin looked reflexively out at the night-dark tarmac for an arriving plane, but there was none. The other side of the concourse, she thought. Maybe Amy heard the sound too: she was looking out the window, her face turned away from Joe and Claudia. A tear crawled lazily down her cheek; she didn't bother to wipe it away. *In another minute she'll be crying*, Mrs. Citrin thought. Wearily she rose and went over to Amy to suggest a visit to the Ladies' Room. The girl looked at her blankly, but let Mrs. Citrin help her to her feet and guide her, comforting arm around her shoulder, toward the bathrooms.

The rumble came again, louder. The floor rippled underfoot, almost knocking Mrs. Citrin off her feet. Amy tripped and slid along the shifting floor, back toward the wall.

Earthquake?

"Kids!" she began. Mr. Quick, the other chaperone, was on his feet looking for the source of the noise.

There was a sudden flash of blinding orange light, near, far too nearby, and the floor heaved a third time, literally throwing a couple of sitting passengers out of their seats. The long wall against which the Rossmore students had been sitting split behind them, and there was a loud creaking sound. Another flash of light. The heavy pane of a picture window exploded inward in a burst of millions of round bits of safety glass, like a shower of gravel raining on those nearest—Mrs. Citrin's students. As another rumble shook the building and dust filled the air around them, the screaming began.

Salem Center

Without thought and within seconds of the ear-splitting alarm Rogue was running down the hall to the Briefing Room, Nightcrawler and Psylocke hard on her heels. As fast as they were, Charles Xavier was faster. As headmaster of The Xavier School for Exceptional Children, Xavier had devoted his life to bridging the gulf between man and mutant-kind. The X-Men were Xavier's greatest triumph, a small cadre of men and women with extraordinary powers, working to help and protect a humanity which regarded mutants with fear and suspicion. He was a mutant himself, a telepath of extraordinary ability. He was also a wise and compassionate man, teacher and counselor to the X-Men from the newest student to the most experienced team member. And no one was more focused in a crisis.

They found him at a terminal, examining data that streamed across the screen. At his elbow was the headpiece that he used to link to Cerebro, the computer which extended his telepathic power even further.

"*Was ist*, Professor?" Nightcrawler peered over Xavier's shoulder at the display.

"A series of explosions at LaGuardia Airport," Xavier said crisply. His resonant voice rang out in the quiet of the computer room, and as his fingers played over the keyboard a hologram of the airport facility appeared in the center of the conference table.

Nightcrawler turned to look at another monitor. "Cerebro assigns a 97.34% probability that the energy spikes there are the product of mutant activity," he noted. "What is troubling is that it does not say *which* mutants."

"Domina and the Neo?" Rogue suggested.

"Magneto?" Psylocke pursed her lips. "What's at LaGuardia he'd want? Unless it's just anti-human terrorism."

Xavier shook his head. "There's been no sign of activity from the Neo's stronghold in Brooklyn, and these blasts carry no energy signature Cerebro has on file—"

"Which lets Magneto out," Rogue said.

"—nor is there a familiar behavioral pattern or modus operandi," Xavier finished. "If it is Magneto, he could be working with someone we haven't encountered before."

"Oh *grand*," Rogue drawled. "Well, right now we need to get there and get the situation under control." She looked at her teammates. "We're the only ones in the house tonight. Y'all up for it?"

Nightcrawler raised two fingers to his forehead in a mock salute. "Do you need to ask?" Behind him Psylocke nodded.

They didn't bother to say goodbye to the Professor as they left. In moments they would be uniformed and in a helicopter, racing the thirty-five miles southeast to LaGuardia airport. Rogue wondered sometimes what it cost Charles Xavier to watch his X-Men go where he, wheelchair-bound, could not. Still, each time they left him she imagined she felt his benediction follow them: *Do good work. Come back safe.* It wasn't a bad blessing to take into a battle with something unknown.

LaGuardia Airport

The floor rippled again, more violently. Over the screams, the protesting roar of concrete and steel being twisted out of recognition rang in Marita Citrin's ears. Everything seemed to be happening in a kind of hyper-slow motion: she had time to watch a baggage jitney that was racing across the tarmac below tip over and skid sideways, sparks spitting upward from the contact friction of metal on cement. She had time to remember where the exits were, and to wonder why the airline representatives weren't already yelling evacuation instructions. She had time to scan the area and count again: seventeen kids, still alive and kicking.

Mrs. Citrin raised her voice over the unbelievable tumult.

"Rossmore! Everybody together *now*!" she yelled. "Don't *worry* about your backpacks!" Mrs. Citrin yelled. "There's nothing in them that can't be replaced! Come on!" She was amused—or would have been amused, if she hadn't been so scared—to see Joe offer his hand to Amy, pull her to her feet and shove her gently in the direction of the huddled group of Rossmore students. Claudia Peña was already with the group, white-faced and trembling.

The explosions stopped, but the tremors and the rumbling continued. There was plenty of other noise too—a frightening creaking from the long wall; the whine of a jet engine nearby; the crackle of fire; and above all, the cries of people all around them. A woman screamed for her child, over and over again. Someone was moaning nearby. Not one of hers, Mrs. Citrin thought with gratitude. She did her best to project calm assurance: they were all right now; help would arrive shortly. She would get them all back to Boston in one piece. She prayed that she was right about all these things. But where were the airport people, the airline representatives, someone official to tell them what to do?

Mr. Quick looked at her meaningfully, nodding his head in a "look over there" gesture which answered one of her questions. The corridor running back to the main terminal was entirely blocked by debris; a chunk of the ceiling had fallen in, allowing a glow of light and a glimpse of dark sky. A tide of cold air from the shattered observation window swept through the hallway; on the tarmac there were only lights and a vague impression of scurrying busyness, none of it apparently aimed at getting to their concourse. For the moment it looked like the Rossmore group and the other passengers at this end of the concourse were stuck where they were.

Mrs. Citrin swore silently—years of watching her language around her students kept her from voicing either her fear or her outrage that this was happening to *her* kids, on *her* watch.

"Mrs. C, I'm going to be sick." That was Glynnie, their wardrobe mistress. A big, doughy girl with pretty eyes, Glynnie was white as a sheet and trembling. "I really am. I need the bathroom."

Suppressing irritation, Marita Citrin nodded. "Mike," she said to Mr. Quick, "I'll take Glynnie. Can you hold the fort?"

Mike Quick looked as though dealing with exploding airports was far more to his taste than handling one nauseated female student. "Go ahead. We'll be okay."

Devoutly hoping that he was right, Mrs. Citrin took Glynnie down the hall. The plumbing, thank God, still worked.

In the five minutes they were away from the group, the worst of the noise seemed to have died down, and the awful shaking of the building had stopped. Pushing through the huddled groups of people at their gate to join the Rossmore students, Mrs. Citrin surveyed the damage. Aside from the blocked hallway, broken observation window, and the cracked wall where her own students had been sitting, there were tiny bits of safety glass and cracked tiles everywhere. At two of the four gates doors hung open onto the empty night air, swinging crazily off hinges: the gantries that should have led to departing planes had split off from the side of the concourse. Vending machines had been knocked over, and a coffee-and-croissant stand, shuttered for the night, had collapsed; the incongruous scent of coffee mixed with those of jet fuel and cement dust.

Joe Nadderley and two other Rossmore boys had gone to help lift a vending machine that had pinned a man in a suit. A couple of the girls were tearing up strips of T-shirt; Mrs. Citrin thought it was some sort of weird panic reaction until she realized the girls were handing them to each other as bandages for scrapes and cuts.

The rest of the students were just sitting, grouped around Mike Quick's feet, arms around each others' shoulders.

"Oh my God, look!" Claudia, one of the girls huddled on the floor, was pointing where the observation window had been, out at the night sky. Mrs. Citrin followed her glance and gasped. A helicopter, a strange, high-tech looking thing, flew purposefully toward the airport; from it a figure had fallen—no, the person was *flying*. As they neared, Mrs. Citrin realized that it was a woman, dressed in green and yellow, visible in the glow of fire and airport lights that tinted the night sky.

"Paranormals," Mrs. Citrin breathed. She'd read about them for years—the Avengers, the Fantastic Four—but never expected to see any of them. "Kids, help's on the way," she said.

As Mrs. Citrin and her students watched, another woman, this one in black and red, swooped from the 'copter, down toward the concourse across the tarmac, where orange fingers of fire were reaching upward, threatening to grow into an uncontrollable blaze. The woman in black and red—could she really have purple hair?—made a gesture with her hand and what looked like a burning sword appeared. Hovering above the opposite concourse, the woman made a gesture with the sword, a quick circle, and—what happened? It was as if the concourse had been enclosed in a glittering bubble. The surface of the sphere that surrounded the concourse gleamed and undulated, then slowly began to shrink. As it was compressed, it compressed the fire burning inside it. Mrs. Citrin watched as the fire receded, then went out entirely. The woman with the purple hair dived through the bubble into the concourse with the first woman, a red-head with a streak of white hair framing her face, following after. They reappeared, a moment later, each carrying a man in her arms, taking him to safety.

"Are they Avengers?" one of the kids asked. "Which ones are they?"

"Why aren't they helping *us*?" Claudia moaned.

Mike Quick, looking up from inspecting a cut on Jamal Dewey's arm, shook his head. "Our situation is pretty stable. The concourse over there was on fire. Don't sweat it, kids: if *they* don't get to us, the fire department or someone will."

"Oh, man, I hope *they* do it. My sister will never believe I got to see *Avengers*—"

A handful of kids began spinning the whole thing into the story they'd have to tell when they got back to Boston—as if exploding airports wasn't enough? But the shaking had stopped now; things did, as Mike had said, seem stable. If imagining what they'd say at school assemblies and to awed classmates kept her students happy until the fire department came, Mrs. Citrin was delighted to have it so.

With the quakes over, a couple of the kids ventured over to grab their backpacks, then to get the packs left by students still too shaken to leave the huddled group. In her head, Mrs. Citrin began making a plan: they would be rescued, probably brought somewhere they could stay the night; she'd have to call all the parents—that she did not look forward to—and tomorrow the airline would put them on a plane to Boston, and it would all be—

The floor lurched. This was different; not a quake, but something below them, something big and structural threatening to give way. Mrs. Citrin looked around frantically for someone who would explain that it was all right, nothing to be alarmed about. All she saw were faces that reflected her terror right back at her. *What is happening?*

A face appeared in the space where the observation window had been: a firefighter, calm and impassive, shouting instructions. They had to evacuate; the structure was unstable. If everyone came forward slowly, one at a time, they'd all get out fine. The man's ruddy, matter-of-fact face inspired confidence. Mrs. Citrin urged the first of the girls to go forward. Behind her she sensed a crowd forming. The firefighter shouted again: *don't crowd, don't push, it's safer to come one at a time.* He helped each of the Rossmore students onto the ladder, waving people forward. A second firefighter, on a second ladder, was helping other people down. Mrs. Citrin counted her students: thirteen—fourteen—fifteen—sixteen down the ladder, one beside her.

"Mrs. C," Glynnie moaned. "I can't. I'm going to—" the girl dropped to her knees, sick again.

Mrs. Citrin waved Mike Quick forward. "We'll be down in a second," she yelled to Mike. After him other people started down, and the firefighters were helping the people with injuries. In just a second she and Glynnie would be on the ladder. Everything would be okay.

The floor lurched again, knocking Mrs. Citrin off her feet. She struggled back up her knees, ignoring the several different aches, and put her arm around Glynnie's shoulder.

"Glynnie, sweetheart, we have to move. Sick or not, we've got to go, honey."

Glynnie retched and cast a piteous glance at her teacher. Scared and at the end of her rope, the teacher yanked the girl to her feet and pushed her toward the ladder. One of the firefighters was gone; the other one grabbed her hand, steered her on to the ladder, and reached out to Mrs. Citrin.

With a roar, the floor pitched, throwing her backward, and the sky fell in.

Dust flew everywhere, impenetrable. She couldn't see what had happened. She'd been knocked sideways by something falling, and she didn't know where the ladder, and safety, were anymore.

There was a soft pneumatic sound and the acrid smell of something pungent. Incense? Sulpher? Brimstone? A smell from Sunday School a million years ago. Mrs. Citrin looked up to see a monster standing beside her, hand extended.

"The ceiling is falling. Give me your hand," the monster yelled above the roar of metal. Its skin was cobalt blue, its eyes malevolent yellow. Its hands and feet were disfigured, and that barbed tail—the thing looked like a demon.

Mrs. Citrin stood paralyzed, gripped by a gibbering under-the-skin reaction to something Other. *Not real,* her mind insisted. Even worse: *not human.*

"I will get you out," the monster was saying. "Please." It reached out to her—two long, gloved fingers and a thumb, extended to enfold her own human hand. "I'll have you on the ground in a second, I promise."

Every single atom in Marita Citrin's body revolted at proximity to this Other, screamed at her to recoil, to get away from the blue-skinned monster. The floor groaned again, shook, dropped. The monster grabbed her hand. The world vanished.

Nightcrawler grabbed the woman's hand and teleported. He did the trip in two stages: first up to the roof for a microsecond, and then, spying a clear space on the tarmac, another hundred yards from the concourse building and sixty feet down. It was far more taxing to teleport—jaunt, he called it—two people than one, and jaunting up or down was harder than making a lateral jump, but this was safest, and he'd deal with the consequences later. When they landed he released the woman's hand. She staggered away from him, more terrified by him than by the threat of death. He let her go, crouched over. Such a jaunt should have taken every last erg of energy he possessed; he was poised to collapse.

But he didn't. Weirdly, Nightcrawler was still at full energy—and while he couldn't understand *that,* he was not going to quarrel with such a gift. Were there more people to be brought out of the concourse? He jaunted back into the terminal. There was no one else he could see, but the debris might make it impossible for him to know for sure. As he searched further he said a prayer, hoping he would miss nothing.

"Nightcrawler!" Rogue's voice came over the two-way radio built into the collar of his uniform. She was barely audible above the protesting roar of the building around him. "That structure's going to *go.* Get out *now!*"

The X-man teleported instantly. Reappearing beside Rogue at the parked helicopter, he heard Charles Xavier's voice over the radio:

"... *the likelihood of mutant involvement now 98.73%.*"

"That may be so, Professor—but there's no sign of hostile mutants from what ah can see." Her drawl, Nightcrawler noted, was thicker and more redolent of Mississippi when she was frustrated. "You certain there's no chance this was a natural disaster, earthquake or something?"

"*According to Cerebro, whatever caused this, it was not Mother Nature,*" Charles Xavier said. "*The energy signatures suggest one, maybe two lifeforms. Probably* homo superior. *What is more troubling is that the signatures are somewhat . . . blurred. I still am not able to pinpoint who our culprit is.*"

"No one has claimed the credit?" Nightcrawler asked.

"*No one, Kurt. Which suggests a number of things.*" Nightcrawler recognized the professor's pause for what it was: the gesture of a natural teacher waiting for his students to supply the answers.

"Whoever did this may still be here to be found," Rogue suggested.

"Or whoever did this did not wish to take credit," Nightcrawler added.

"Or maybe . . . whoever did this didn't *know* he'd done it. I mean, there's a lotta damage, but—" Rogue's voice trailed off thoughtfully.

"*But?*" Charles Xavier's question echoed Nightcrawler's own.

"I can't figure out the point of the damage. All it knocked out were the concourses—a Godawful expensive mess, but not the kind of thing you'd do if you wanted to sabotage operations. No strike at the flight tower or the runways. If you want to kill people you'd blow things up at a peak hour, not midnight. So what is our villain accomplishing?"

Psylocke alit beside her teammates, looking around her, as if doing so would explain the part of the conversation she'd missed.

"The last people have evacuated from this concourse," she reported.

"And at the other one as well," Nightcrawler chimed in. "Though that was mostly the fire department. Why was there fire in one concourse and an earthquake in the other? I wonder—"

Charles Xavier seemed to pick the thought out of Nightcrawler's mind before he could articulate it. "*Yes, you might be able to discern the damage vectors of the event if you got far enough up.*"

"I'm on it!" Psylocke used her telekinetic ability to soar upward several hundred feet. She hovered there for a few moments then dropped down to join them again.

"Only the two concourses and the tarmac between are seriously damaged," she reported. "The angle suggests destructive energy originating somewhere inside the northern-most concourse, the one with the structural damage, with the force shooting southward across the tarmac to the other concourse. That one doesn't have nearly as much structural damage, and I'd be willing to bet that the fire was a side-effect of whatever energy caused the quake-effect."

"So our culprit is not a fire-manipulator. What other sort of power could achieve this kind of devastation?" Nightcrawler squatted down, peering thoughtfully at the night scene below them: the rescued victims being shepherded toward the main terminal, the firefighters furling hoses and refastening ladders, the swarm of uniformed personnel already assessing damage and repair. "It seems we are most likely dealing with a mutant with telekinesis or some other matter-manipulative ability. Very powerful. And if Rogue is correct and this was not a deliberate attempt at sabotage or terrorism, but a—what would you say? A tantrum? Then we had best find out who it is before he loses his temper again."

AeroMotel, Grand Central Parkway, Queens, New York.
Three A.M.

The airline had found rooms for them—five doubles at a nearby motel which could most charitably be termed a discount joint — but it was passably clean, and the kids didn't care as long as they were away from the airport. Mrs. Citrin and Mr. Quick had settled the Rossmore students into their rooms, then taken to the phones, calling parents, explaining, soothing, reassuring. It helped to be able to tell them that none of the kids had been seriously hurt. Mrs. Citrin had finished her last call and then gone across the hall to the postage-stamp sized balcony that overlooked the highway, to lean on the rail, take a few quiet breaths of night air, and tremble a little on her own.

Seventeen students, still alive and well, if shaken up. Most of them were asleep, but a few were too keyed up; she'd seen them sitting cross-legged in the hallway outside the rooms, whispering. It was useless to scold or insist they get some rest; Mrs. Citrin didn't even try. She had things to think about on her own.

She could not get that face, the demonic, terrifying face of her rescuer, out of her mind.

All of her life Marita Citrin had considered herself both tolerant and liberal. When the Sunday morning pundits debated whether mutants should be allowed to live among regular humans, she turned the set off and went to Mass. The question was academic for her, anyway; she'd never heard of any mutants in the upscale Boston suburbs where she lived and taught. *Live and let live*, she thought.

That was before she'd come face to face with a demon. Before the demon had saved her life.

She was stunned by the primitive horror that had flooded her at the sight of the creature. She did not like knowing she was capable of such unthinking, unreasoning repulsion. The dark blue pelt, the yellow glow of his eyes, the elfin twist and point of his ears, the grotesque two-fingered hands and taloned feet and the barb-tipped tail, looked like something from a child's storybook: *once upon a time there was a demon.* And even when the monster held out its hand to help her she had felt only revulsion and terror at how different, how frighteningly different, it was. Even its voice, the faint, gutteral foreignness of its accent, had terrified her. In that moment she had wanted, with an instinct deeper than civilization or reason, to smash it, drive it away or better still kill it, rather than have to confront the terror it woke in her.

And when it had touched her hand and done . . . whatever it had done to get her out of the concourse building, her terror had been swallowed up by something different, a weird hollowness that felt as if something was being drawn out of her, her soul or her energy or something she did not have the words for. For a long second it had seemed as if that soul-energy had mingled with that of the monster.

That was the worst horror of all.

Marita Citrin had always been, not an activist, but at least actively tolerant of others, whatever their color or religion or outlandish opinions. She had tried to live her ideals, to set a good example for her students. And now, staring out onto the highway on which, even at this hour, cars still plied the route between Queens and Manhattan, she had come face to face with her own bigotry. She didn't like it.

"Mrs. C?"

Mrs. Citrin started. Amy Langel had come up quietly behind her and stood, her back pressed against the stucco of the motel's exterior wall.

"I don't feel very well," Amy said. She looked rotten: dark shadows under her eyes, pale in the harsh light of the pink halogen streetlamps, her dark hair in untidy wisps around her face. "I feel —weird. I don't know."

She took a step away from the wall and Mrs. Citrin shifted over to make room by the railing. When Amy stepped near, the teacher felt her forehead and took her pulse, not so much because she thought the girl was sick, but because going through the motions of checking was calming for both of them.

"I think it's just shock, Amy. It's been a rough night."

Amy nodded. "A rough *week*," she said, and Mrs. Citrin remembered (how could she have forgotten?) that Amy had been upset before the disaster hit the airport.

"We're safe now," Mrs. Citrin said reassuringly. "Tomorrow morning we'll take the train back to Boston. Your Mom's going to meet us at Back Bay Station . . . and by next week this will be a great story, not a scary event. How you lived through an earthquake and got rescued by—" she faltered. "By—"

"They were mutants, weren't they?" Amy asked softly. "The woman who put out the fire had purple hair and a—a mark on her face, like a scar or war paint or something. Do all mutants look that weird?"

"I don't think so." Mrs Citrin tried not to envision the face of her rescuer, cobalt blue, demonic, but smiling at her. *Set a good example*, she reminded herself. "That's why some people are scared of them: most mutants look just like everyone else, and people are fearful because they can't be sure of who they're dealing with. Or what they want."

"God, imagine finding out that you're not *human*! Everyone being afraid of you. Not having a normal life—" Amy shook her head and added with a hint of humor, "It's hard enough being a teenager!"

As if on cue there was a burst of laughter from the hallway inside, then a mumble of conversation. A girl's voice, then a boy's, then the girl again, not loud enough to overhear, but loud enough to identify: Joe Nadderly and Claudia Peña. Another laugh.

Mrs. Citrin felt Amy go rigid beside her. She tried to think of the right thing to say to the girl.

"Next week *that* won't hurt so much either," she said at last. "I know it doesn't feel that way now—"

Amy looked at her teacher with fierce dark eyes.

"What did I *do*?" she demanded. "He won't even tell me what I did wrong!"

"You probably didn't do anything wrong. And he's probably afraid to say anything to you," Marita Citrin said gently. "He knows he's behaving badly. He's probably afraid you'd cry, or yell at him. Seventeen-year-old boys don't always handle relationship stuff well, especially—" she hesitated. "Especially the break-ups.

I've seen a lot of this over the years, Amy. I don't think he wants to hurt you, but—"

"Well, he has!" Amy stared out into the night, her jaw set with anger. "He's been a—a—" her voice climbed as she sought a word bad enough to convey her outrage. Mrs. Citrin pursed her lips together to contain a laugh, more from exhaustion than lack of sympathy. Her whole body ached with fatigue; for a brief moment she even felt the balcony sway beneath her. *Physical memory*, she thought. *The body reliving the sensation of the quake.* She was way too tired to be dealing with Amy's relationship woes right now.

"Listen, honey, what we need right now is sleep," Mrs. Citrin began. Then stopped.

The few cars on the highway below them were behaving oddly. One slid sideways across the lanes, the brake lights unnaturally bright in the darkness; another spun half a turn and stopped, juddering backward, almost as if it were hopping across the asphalt. Before Marita Citrin could form the words *not again*, the surface of the multi-laned highway began to shimmy side to side, then to ripple. The balcony shook again. There were shrieks from the hallway behind them in the motel.

Amy stood, clutching the railing, tears running down her face. Mrs. Citrin grabbed the girl's arm to drag her into the motel—that had to be safer than standing on a balcony six floors above ground.

"Come on!" she shouted.

Amy started to turn, then stopped. "Mrs. C!" she screamed.

The three westbound lanes of the highway broke clean across and, impossibly, one end of the broken pavement reared up like a snake, thrashing back and forth, side to side. The two cars which had been caught on the road were hurled up and off the highway to land who knew where. The few other westbound cars were skidding, jamming on the brakes, sliding helplessly backward. The rearing, broken end of the road rose up, then lashed sideways at a big, square factory building, sweeping through a row of darkened windows as if trying to wipe a whole floor out at once. The structural support below them gone, the upper floors collapsed downward, spraying broken glass like powder. The streetlamps nearest the building shattered.

For a moment Mrs. Citrin had been mesmerized by the destruction, unable to look away. Then, as the balcony shuddered again, she grabbed Amy Langel and pulled her inside. It was like dragging a piece of furniture; the girl was rigid, eyes closed, shuddering with terror. Over Amy's shoulder Mrs. Citrin saw a halo of light as the motel's neon sign exploded in a cascade of multi-colored sparks.

"Amy," the teacher yelled. "Amy!" Other students were swarming around them in the hall, yelling. Mrs. Citrin tried one more time: "Amy!"

The girl's eyes opened slowly. Tears sheeted down her face.

Mike Quick appeared in a doorway. "I've got all the boys!" he yelled to her. That was her cue to hand Amy to one of the girls clustered around them and go check for stragglers in the girls' rooms. As she went, Mrs. Citrin tried to count that magical seventeen, but it was too confusing: people were milling everywhere, and the motel building was shuddering. As she slammed into the first room Kryssie Sattemeir squeezed past into the hall, crying. Mrs. Citrin checked the bathroom and the closets—no other kids. Into the second room, the same sweep of the closet, bath, bedroom—no one. She thought, as she darted into the last room, that the quake was beginning to subside; the trembling was becoming rhythmic and gentler. No one in the closets, no one in the room proper, but she couldn't open the bathroom door. Ignoring the panic that lanced through her, Mrs. Citrin pushed against the door—not locked, but blocked by something—until it moved enough for her to get her head in and see Glynnie, the wardrobe mistress, out cold and curled fetally, half-way under the sink, her back against the door.

Mrs. Citrin gave an heroic shove that slid Glynnie in far enough so she could squeeze through the door, and dropped to her knees to check the student. There was no mark, it didn't look like the girl had been knocked down. Probably a faint. Mrs. Citrin patted Glynnie hard on both cheeks, not quite a slap (*you never strike a student*) and the girl moaned, eyes still shut. It seemed to take forever to wake Glynnie up and then to get her on her feet. Glynnie was a big girl, tall and softly fleshy; as groggy as she was, she was barely carrying her own weight. Once she was on her feet Mrs. Citrin draped Glynnie's arm over her own shoulders and started them shuffling out of the bathroom, out of the room, into the hallway filled with Rossmore students and other motel guests.

"Everybody here?" she called to Mike Quick.

Over their heads he nodded. "With Glynnie that makes seventeen," he said. "Let's get out of here. She okay?"

"Fainted." Mrs. Citrin didn't argue when Jamal and Joe took Glynnie's almost dead-weight from her shoulders and, one on each side, followed Mr. Quick and the other Rossmore students down the hall toward the Emergency Exit. The rumbling had stopped, the floor stayed still now, and aside from the weeping of some of the students the hallway was hushed. In the stairwell the footfall of motel guests echoed dully, people talking in whispers as if they were afraid a sound would start the tremors again. Mrs. Citrin found herself counting the group again, reassuring herself.

She got sixteen.

Counted again. Sixteen. Counted and named each kid silently, praying that the missing one would appear suddenly. Still sixteen.

Amy Langel was missing.

Rogue's team had started back to Westchester when the second strike began in Queens. Before the radio report finished, Nightcrawler, his two long fingers playing easily over the controls, had accelerated and banked the copter sharply, turning east again. Lit only by the low lights of the control panel, his blue fur looked almost black. His lips were moving slightly; praying, Rogue realized. For help? Guidance? She sometimes wished she had his faith.

Especially being team leader, it would be nice to feel that someone, *something* was with her when she made decisions, sent friends into danger, on little more than her own instincts.

As if on cue Charles Xavier's voice crackled on the radio: " . . . *again, there's no evidence of geologic causality. It appears to be telekinesis at work. Cerebro—gives—*"

"A high probability of mutant activity," Rogue finished for him.

"*Yes, but again, the activity is masked in some way. I've run diagnostics, and I don't believe the problem emanates from Cerebro. It's our culprit, somehow masking the signatures.*"

"So we still can't determine who's responsible. Professor, do you have a visual fix on the site?"

"*Negative. It's west of the airport along the Grand Central Parkway, perhaps a mile or so from the last site. If you can follow the highway itself, you should be able to—*"

"We have visual," Nightcrawler broke in. "*Heilig Mutter*, what did *that*?" he added. "The highway looks like a pile of bootlaces."

"Ah was thinking worms, myself," Rogue said slowly. She toggled a searchlight to play over the highway and the wreckage of buildings on its north side. "Psylocke, there anyone alive in there?"

She asked out of long habit, without thought, but the moment the words were out Rogue wanted to bite them back. Without her telepathy, Psylocke couldn't know if anyone was alive, and she'd been fretting about it earlier. *Some kinda great team leader I am*, Rogue thought. She tried another spin on the same question. "Your vantage point is clearer than mine. See anything moving?"

Psylocke flashed her a look that might have been gratitude. "I can't tell anything about the building wreckage yet, but some of the occupants of the cars are alive, I think. We need to get them clear."

"I thank God this happened at three in the morning, not eight A.M.," Nightcrawler said. "Do you two want to hop out here? I'll land the chopper."

"Do that," Rogue said. "Come on, Betts, let's head on down there."

Rogue swept out of the copter, diving straight down for fifty feet to avoid the air currents from the chopper's powerful rotors, then caught an updraft and glided down toward the highway, sweeping past each of the cars that stood scattered across the lanes. All abandoned, thank God. No one to pull from the wreckage and keep alive. In the distance there were flashing lights and the high, thin wail of an ambulance siren, probably headed this way.

Psylocke, flying down behind her, had dropped below the highway to check wreckage there. Rogue swooped over the highway's edge and lit beside an old Volvo so damaged it looked as though it had been crumpled up by a giant hand. On the driver's side a grizzled older man sat, slumped to one side and held in place by the seatbelt. He was unconscious and there was a huge bruise on one side of his face, but his pulse was strong. Rogue pulled the door off the car—always good to make life easier for the paramedics—but didn't move the man. She knew enough to know you only moved a victim when there was no alternative.

"Rogue!" Psylocke's voice rose over the increasing wail of approaching ambulances. Rogue turned to see her teammate wielding the eldritch sword which was the physical manifestation of her telekinetic power, cutting open the cab of an old blue pickup truck. "I need help here!"

The pickup and the street around it were covered with shards of glass, fragments of brick, and dust so thick it lay like a coat of paint over everything. As Rogue reached the pickup, part of its cab fell to the pavement with a wrenching noise; a man in mechanic's overalls was inside, pinned against the door by the steering wheel, alternately moaning and trying to twist around enough to check on the little boy beside him who drooped against the confining seatbelt. Rogue's heart fluttered as she reached in, touched the boy's neck to feel for a pulse—and the boy snored. *Sleeping*, she thought. She didn't know whether to be amazed or amused.

"He's okay, sir. You sit still, now, help's coming," Rogue told him. Behind her she heard an ambulance skid to a stop, the siren's wail abruptly cut off. A hundred feet away, Psylocke had gone on to the last car, which lay on its side just below the bizarre tangle of asphalt which had been the westbound lanes of the Grand Central Parkway. As Rogue joined Psylocke the unmistakeable stink of gasoline rose up almost visibly from the shattered pavement beneath the car. On a count of three Rogue gently lowered the car back onto its tires while Psylocke lifted and cradled the driver and passenger in an unseen telekinetic brace.

There was footfall on the asphalt: EMS workers running to assess the victims. Rogue left Psylocke and sped across the road to examine the half-demolished wreck of the factory. Nightcrawler, she saw, had parked the chopper in the parking lot of an airport motel across the highway.

Then, disconcertingly, he was beside her. Rogue's nose wrinkled at the smell of brimstone caused by Nightcrawler's jaunts.

"See anything?"

He jerked his chin upward to indicate the remaining highway. "From up there, it looks as though the force, whatever it was, came from the south, which suggests the motel over there. There's an arc of damage. And this is interesting: the motel has been evacuated and everyone is standing in the parking lot. I'm certain I saw some of the same people at the airport earlier."

For a moment the import of the statement was lost on Rogue. "Guess the airlines had to put them up some—oh. *Oh.*" She looked at him, comprehending. "There's our link. Either somebody is targeting someone in that group—but you say the damage patterns move *out* from the motel? More likely then that one of those people is doing the damage."

"It looks that way," he agreed.

"Doing it deliberately?"

"That I cannot say. No, actually, I don't think it's deliberate. It's too—"

"Uncontrolled?"

"*Ja.* That's one way to put it." Nightcrawler smiled mirthlessly.

"It's—what did you say earlier? It feels like a tantrum. What do you want to do?"

Rogue felt an instant of that immobilizing dread: why do you have to ask *me*? Common sense rescued her. "I'm going over and see if any of those people saw anything. Can you use that charm of yours to sweet talk the authorities so they don't decide *we* did all this?"

She did not wait to hear Nightcrawler agree. Rogue flew over the wrecked highway and dropped down into the parking lot of the AeroMotel. There were several hundred people standing in the lot, many fully dressed, others in pajamas or robes or with blankets draped like togas or stoles. *Get to know your fellow man,* Rogue thought. *Who wears pajama bottoms, who wears the tops.* Most of them were dull-eyed in the aftermath of fear, but all turned their heads to listen as she yelled a couple of questions.

"Was anyone here at LaGuardia Airport during the earlier—" what to call it? She fell back on cop-speak. "The earlier incident there?"

A bristle of hands went up at one side of the crowd, perhaps twenty people, most of them teenagers. A man with a graying brush cut raised his hand. The kids looked to him—a teacher, Rogue thought. Coach. Someone in authority. The group of kids and teacher were the only ones who seemed to know what she was talking about, or to care.

"Sir, can I ask your group some questions?"

"I guess so," he said. "Is it over?"

"I don't know. I think so. Hope so, anyway." Rogue steered the group away from the rest of the weary, miserable looking motel guests and got them all leaning against cars in the parking lot. Sixteen kids, she noted, and one adult. *That's one brave grownup.*

"This your whole group, sir?"

The teacher shook his head. "One of the kids is missing; the other chaperone went to find her." He looked past Rogue. "Marita! Over here!"

A pretty, harried looking woman looked up at the call. She

looked to be in her thirties: chestnut hair, narrow face and small-lensed glasses, pressed jeans and a sleeveless lavender polo shirt. Her expression was hopeful for a moment and then, as she realized her colleague had not found the missing child, grim. She joined the group but spared Rogue only a brief glance before she went back to peering at the crowd.

"*You* haven't seen a girl, sixteen years old, chin-length black hair, in a green tank top and jeans, have you? Looking upset? I've got to find her—"

"I just need a minute, ma'am," Rogue assured her. "I'm trying to find the source of these incidents," Rogue began. *Incident.* What a word for this devastation. "When your group was at the airport, did you notice anyone acting strangely?"

The male teacher shook his head. "Everyone was scared, there was a lot of noise, yelling, but—those are things you'd expect. What do you mean, strangely."

Frustration brought out the Mississippi in Rogue's speech as she sought to explain. "Anyone look like they were upset before things started happening, or like—like something strange was going on with them?" How could she know how a mutant's powers would manifest? Glowing eyes? Destructive rays coming out of the fingertips? "Anything . . . unusual? Weird?"

The other teacher, the woman, was on her toes trying to look over the crowd. "She can't have gone this way," she was muttering. "Could she still be in the motel? I'm sorry, I have to look—" She turned away. Rogue stopped her, grabbed her arm. A jolt of impatience went through her, made her want to shake the teacher.

A thought occurred to her. *If I could touch her, I'd know her memories, see what she's seen.*

Of all the thoughts in the world, this was the one Rogue guarded against most vigilantly, but for a moment it seemed like the most reasonable thing in the world. Take off her glove and touch the other woman, draw out her memories. Never mind the danger to the teacher: *just a touch*, she thought. But in her imagination she saw herself barehanded, holding the teacher's hand, reveling in the sensation of power that flowed into her with the woman's memory and strength, the pleasure of drinking her dry, taking the last drop of life itself.

At almost the same moment Rogue and the teacher pulled away from each other. The woman said "I *can't*," over her shoulder and disappeared in the direction of the motel staff, who were clustered around the doors to the building. Rogue stood stock still, feeling her own shock and horror at what she had contemplated. The feelings, her revulsion and, beneath it, the need to touch, ebbed slowly. *What the hell was that*? she wondered.

She turned back to the man. Neither he nor his students had noticed anything peculiar, and none of them seemed to be able to help. The kids were wide-eyed and astonished at their proximity to a real paranormal; several of them giggled nervously as they repeated the same story. At the airport they'd all been talking, reading, waiting. No one had seen anything peculiar. No one had been upset, just tired and ready to go home.

"Nothing unusual at all," Rogue insisted. There was silence. She turned to go.

"Amy was crying," a heavyset girl threw out as an afterthought. One of the boys gave her an uncomfortable look. "I mean, *before* the quake and everything started happening."

The tall boy in the blue sweatshirt shook his head violently. "Come on, she was okay," the boy said.

An exchange of looks heavy with adolescent meaning. Rogue instantly remembered sitting through just this sort of silent conversation among Charles Xavier's younger students, mutants just coming into their powers: an eyebrow's lift, the droop of a mouth's corner, the scornful turning of a head. So much going on with kids this age, how could they be expected to see anything but themselves?

"She was a mess, Joe," the heavy girl insisted. "All the way home."

The boy made a dismissive noise and turned away. The girl glared after him. Rogue gave up, thanked the group and their teacher, and flew up to survey the scene: the motel, guests milling around in the parking lot—she noted the female teacher talking agitatedly with a group of uniformed motel workers. The highway was ripped and twisted; that was going to make the morning commute a nightmare, she thought.

"Rogue!" Psylocke's voice cut through her reverie. "I need a hand here!"

British understatement, she thought grimly. The building on the far side of the highway, in which several upper stories had caved into a horizontal slice across its face, was beginning to shift forward, threatening to collapse toward the street. Psylocke had formed a telekinetic brace against the side of the building, but Rogue knew she wouldn't be able to hold the building for long. The drain on her teammate's power would be too much. They needed to shore up the side of the building, but with what? She surveyed the highway, hoping she could turn debris into some sort of brace.

Stanchions—the structures of girders and cement which held the highway up. The ones which had been supporting the stretch of twisted highway weren't pretty—they were ragged and torn—but they were still solid. If she could get some of the girders loose from the stanchions themselves, they'd make the start of a support for the face of the building. And guard-rails. They weren't very strong, but they were strung together with high-strength cable that would serve, and God knows they weren't doing anyone any good lying in the wreckage of the highway.

"Betsy, can you hold out for a couple more minutes?" she called out.

"A few more," Psylocke agreed.

Rogue was already on the highway, straining at the girders that formed the support stanchions. Thank God a few of them were already loose. Rogue pulled one up, planted it into the sidewalk and bent it upward so it leaned into the factory wall. She went back for another, and repeated the process until she had put six girders in place, rising up like flying buttresses to hold the side of the factory up. Then, loosing cable from the guard-rail posts, she circled the factory and the girders once—that was all the cable she had—to tie them together.

"Clever!" Nightcrawler appeared on the roof of the building and looked down, examining the structure. "I think it will hold."

"Guess we better find out," Rogue called to him She alit on a part of the highway still standing. "Psylocke, let it go!"

The building sagged forward with a high, protesting sound too loud to be called a creak. Rogue held her breath—but the jury-rigged supports held. It might be that all she'd done was save the building for the wrecker's ball—but at least now a demolition crew could approach it safely.

Psylocke joined her on the highway, and then Nightcrawler as well. Rogue frowned as her mind returned to chasing a thought, an almost-put-together idea which had come and gone as she'd worked to put the supports in place. Before she had shored up the factory she had been talking to those kids and their teacher. No, teachers. But one of them had been too distracted to be of much use.

"Hang on a second," she told her teammates.

The student group was among the last of the motel guests straggling back into the building. Rogue flew down and stopped them for a moment, asked a question, then another. Satisfied, she went back to her teammates.

"I think I've found our culprit. I mean, I know who she is."

"She?"

"Girl named Amy, one of the kids we pulled out of the airport. She had a hard time on the trip, broke up with her boyfriend—just the sort of adolescent angst—"

"—to create a crisis that could evoke latent mutant abilities," Psylocke finished. "Poor kid. Although with abilities like this, I'm surprised nothing ever happened before And that she didn't make it onto Cerebro's radar."

"In any case, I don't think she's doing this deliberately—"

"But we better stop her before she does it again," Nightcrawler rolled his eyes. "Her teachers won't want to hand her over to us. We're not what you'd call 'the authorities.'"

"It isn't even that simple, Kurt. She's not with the group. She's run away."

"Probably scared to death, poor girl," Psylocke said. "But where would she have gone at—what is it, 4:30 in the morning. In *Queens?*"

For a moment the three X-Men scanned the horizon looking without much hope for some sign of a lost teenager.

Like looking for a needle in a haystack, Rogue thought. *If you find it, it's probably because it's done some damage. Look for damage.* She stared to the west and saw nothing but the lights and towers of Manhattan in the distance and, nearer by, streets and streetlights and nothing much else. She looked south, blinked, looked again.

"Oh, damn," she said, the Mississippi drawl thick as mud. "Ah got her."

Her teammates followed her gaze. To the south, a mile or so away, a funnel of gleaming gray *things* was rising shakily above an open space, dancing in a circle. It took a moment to understand what they were seeing.

"Gravestones," Nightcrawler murmured. "*Heilig Mutter.*"

As they watched, the stones spun faster and faster, rising above the graveyard in a perfect column that glinted in the pre-dawn light.

St. Astrid's Cemetery, Queens, New York. 4:52 A.M.

Marita Citrin paused to catch her breath and look around. The streets in this neighborhood were largely lined with faceless old buildings, warehouses or factories, by the look of them. She hadn't seen another soul since she'd started walking south from the motel. The last person she'd talked to—it would be the last one, she thought bitterly—was one of the motel janitors, a man whose English got tangled up in a middle-European accent. She had managed to get her question across to him, though, and to understand his answer: he had seen Amy Langel running south away from the motel, perhaps fifteen minutes before.

For one endless moment Mrs. Citrin had felt defeated. She wanted to sit down on the broken cement of the sidewalk and cry. What was she going to say to Amy's parents? How on earth would she find the girl in a place she didn't know, in the middle of the night, exhausted as she was? The one question she didn't ask herself was why Amy had run. Mrs. Citrin was sure she knew the answer to that one, and it scared her.

She turned around to look back at the motel and could no longer see it. Only thing to do, then, was to go forward. She started walking again, wondering what she would do when she found her student. If she found her student. What could she say to the girl? *I know what you are, but it's okay? Somehow you blew up an airport and a highway, but honest, sweetie, that's okay, it's nothing anyone's going to hold against you?* And the most frightening, damning thing of all: *you're a mutant. You're not human. Your life will never be the same.* There had been a moment, standing on the balcony with Amy as the highway had begun to twist, when Mrs. Citrin had been aware of something *flowing* from the girl, of an intense force pouring out of her. Amy was connected to the destruction, but was she doing it deliberately? Scenes from old horror movies played in Mrs. Citrin's head—*Carrie*, particularly — but she couldn't believe that Amy, a good student and a responsible, sweet-natured kid, would cause this kind of destruction deliberately. Unless finding those powers had changed her, made her as inhuman as that blue-furred monster she'd met earlier.

"Stop that," she muttered to herself. The neighborhood around her was changing; instead of blockish warehouses she was now walking through two- and three-story houses, lit by streetlights that made everything a warm gray. Up ahead she saw a park, gray-green trees rising up behind a tall wrought-iron fence. It seemed like the sort of place a frightened, deeply upset teenage girl might go. Her feet hurt, her mouth was dry and she was as tired as she had ever been in her life, but Marita Citrin went onward, praying she would find her student there.

A block closer and she realized it wasn't a park but a graveyard. A wrought-iron arch above proclaimed St. Astrid's Cemetary; under the arch, one of the wrought-iron gates had been knocked off a hinge and was hanging open.

Mrs. Citrin swallowed a lump in her throat. She had come to the right place.

"Amy?" she called out waveringly. She coughed to clear her throat, trying to keep the fear out of her voice. Her student needed someone calm, dispassionate and sympathetic, not a scared woman newly in touch with her own anti-mutant bigotry. "Amy, it's Marita Citrin. Sweetheart, let's go back to the motel. Everyone's getting worried."

No response. Reluctantly, Mrs. Citrin went through the damaged gate and started to follow the driveway, turning her head back and forth, searching for the sight of her student.

"Amy?" she called again. "Come on, honey. It's been a long day; you need to get some sleep."

She heard a sob off to the left. Peering through the darkness she saw a bit of bright green in the shadows: Amy's tank top. She took a few steps closer and could make out the form of the girl sitting curled up against the door of an immense old mausoleum, arms wrapped around her knees and head down.

"Go away!" The girl cried. She kept her face turned from Mrs. Citrin.

"You know I can't do that, Amy. Please, I know what's happening is scary, but you have to come back with me. Your parents—"

"They aren't my parents!" Amy wept. "They can't be. My parent's aren't monsters! *I'm* a monster!"

"No, no," Mrs. Citrin said soothingly, but as she stepped closer to the girl she realized that she was trembling. *Maintain*, she thought. Keep calm. "You're not a monster, honey. You're scared, it's been a rough night—" She was only a few feet from Amy now, and kept moving forward slowly, gently. Now she could reach down and push a lock of dark hair out of Amy's eyes, stroke the hair back from her forehead, talk soothingly, reassure the girl, get her back to the motel—

"LEAVE ME ALONE!" Amy howled, sitting bolt upright. Mrs. Citrin felt Amy's anger pour through her and was powerless to pull her hand away, as if she had touched an electric current. A moment before the air had been filled with the sort of small noises that go unheard in cities except in the dead of night: distant traffic, the haunted wail of a city bus's brakes, insects humming nearby, the dry whisper of breeze among the trees, and the rattle of stones and twigs underfoot. Now there was only a soft, unnatural hush, as if the two of them had been encased in cotton. Mrs. Citrin, her hand still on Amy's shoulder, began to feel the world receding from her, leaving her in a bubble with Amy and the buzzing in her own head. Her peripheral vision began to close in, reducing what she could see to a bright center: Amy's face in a grimace of misery with tears coursing down it.

She shook her head hard and her vision cleared. Nothing magical about that, she thought grimly. Just the beginning of a faint. But the hush continued, and when Marita Citrin spoke, her voice sounded weirdly loud and close.

"Amy, you have to stop this now," she said firmly. "You're upset, and you have a right to be, but this is not the way—"

"Stop it stop it stop it stop it!" Amy's hands covered her ears and she shut her eyes hard. Mrs. Citrin, released from the unseen force which had kept her touching Amy, dropped to her knees and threw her arms around the girl, as if by containing her pain and shock she could contain the destructive energy as well. The ground trembled underneath them; Mrs. Citrin looked up and saw tombstones rocking back and forth, uprooting, dancing upward five, ten, twenty feet into the air, higher, moving in a circle, spiralling upward.

If she drops them we'll be killed, Mrs. Citrin realized. Was that Amy's intention? To rain those several-dozen stone slabs down on their heads and crush them? The girl might want to die at this moment, with this frightening revelation about herself, but Mrs. Citrin didn't want to die. She was way out of her depth, she knew, but who else was there to help the girl? She did the only thing that made any sense to her: she grasped Amy tighter, willing her student to feel the affection and comfort she was trying to give her, praying the girl would not sense her fear. That same fear of the unknown that had overwhelmed her with the blue-furred mutant was coursing through Mrs. Citrin now like a charge of electricity, but she would not, could not, give in to it. *Come on, Amy,* she thought. *Come on, sweetie, calm down. It's okay. It's going to be all right.*

But when Mrs. Citrin saw Amy's eyes, glazed and unfocused, and the twisted expression of pain and outrage on her face, she knew it wasn't true. Above their heads the spiral of gravestones spun faster.

In the moments it took the X-Men to reach the graveyard the funnel of gravestones had risen high into the air, forming a tower eighty feet high. The three mutants hovered, a hundred feet up and about the same distance away from the tower of gravestones, assessing the situation. Directly under the whirling stones were two figures crouched together. The older woman had her arms around the girl, her shoulders drawn up defensively and her face hidden. The girl had her arms wrapped tightly around her knees, her face turned upward toward the spiral of granite.

"At the speed those stones are moving, even if she lets go they're going to go flying. Some of 'em could go half a mile before they smash something," Rogue yelled. "We can't just make her stop; we have to get the stones down first. Psylocke, can you throw a telekinetic bubble around all that?" She gestured toward the spinning mass of stones above their heads.

Psylocke shook her head. "I'm still recovering from holding that building together. If even one of those stones broke through—"

Rogue nodded grimly. "I don't suppose just going up and asking her to stop would do it."

"That's worth a try." Psylocke grinned. The tattoo that masked one eye made it look as if she were winking. "I'll take a shot."

She leapt into the air and came down a dozen paces or so from the girl and her teacher. Neither one moved. This close, Psylocke could see that the girl's eyes were closed and tears were streaking a path through the grime on her face. In the old days, Psylocke thought, I could have taken control of her for a minute, got her calmed down, stopped the threat.

The old days were gone. She'd have to try the old-fashioned way. She cleared her throat and said hello.

At the sound, the girl shuddered. The teacher didn't move at all—appeared to be under a spell, frozen in place. If it came to force, the teacher might get hurt. We'll have to get the woman away from the girl, Psylocke thought. Start talking.

"I'm here to help," she said quietly. She took a step closer. There was a field or aura around the girl that sent a shiver through her, but she kept going. "But we have to get those stones down first. People might get hurt; you don't want that." She kept her voice gentle and low pitched. "Whatever has happened, we'll help you. You're not alone—"

Something slammed into her from behind. Psylocke rolled to one side and was up on her feet in an instant, the glowing eldritch sword which was a focused manifestation of her telekinetic ability already in her hand. A stone angel came flying toward her; with a stroke the telekinetic sword reduced it to dust. A barrage of granite—statues, footstones, ornaments—followed the angel. It was all Psylocke could do to keep up with them. The telekinetic sword blazed as if it had a life of its own, seemingly swinging itself as it blocked and destroyed the chunks of granite. The barrage stopped, but the sword kept arcing wildly, taking Psylocke with it, slicing through the door of an elaborate mausoleum, shattering the stone around the door, swinging upward to strike again.

Psylocke felt a stab of fear as she wrestled with the telekinetic sword. It swung so hard she wrenched her shoulder pulling it away from another block of granite. *Got to get away from here*, she thought, and leapt upward. The sword caught the bough of a tree as she went, cutting it off. Then Betsy was in the sky, hovering just out of range of the tower of spinning gravestones, and the horrible out-of-control feeling was gone. She caught her breath and flew back to Rogue and Nightcrawler, now standing on the ground near the cemetery gate.

"It's more than just destruction," she told her teammates breathlessly. "She's got some sort of field or aura. I felt it—I could barely control my telekinesis. It was frightening. I went from coping with a threat to feeling I was *becoming* a threat."

"And this aura—what? Boosts your powers?"

Psylocke nodded. "I'd swear it. For a minute it felt good, very powerful. Then it started to get too strong. If the girl's capable of causing *that*—" She shuddered. Even the memory of that surge of frightening power was unpleasant.

"No." Nightcrawler said it flatly, emphatically. His dark brows knit thoughtfully. "You're the only one who has been near the girl, but I've had the same sensation, and I would guess," he looked quizzically at Rogue, "that our Leader has, too. With the teacher."

Both women turned to look at him.

"But I felt her power just now, when I approached her," Psylocke objected.

"Y'all saying that *both* of 'em have telekinetic powers?" Rogue's drawl had asserted itself again.

"No. I'm saying the two of them play off each other. That each has a different power. I wondered earlier why, if this child is so powerful, there had been no sign of her ability before this—"

"Play off each other how?" Rogue began.

"Listen," he said urgently. "When I jaunted the teacher out of the airport, it was too easy. Two jaunts, and no drain on my energy or abilities. I could have gone on forever. I *wanted* to—until I put her down and went back to look for other victims. The girl has telekinetic ability, beyond a doubt. But the teacher is—" he paused, pursed his lips, sought the right word. "The teacher is *katalystor*, a potentiator, someone who enhances the power of another mutant. Without the teacher there, perhaps the girl would have done nothing more than rattle garbage cans or break dishes. With the teacher there—Boom! And I wonder if perhaps that is why Cerebro couldn't sort out who was the—" he looked up at the spiral of granite stones—"*Himmel!* At the top!"

Psylocke forllowed his glance. At the highest point of the spiral, three gravestones were beginning to wobble as they spun; in another moment they might break free of the spiral and go spinning up and out, landing with killing force somewhere among the sleeping homes.

Rogue was already in the air. She called into the microphone in her collar: "Kurt, get the teacher away from here! Betsy, are you recovered enough to throw a shield around the stones while he does it?"

She didn't wait for a response, but flew upward, hovering just above the stones, and plucked the three unstable ones out of the air one at a time, hurling them with controlled force back to the ground. The turbulent air at the top of the funnel buffeted her. Twice she was almost knocked away by stones whipping at her. *Like cuddling up to a hurricane,* she thought. The air howled past, and anything she might have yelled to her teammates, or they to her, was lost in the sound.

Then, abruptly, the spinning stopped.

The stones hung, suspended in air above the graveyard, but Rogue, who had been caught up in the cyclonic air currents as she flew, was flung half a mile out of the graveyard by her own momentum. She landed ingloriously but luckily on one hip in a playground, so hard that she left a dent in the foam play-surface. Wincing slightly, she was back in the air seconds later, peering in the graying darkness for a sight of Nightcrawler or Psylocke. The stones still hung in the air, but had stopped their frightening spinning. Below, shimmering slightly in the fading moonlight, a telekinetic bubble enclosed the girl, Amy. Nightcrawler must have jaunted the teacher away, she thought, for the girl was alone, sitting curled up in a pose of pure desolation. *Poor kid*, Rogue thought. Then reminded herself: *dangerous kid.*

As Rogue watched, Psylocke approached the bubble and moved *through* it to join the girl trapped inside. The team leader murmured a prayer that the girl, without her teacher's potentiating influence, would listen to Psylocke. Just in case, she stayed hovering above them, plucking gravestones one by one from their frozen positions and dropping them on the ground.

Marita Citrin knelt, her arms still wrapped around Amy's shoulders, unable to move. *Rodin*, she thought wildly. *Some sculpture by Rodin, that's what we look like.* Except that Rodin didn't sculpt his subjects with their hair flying around their heads, sparking with electricity. The current between them was literally electrifying, Mrs. Citrin thought she smelled ozone on the night air. She was frozen in place, feeling rather than seeing the gravestones whirling above her head. They did not frighten her as much as the feeling that flowed between her and her student, an awful, draining feeling that in offering Amy comfort, she had given away her own life. *I'm going to die*, she thought. Prayers she hadn't thought of in years—hadn't said aloud in more years than that—came back to her. She said them silently, over and over. Her lips would not move.

Then, mingled with the ozone, the acrid smell of brimstone. Mrs. Citrin felt rather than saw the new presence behind her. Amy must have felt something too, for the exchange of energy between them faltered for a moment and Mrs. Citrin was able to drop her arms.

The moment she did that she was gone. Someone held her around the waist, dragged her away, and then she felt that hollow, awful feeling again. Her shoulders prickled, and she knew that when she opened her eyes the hands that clasped her would not be normal human ones, but the weird two-fingered hands of the demon-man. She was praying aloud now, her face clenched up tightly so that she would not have to open her eyes.

The blue man was saying something. She didn't understand at first; he wasn't speaking English, but the cadences were familiar, dovetailing in some way with her own words.

"Gegrüßet seist du, Maria, voll der Gnade,
der Herr ist mit dir.
Du bist gebenedeit unter den Frauen,
und gebenedeit ist die Frucht deines Leibes, Jesus.
Heilige Maria, Mutter Gottes . . ."

The hands at her waist released. She turned to face her abductor.

"You're Catholic?" he asked quietly.

She nodded.

"I too. I'm sorry to have given you a fright," he said gently. "But we had to separate you from the girl. This was the quickest way."

"What do you mean, you *had* to separate us? What are you going to do to her?" Responsibility overcame fear. Mrs. Citrin cast a quick look around her; he had brought her to a granite enclosure, spare and unfurnished but high ceilinged, with open slats near the roof to let in air and light from a streetlight outside. Enough light to make out shapes and the expression on the blue man's face. It was an outdoor chapel, she realized. Still in the cemetary. "She's my student," she told the blue man grimly. "I have to stay with her."

"If you want to help her," the demon said quietly. "The best thing you can do is stay away from her."

"You don't understand," Mrs. Citrin said. It took all her courage to face him. Despite his apparent gentleness, it was hard to speak past the lump of terror in her throat. "Her parents put her in my care. I'm responsible for her. What she *is* doesn't matter, even if she's—she's . . ."

"A mutant? You're right. What matters at this moment is helping her to control her abilities so that no one gets hurt. We have—"

he chuckled softly. "We have a good deal of experience in dealing with new mutants. And, if you will pardon me, *we* are sympathetic to the problems she faces."

"I—"

"Would make matters worse," he finished. "Have you not realized? The girl's powers only got out of control when you were close by. Something about you—I felt it myself. You . . ." He paused, seeming to seek the right word. "You are a catalyst of some kind. A potentiator. Your gift is to magnify the gifts of others—"

"Gift?!" She ignored what he was implying about her. "But magnify how? I don't *do* anything."

The blue man gave a courtly, ironic bow. "Your charming presence, I think. Nothing deliberate. Just now, when Psylocke came near you and used her telekinetic sword to smash the debris your student was hurling at her, the sword—a manifestation of her power—was larger than I'd ever seen it, and her control of it was erratic. My other comrade experienced something similar when she spoke to you. And when I brought you out of the airline terminal— it's normally very hard for me to teleport another person, That jaunt, up and then across, should have exhausted me. Instead I was energized by it. The same thing happened just now—and the minute I teleported you away from her, the girl's power dipped. The danger stopped."

Mrs. Citrin covered her mouth with her hand. "You're saying it's my fault—"

"No." His eyes, those eerie yellow eyes, were sympathetic. It was true: he was not holding her responsible. "Not your fault."

"*You're saying* I'm *a mutant*," she whispered. She backed away from him, felt the abrupt bite of a concrete bench behind her knees, and sat down, hard.

"It does seem that way." Nightcrawler sat down at the other end of the bench. She was aware that he was giving her space, trying not to force his presence on her.

"You could be wrong," she insisted.

"I could," he agreed. "I'm only human."

She sat up and stared at him, trying to read his face, looking for sarcasm.

"How could I not know I was *different*?" she asked. "How could I be a mutant and not know it?"

The blue man tilted his head thoughtfully. "There have probably been signs of it all along. You're a teacher, yes?"

"English and drama."

"You get good performances from your students? Good work? Your students do their best for you? People remark upon it?"

Mrs. Citrin nodded, recalling more than a decade's worth of teacher evaluations. "I thought that was because I was a good teacher," she said at last, rather sadly. Was that going to be taken away from her too?

"I think you *are* a good teacher. And that you're lucky to have a gift that reinforces that talent."

That was kind, Mrs. Citrin thought. He'd understood. There was something human about him, whatever he looked like. But that didn't mean she wanted to accept what he was saying, wanted to be what he was.

For a few moments Mrs. Citrin thought of students whose performances had surprised her and themselves; kids who had seemingly blossomed in their classes. More than a decade of bringing out the best in her students. And then Amy, blowing up airports.

She turned back to the man at her side and, her eyes adjusted to the half-light of the chapel, studied him. His face—if you did the impossible and ignored the blue skin, the yellow eyes and elfin ears—was actually attractive. Good bones, and that wide, white smile. It was possible to see, or at least imagine, kindness and intelligence in those eyes despite their malevolent color.

"Were you born like that?" she asked. Immediately she regretted the question, afraid that she'd offend him, make him mad. But the blue man did not seem to be troubled.

"Looking this way? Yes. I was lucky; as an infant I was found and adopted by Gypsies—a people who know a little something about being outcasts. *Normal* people might have drowned me or burnt me at the stake or left me to the elements, as suits an abomination. But my adoptive family brought me up with love and kindness. They trained me as a performer, an acrobat. I have been lucky, but I cannot say I have not met people who held my looks against me."

"But don't you hate that? Don't you wish you were normal? Don't you want to . . . rail at someone sometimes?"

"At God?" Now the blue man shrugged. "God made me what I am. I have tried to do good with the gifts He gave me. Even so . . . " His voice trailed off thoughtfully. For the first time Marita Citrin saw the blue man unsure.

"Even so what?"

"I left the X-Men to go to seminary, to become a priest. But even there, there are those who are *uneasy* with me, who find me fearsome."

"So you left?"

"Yes, but not because other students were afraid of me. A friend needed help and I came home. Now I wonder sometimes if this is not where God wants me to be, where I was made to be."

Mrs. Citrin tried to imagine the blue man as a priest, wearing the vestments, performing the sacraments, hearing confession. If she closed her eyes and listened only to that gentle voice with its faint burr of accent, she could do it. When she opened her eyes and looked at him—it was more difficult. But possible, if you looked beyond his appearance and saw the kindness in his eyes.

"What are you going to do?" she asked.

"Now?" The blue man grinned again. "Take you back to the motel, I think. You and Amy must avoid each other—"

"But what's going to happen to *her*?"

"I think, first, we will bring her back to her parents. After that, if she likes, she can be helped to control her abilities. And helped to come to terms with them. Your Amy has a lot of adjusting to do."

"Don't we all," Mrs. Citrin said wryly. She felt wobbly and tired.

Too much had happened to easily digest. But she was no longer terrified.

"What's your name?" she asked the blue man.

"I am called Nightcrawler," he said, sketching a bow. His barbed tail echoed the flourish of his hands. "Oh, my given name? Kurt."

Marita Citrin smiled. "Thanks, Father Kurt," she said. Looking at the blue man she knew that of all the things she could have said, this was the right one. "You *are* going to calm down, aren't you?" Psylocke maintained the field integrity of the telekinetic bubble around the girl, but allowed herself to phase through it, a neat bit of showmanship. She tried to project an aura of calm authority, let the girl know who was in charge, without being menacing. Maintaining the bubble was tiring her out faster than she liked. If Kurt was right and the girl's powers would be lessened by taking the teacher away, then maybe the telekinetic bubble wasn't even necessary. Psylocke was not willing to take that chance while the gravestones still hung overhead.

The girl was sitting, hunched over, with her head resting on her knees, still teary and shuddering. She did not look as if she could be responsible for the destruction at the airport, at the motel, and now here in the graveyard. Psylocke knew better than to let her guard down, though. *If only I could* . . . the thought began. Forget that. It was time to mourn her lost telepathy and get on with her life. Begin by seeing what regular old talking could do.

"What's your name?" she asked.

No response.

"*My* name is Betsy," she tried again.

The girl raised her head from her knees and stared at Psylocke in disbelief. "*Betsy?*" Her voice climbed an octave. "*Betsy?*"

Psylocke nodded.

The girl giggled wetly. "Betsy the super mutant. Wow."

"My full name is Elisabeth, but I'm not sure that sounds any more heroic. When I'm working, I'm called Psylocke. My brother Brian used to call me Betts. You can call me Betsy if you like."

"I'm Amy." For a moment it seemed as if the ice were broken.

But then the girl's head dropped dejectedly onto her knees again.

"This is a hell of a way to find out you've got—" Psylocke searched for a neutral term—"abilities," she finished.

"*Abilities*! I'm a mutant!" Amy said bitterly. "A freak. Destructo-girl. My parents won't even want me in the house—jeez, if someone comes after them to pay for all that damage, they'll lose our house, Mom'll lose her business, the neighbors will . . . . And me! No one'll ever want to see me again—"

"Shshhh." With the feeling that she was working without a net, unsure whether the gesture was a safe one or would start the girl up again, Psylocke put her hand on Amy's shoulder. The girl looked up at her through teary eyelashes. "Shshhh. There are ways to deal with all of this. I work with someone who's been helping kids with special abilities for years. He's good at it, actually runs a school. This needn't be the end of the world, you know."

"It is for *me!*" Amy said venomously. Psylocke could feel the sudden pressure of Amy's power against the telekinetic field that still surrounded them. Lucky she hadn't dropped the bubble. "I wanted to be an actress! I had a plan. I knew how my life was going to go!"

"*No one* knows that," Psylocke said. She thought of the changes in her own life—the pain and loss and love, the exchange of telepathy for the power and growing strength of her telekinetic abilities. Deaths of friends. Deaths of family. Love. "Life hands you any number of surprises—"

"It's not the same for you! You're—you're used to it—"

"Now, maybe. But I was a teenager when my powers manifested. I was a *brat*. And I learned that it was through pain—literally through pain—that my powers grew. I lost my brother. I lost my *self*—it's a long story, and some of it has been distinctly unpleasant. But I survived. I've done some good. Some of it has even been fun."

"Fun?"

Psylocke wanted to laugh at the absolute incomprehension in the girl's voice. She simply nodded her head.

"Fun being a *mutant*? Someone people pass laws against and scream things at? Even Mrs. C thinks I'm a freak. You saw her face—"

"Your Mrs. C was dealing with her own problems," Psylocke said.

"Yeah, like what she's going to tell my parents—"

Psylocke hesitated, not wanting to *out* the teacher, but knowing that Amy would have to understand the deadly combination that she and her teacher made—at least until she had learned to control her abilities.

"We think your teacher has some sort of mutation also, something that exacerbates—" she paused, looked at the girl to make sure she understood the word—"the powers of mutants near her. Her ability is not as remarkable as yours, but when the two of you got together in a highly emotional state—well, the results were messy."

Amy stared at her.

"It wasn't just me?" she asked.

"No. Bad luck, bad combination. If you calm down and stay away from your Mrs. C, you can learn to control your ability. No one need know that you're a mutant unless you decide to use the power, as we do."

The girl thought for a while, her eyebrows knit in concentration. Psylocke, sensing an ebb in Amy's power, relaxed the telekinetic bubble. She was instantly aware of her own exhaustion. Psylocke sat back against the wall of the mausoleum and sighed.

"Can I ask you something?" Amy asked tentatively.

"Anything you like," Psylocke said.

There was a pause, as if Amy were trying to get up her nerve. *Must be some question*, Psylocke thought.

Amy gulped and pushed her dark hair out of her eyes. "Is that your natural hair color?"

Psylocke stared at her. Of all the questions she'd anticipated, that was not one. She laughed.

"*Now*, it is. It's a long story—"

"An awful lot about you guys is a long story," Amy observed. She was comfortable enough now to sound a little irritated.

Psylocke laughed again. "You've got that right. But if you mean, do I have to have my hair done to get it this color, no. The sun rises every morning and my hair is purple. The blaze over my eye, on the other hand, is a tattoo, which is part of the same long story. Neither one really has anything to do with my abilities."

She thought the girl looked a little disappointed. "At least if my hair turned some really interesting color I'd be getting something out of this," Amy said.

"Listen, Amy. You can't know what you'll get out of this. Some of it probably won't be much fun—but a lot of life really isn't much fun either, even if you're as normal as—I don't know, what's normal? Pie, perhaps? But you get through it. First, you'll learn to control the power. Then this ability—this gift of yours—may be something you can use well. You could make a difference. That's up to you."

Psylocke stood up and offered to pull the girl to her feet. "Up you get. Now, my dear, I think we'd best take you back to your group."

Amy pulled away. "No! They know—"

"That you panicked and ran away. The only ones who know what you can do are your teacher, my colleagues, you, and I. We won't tell anyone—not even your parents—unless you ask us to, although I think you might like to talk to the Professor."

"He taught you to control your powers?"

"Charles Xavier. Yes. He's helped a lot of kids in just your situation over the years. Now, would you rather walk back to the motel, or fly?"

Amy's eyes lit up. "Fly? *I can fly?*"

Psylocke imagined a whole new world opening up inside the girl's head. She hated to squash it, but, "I don't know if you can or can't, but for now I was offering a lift back to the motel. If you don't want your classmates to know about your new abilities, you probably don't want to fly back on your own power."

"Omigod. Okay, I'd better not try to fly." Still, something about the idea must have pleased her; the corner of her mouth turned up in a tiny smile. Psylocke asked what it was.

"My boyfriend—I mean, my *ex*-boyfriend. God, if I could see his face when I *flew* back . . . ."

Psylocke managed not to laugh. Had she ever been that young? However much she might understand the feeling, though, she couldn't officially bless using alpha-class mutant abilities to make an old boyfriend *sorry*. She held out her hand.

"Come on, love. Let's get you home."

In the east, the night sky was graying. A rosy glow was stealing over the westernmost reaches of Queens. Sounds came to Psylocke as she rose, carrying Amy Langel, and flew north toward the AeroMotel. The whine of a bus, the rattle of the elevated subway, the sounds of footfall and distant, unintelligible voices, the slow start-up sounds of another day in the city. Silence is a funny thing, she thought. If you listen through it you can hear a lot. If you know how to listen, silence can connect you with the world. Not a prison but a gift.

Psylocke smiled.